Emily Critchley gained a first class degree in Creative Writing from London Metropolitan University. She is now studying for an MA in Creative Writing at Birkbeck, University of London. She lives in North London.

Notes on my Family

Emily Critchley

Published in the UK by Everything with Words Limited
3rd Floor, Premier House,
12-13 Hatton Garden,
London EC1N 8AN

www.everythingwithwords.com

This edition published 2018

Printed and bound in Great Britain by Clays Ltd, St Ives Plc

A CIP catalogue record for this book is available from the British Library.

ISBN 978-1-911427-07-0

To Gary for his love and unfailing support
and to my parents
for not being the Coulsons.

1

It's 7.00pm and we're sitting around the dinner table. There's me, my brother, my sister and my mum and dad. I'm the youngest. My dad likes us to eat together in the evenings so we can 'catch up', and 'talk about our days'.

We're eating chicken Kievs with new potatoes, carrots and peas. I have extra carrots as it's a Tuesday and Tuesdays are a good day for orange foods. I don't have any potatoes as I don't eat starch and protein together.

The chicken Kievs are pre-made. Mum doesn't cook much. To her, this is cooking. There's five of us and, because you have to buy the chicken Kievs in twos, there's one left over. It sits on a plate in the middle of the table. We're already eyeing it up. Probably my mum will offer it to my dad who will either give it to my sister because she's his favourite, or he'll suggest my brother and sister split it because my brother's a little skinny, and he needs the sustenance. Either way, it's unlikely I'll get it. I'm the smallest and the youngest, and a girl, so it's assumed I don't need a second chicken Kiev, or even a half, even though I don't have any potatoes.

We're eating in the kitchen. It used to be the garden until my parents had the extension built two years ago. Before that we had a smaller kitchen and ate at a dining table at the back of the living room. Now we have a big kitchen, all fake oak cabinets painted green, with a large square table in the middle. There's a new television that hangs on the wall in the corner by the kitchen doors that open out into the garden that's now slightly smaller because the kitchen's bigger. *I waited ten years for this kitchen,* my mum always says when anyone comes to the house for the first time.

We've lived in the house for thirteen and a half years, exactly the same amount of time that I've been alive. We moved when Mikey was two, so he doesn't remember the old house but Sarah does. We call Michael Mikey. Dad still calls him Michael, or Mike, because he thinks it's more masculine. He's never said this but I know that's why. Mum was the one who first called him Mikey. Most of the time now Dad forgets and calls him Mikey too.

My mum had my brother and sister close together. She was very happy to have a girl and a boy. It's what she'd always wanted. Only then I came along. I was 'a happy accident', which is what Mum said when I asked her why they decided to have me as well.

Dad isn't eating much, which is unusual. My dad's a P.E. teacher and, like Mikey, he also needs sustenance. He works at our school which is unfortunate, although he tries not to embarrass us. It's mostly Sarah who gets embarrassed. She looks the other way if she ever sees him in the corridor. Sarah doesn't have to do P.E. anymore because she's in the sixth form. Mikey doesn't have to do that much P.E. because he's doing his GCSEs and he doesn't like sport. In fact, none of us like sport very much which is a shame for Dad.

Dad clears his throat and puts his knife and fork down. 'There's something I've got to tell you all,' he says.

This is it, I think. They're getting divorced. Sarah and Mikey stop eating. I know they are both thinking this too. The reason we are all thinking this is because Dad has been sleeping on the sofa for the last three weeks. At first when we found him there he'd tried to come up with excuses. *I was snoring. Your mother couldn't sleep,* or *I wanted to stay up and watch television.* After a few days of this he gave up with the excuses and we got used to seeing the spare single duvet folded up neatly on the sofa arm in the mornings. It had one of Mikey's old duvet covers on it. The one with the frogs.

It's difficult to tell as our parents both work full time and often these dinner gatherings are the only time we see them together, but I'm pretty sure they aren't even talking to each other anymore. For the first few days after Dad started sleeping on the sofa, Mum had looked mad, and a little shocked. Then she'd just looked normal again like a prisoner who, after the initial few days in her cell, has come to accept her fate.

Dad looks down at his chicken Kiev. For some reason we all look at Mum. She puts down her knife and fork and takes a small sip of water. I can't tell what she's thinking.

'Are you getting a divorce?' Sarah asks.

'We're having a trial separation,' Dad says. 'With a view to permanent,' he adds, just to make sure we've all got it.

Sarah drops her knife and fork onto her plate. 'I knew it! This is so unfair!'

This is typical of Sarah, ever the drama queen and always thinking of herself. She's seventeen but often behaves as if she's seven. Mum says it's hormones. That's what she told me when Sarah was fourteen and she pushed me down the stairs because she thought I'd used her hairbrush and given her nits. *She's going through a difficult time. She's hormonal. You need to be patient, Lou.* I have been patient my entire life. We've all been patient. Sarah's mood has never improved. *It's a phase,* Dad says. In my opinion Sarah's moods aren't a phase, more of a personality malfunction.

Mikey looks really upset. Mum puts her hand on his shoulder. 'We all still love you very much.' She says this like it's something she's read in *Psychologies* magazine. 'Some people just love other people too now.' She glares at Dad.

This is something new. We all look at Dad. He looks uncomfortable.

'You might as well tell them, Eric. They'll find out soon enough. Better Sarah hears it from you first.'

Sarah's wide-eyed. 'What's this got to do with *me*?'

Dad coughs. 'We're all adults,' he says, glancing at me. 'Well, nearly all. The truth is I've been seeing someone else. Now, I don't want you to think this person is the *cause* of your mother and I's - trial separation.'

Mum makes a snorting sound like a horse.

'She's a very special person, and I'm sure you'll all come to like her very much.'

'She's a school girl,' Mum says, carving a small piece of chicken Kiev and popping it into her mouth.

Dad sighs. 'She's in the sixth form. The year above Sarah.' He can't seem to look at any of us. 'It's legal,' he says as if this was the first thing that entered our heads. 'Perfectly legal. She's eighteen. In fact, this she's leaving school this summer.'

'What?' Sarah says. 'Sorry. Is this a joke?'

'Our school?' Mikey asks.

Dad nods. 'Yes,' he says, answering Mikey's question.

I look around the table. Dad and Mikey are staring at the tablecloth. Sarah looks as though someone's slapped her in the face. Mum's the only one still eating, calmly carving chicken Kiev and cutting little circles of carrot in half.

'You had an affair with a student?' I say, feeling I need to clarify this point. Legal or not, to me, this all sounds pretty controversial. My dad is not controversial.

Dad frowns. 'I'm entering into a new relationship. A new phase of my life. I do hope, in time, that you'll all be happy for me.'

'Who is she?' Sarah whispers.

Dad clears his throat. 'Her name's Kaylee. Kaylee Deal.'

'Kaylee Deal!' Sarah screams. 'That's gross! That's totally fucking gross. I mean - she's *hairy*!'

Dad doesn't deny this and I know he must be feeling pretty bad because he doesn't tell Sarah off for her use of bad language.

I try to think who this person is, this hairy person, but I can't get an image. I wonder if Sarah's ever brought her home for dinner. I expect she hasn't. You don't usually call your friends hairy, and Sarah's very particular over who she associates with in the sixth form as it's important for her to be popular. This is not something we have in common. In fact, for two people born to the same parents who have been forced to share living accommodation for the last thirteen and a half years, we have very little in common.

Mikey looks worried. 'Does anyone know?' he asks.

'Not too many people yet,' Dad says. 'We were trying to keep it quiet until she's finished school. For obvious reasons.'

'Do her parents know?' I ask, trying to picture it from their point of view. Perhaps they'll be totally fine about it. Chilled. Perhaps they're chilled people who let boys stay over at the house and tell the school that Kaylee's sick when they want to take a week off to go on holiday when it's cheaper. Perhaps they smoke a little cannabis at the weekends and have always encouraged the mild use of substance abuse so that Kaylee and her brothers and sisters, if she has any, don't get hooked on weed and destroy their brains before they're twenty-three. Perhaps, I think, they can only blame themselves.

'No, but... She's planning on telling them. Soon.'

I wonder how this all started, then I decide I'd rather not know. I can't help but think of the P.E. equipment cupboard next to Dad's office.

Sarah bursts into tears. Dad looks distressed. Mum pats Sarah's shoulder as if to say, *You think you've got it bad. Welcome to the real world, sweetheart.*

It's difficult to feel sorry for my mum because she married my dad, but still I wonder how she'll cope with this. She seems to be taking it all in her stride, like Dad had announced he'd decided to take up match box collecting or something. I look at her closely. Her eyes seem a little glazed. I wonder if she's back on the Diazepam. I know she's taken anti-depressants as I have seen them in the bathroom cabinet. Sometimes Mum feels depressed and overwhelmed with her life. When this happens she goes into the doctor's office and cries and he gives her drugs. I know this as when I was younger she used to have to take me in with her. The doctor used to give me a lollipop and pat me on the shoulder and say, *Take good care of her.*

'How will this affect our lives?' Mikey asks.

'Are you having a mid-life crisis?' I ask Dad.

Dad ignores me and turns to Mikey. 'We both intend to make sure our new situation doesn't affect your lives any more than it has to. It's a positive change for me. It won't affect you.' He looks down at his chicken. 'I have to do this,' he says firmly, as if justifying it to himself.

Of course it will affect our lives, I think.

'Why are you telling us now?' I ask. 'Why didn't you wait until she'd left school?'

Dad scratches his head. 'That was the original plan. Only we were seen.'

'Seen?' I say.

'Yes. Seen. Together.'

Clearly this is all the information we're going to get. I think once again of the P.E. equipment cupboard. Perhaps they were caught when someone went looking for a shuttlecock. Perhaps they were seen holding hands by the bike sheds or passing notes to each other during assembly.

Sarah finally stands, pushing back her chair so it screeches across the new tiles. Mum winces.

'I'm *never* speaking to you again,' Sarah says to Dad. She leaves the room and we all listen to her footsteps on the stairs and then, the slamming of her bedroom door.

Dad tries to smile at Mikey and me. 'She'll be all right in a few days,' he says helping himself to the last chicken Kiev. 'She'll come round.'

No one believes him.

NEWS TRAVELS FAST and, by Friday, everyone at school knows about Dad and Kaylee Deal. Everyone in the sixth form anyway although I'm sure the scandal is traveling downwards as I'm given some funny looks at break time.

I long ago developed a method for survival at school. It's quite simple really. Never make eye contact. If someone calls your name or calls you *a* name, don't ever look up. Pretend you're deaf, blind, dumb, whatever the occasion calls for. Never react. If someone pushes your books out of your hands in the corridor, look the other way. Bend down very slowly and collect them, still looking the other way. Do it as if it happens to you all the time. If you get kicked when you're down, stay down. Don't react. Pretend it didn't happen. Pretend you didn't feel anything. Eventually they'll get bored and move away. If they think they can't hurt you, they won't hurt you.

This is how I survive the looks at break time and why I pretend I've heard nothing when a boy in Year Ten shouts in my ear by the soft drinks machine, 'Your dad's having sex with Kaylee Deal!'

I'm on my way to the toilets at lunchtime when I see Sarah and her friends. The girls here go to the toilets in packs. I prefer to go it alone and go as little as possible. Most of the time there's a crowd of girls around the mirror, some applying lipstick, others texting or plucking each other's eyebrows. I've never plucked my eyebrows. I'm working towards a uni-brow so that I can look moody and interesting, and perhaps slightly threatening, like the Mexican painter Frida Kahlo, although so far it hasn't really happened. My eyebrows are too light in colour, and they refuse to grow.

The toilets always smell of either cheap celebrity endorsed perfume or cannabis. Of course sometimes they just smell of shit. Mum tells me off for stating the obvious. She also says I'm too literal. *You always state the obvious Lou. You always say what everyone's thinking but should never be said. You were always embarrassing me when you were little.*

You never know quite what you're going to enter into

when you go to the toilet at school, which is why I also adopt the 'avoid eye contact' rule. I've witnessed a fight, an assault, a girl standing next to the sink with a pregnancy test crying, and once a girl trying to escape through a window. She appeared to have got stuck and was shouting to a boy called 'Tubz' on the other side to pull her through.

I'm on my way in when I spot Sarah and her followers on their way out. Sarah has a group of friends. There's about five or six of them, sometimes more. I don't know how it works, but it seems to me that they have a leader. I don't think they elect a leader, it just sort of happens. The leader decides who's in and who's out and the other girls follow her around. Every few months it changes and another one of the group, whoever's in favour for some reason or another, becomes the leader. Recently I've noticed it's Sarah who seems to have taken over the position.

'Come on girls,' I've heard her say in the corridors to the others. She herds them through, kind of like a sheepdog.

Today she's linking arms with one of the girls, a large-chested red-haired girl called Ruby who everyone knows had sex with her second cousin when she was fifteen. The others are following close behind them.

'What are you going to do?' One of the girls whispers to Sarah as they walk past me.

'I probably won't ever speak to him again,' Sarah says nonchalantly.

I assume she's talking about Dad.

They pass me by. Sarah pretends she hasn't seen me which is fine with me.

Once I'm out of the toilet, I join the burger queue.

There was an incentive a few years ago to supply kids with healthy school meals; a campaign by a local chef. It didn't really catch on at our school, although you can get salad as well as chips now. I've seen the dinner ladies throwing away the limp lettuce at the end of the lunch break. Sometimes I make my own lunch as I like to save my dinner money for 'important purchases' but there wasn't much in the fridge this morning. It'll have to be a burger although, because I don't eat starch and protein together, sometimes I eat the burger and sometimes I eat the bun. Today it's the bun.

I put the burger wrapped in greaseproof paper onto a green tray and scan the hall for somewhere to sit.

I often eat alone which is considered a little weird. This doesn't bother me. To be honest I don't have many friends. I find people intense. I prefer to observe from a distance rather than communicate directly. I do have one friend, Sam, but he's off sick today. He's often off sick. He has a fragile immune system. He's allergic to pretty much everything, which can be awkward.

I finish my lunch and reluctantly throw the burger part away. If it's a day when I eat the burger, I'll wrap the bun back in the greaseproof paper and keep it in my blazer pocket until home time so I can feed it to the ducks. I've never fed the ducks the burger. I'm not sure if ducks should eat cow. It doesn't seem like the natural order of things.

After lunch I head back to my locker to collect my books for the afternoon. I have a bottom locker which means I get trampled on four or five times a day. I squeeze my way in through a tangle of legs and try not to look up anyone's skirt. The boy to the upper left of me drops a football on my head.

Whether you get a top or bottom locker is all down to luck. Top or bottom, there's no in-between. A little like life. I've had a bottom locker two years in a row. They don't have lockers in sixth form. They're allowed to carry their bags around with them. Sarah had a top locker for her entire five years of locker ownership. Sarah can be quite intimidating. My guess is that she made someone swap with her.

I have maths, followed by religious studies. I'm in top set for most subjects. This isn't because I'm particularly clever. I'm not a child prodigy or anything. The fact that I'm in top set is more because I'm conscientious. I apply myself. I also like being in top set because the kids in the classroom are generally nicer. They're too busy trying to please their parents and get a good report so they'll earn a trip to *Chessington World of Adventures* at half term to notice anyone else.

I hate theme parks. They're on my list of things I hate which includes: noodles (difficult to eat) dentists (very invasive) balloons (you never know when they're going to pop) escalators (difficult to get on and off) and the colour purple. Not the book, *The Color Purple,* which is actually very good, just the colour.

In religious studies we get to watch a film about Jesus Christ starring Mel Gibson. Our teacher, Miss Briggs, sits at her desk texting. She's holding the phone under the desk as if, by doing this, we won't notice she's texting. I'm pretty sure she's got relationship trouble, that she feels too depressed to teach us today, and that's why we're watching the film about Jesus Christ starring Mel Gibson.

Miss Briggs is wearing her old Timberland boots again which is bad news. Miss Briggs has short hair and she used to always wear baggy sweatshirts with leggings and Timberland boots, except on parents' evening when she'd wear a pair of trousers and put a suit jacket over the sweatshirt. Someone obviously told her to dress up. A few weeks ago she got her hair done. She started wearing proper trousers, new sweatshirts, shiny black boots with a small heel. I think that's what happens when you fall in love. You think, *this person's interested in me?* Instead of thinking, *well so they should be,* you think, *Why?* and then, *they could leave me.* So you make more of an effort with your appearance, and then they leave you anyway.

I study Miss Briggs carefully. Along with the Timberland boots, she's wearing her oldest sweatshirt. Her eyes are red and she's got little pieces of hair sticking up behind her ears. It's definitely over. For a moment I feel sorry for her. I wonder if she realises she's showing a DVD with an eighteen certificate to a class of thirteen and fourteen year-olds.

When I arrive home from school Mikey's the only one in. He's wiping something white and powdery off the kitchen worktops. The sink is full of washing up. Mum's usually home early on a Friday but there's no sign she's been in. There definitely wouldn't be washing up in the sink if Mum was home already. She's probably at the hairdresser's. That's usually where she is if she's ever late home on a Friday, although she did say that next time she went she'd take me with her so I could get my fringe trimmed. My fringe grows quickly and I keep having to flick it out of my eyes by jerking my head in a way that makes me look like I've got a nervous twitch. Mum has long hair like Sarah. Brown and shiny. Sarah's dyed hers now. She has stripy highlights which remind me of a jungle animal. My hair only reaches my shoulders. It's a sort of lightish brown colour. The colour of a rich tea biscuit when you dip it in a cup of tea. It's a bob, although 'bob' indicates a style. I don't have style.

'What are you doing?' I ask. It's unusual to see Mikey in the kitchen. He's usually upstairs in his room, watching music videos by female divas on his laptop.

'Baking,' he says.

'For Home Economics class?'

'No, just because.'

He goes to the oven and peers through the door. I stand next to him and we both stare at the tray of rising fairy cakes.

'You can have one,' he says. 'When they're done.'

'Thanks,' I say.

I notice a pile of cookbooks on the kitchen table. Library books. He must have taken out the whole section. A shame for anyone else who wanted to bake a cake this weekend. I study the top three on the pile. Mary Berry's *Baking Bible,* Nigella Lawson, *How to be a Domestic Goddess* and *Saved by Cake,* Marian Keyes.

Mikey's gay. I'm not mentioning this because of the cakes. That would be like associating every man who does a 'once thought of as female occupation' as being gay. That's ridiculous. But Mikey is gay. No one knows. I'm not even sure if Mikey himself knows. I'm pretty sure Mum suspects and is secretly pleased. If Dad suspects he tries very hard to ignore it. Mikey's friends are mostly girls and, on the odd occasion Mickey brings them round to the house, after they've gone, Dad says things like, 'Popular with the ladies, Michael!'

Dad hoped Mikey would be sporty. He hoped we'd all

be sporty. Sarah's on the school netball team but she's not very good. They only took her because she's tall and all her friends come to watch the matches if she's in them so it looks like our school supports team sport. Actually, the boys just want to stare at Sarah's legs.

I'm not at all sporty. I don't see the point of it. Also I don't like taking my glasses off as I can't see very well without them and sport is usually a dangerous occupation for people who wear glasses, although tennis players seem to manage. They often wear designer sunglasses. I expect they don't have much choice. They need the sponsor money.

Dad used to take Mikey to football matches with him when he was younger, to the family seats where there's supposed to be less swearing, only there isn't. When he was very little Mikey would fall asleep. When he was older, he'd listen to his iPod. Dad gave up in the end. He took Sarah for a while when Mikey was a baby. She only went for the free hotdog at half-time. Sarah likes junk food.

Dad never took me to watch the football. I can't even catch a ball. When we play rounders at school I always opt to be a fielder. This means I go very far away, stand on my own at the bottom of the school playing-field and pray the ball doesn't come my way.

I think I might have something called dyspraxia, or a mild form of it. It's never been officially diagnosed. It took me a long time, when I was little, to learn how to use a knife and fork. I always used to hold the fork in a funny way. It also took me a long time to learn how to hold a pencil properly, and I have terrible co-ordination. I'm always bumping into things which may be partly because I don't see very well or partly because of the undiagnosed dyspraxia. It was my primary school teacher, Miss Wright, who said to Mum. *I think Louise might be dyspraxic,* as if it explained everything. Mum mentioned it to the doctor who said, *Probably. We can send her for tests if you like.* Mum said no, it was okay. She was always against putting us through any kind of unnecessary trauma. She considered herself the ultimate un-pushy parent, or perhaps she just had other things on her mind. This is why I didn't take the eleven plus and why I don't go to a better school. *Your father and I don't like the thought of the unnecessary strain it will place on you.*

I know that there are other ways in which I am different to other people. A lot of things make me anxious, and sometimes when I get anxious I scratch myself or I can't breathe or speak, and sometimes I am even sick. When this happens it means I am having a meltdown. Most of the time it doesn't come to that because I am usually able to find somewhere safe where I can be quiet. I am a person who likes to spend a lot of time by myself and I am rarely bored. I like to spend a lot of time by myself because I find it difficult to talk to other people, especially more than one person at a time and especially if I don't know them very well.

I guess it's a shame for my dad that none of us are sporty. I wonder if Kaylee Deal is sporty. Perhaps she represents the daughter he never had. That's too gross even to think about.

The kitchen smells like cake. It's a comforting smell. Mum used to bake cakes when we were little, bread sometimes too. She gave up baking when she went back to work full-time. The smell in the kitchen reminds me of rainy days and birthday parties. I like birthdays but I never liked birthday parties very much when I was younger because they were always noisy and confusing. I find a lot of life noisy and confusing. But I do like cake.

The alarm on Mikey's phone goes off and he reaches for the oven gloves. He takes the cakes out then carefully slides each one onto a ready prepared cooling tray. We both admire them. I can tell he's pleased.

'They look great,' I say.

'I've got to decorate them yet.' He reaches into a Lakeland bag. He lines the cake decorating things up on the kitchen worktop like he's about to perform surgery.

'When did you go to Lakeland?' I ask.

'Mail order,' he says. 'Dad's PayPal.'

I leave him to his cakes.

Upstairs I sit on my bed and stare at the poster I have blu-tacked to the back of my bedroom door of the three-toed sloth. I bought it from the zoo. There were more posters of the three-toed sloth left in the box than any of the other animals. *Are you sure you don't want the panda?* Mum had said. I liked the sloth.

In fact, I like most animals, although I have more interest in some than others. I particularly like farm animals and animals that are native to the British Isles, especially small mammals.

The three-toed sloth is not native to the British Isles which is why I saw it in the zoo. The three-toed sloths are tree-living mammals that can be found in central and South America. I have never been to central or South America. The furthest I have ever been is Lanzarote on holiday with my family three years ago where I reluctantly rode a camel. The three-toed sloths are quite ugly, but it should be remembered that this is not their fault.

I always keep my bedroom tidy. It's the smallest room in the house after the downstairs loo. It's also probably the tidiest. I have a blue clock on my wall that glows in the dark so I always know what time it is. I have a single bed pushed against the window to make room for my wardrobe, chest of drawers, and a very small desk. I don't keep any things on the desk apart from my laptop which is quite old now as it used to be Dad's. I have one desk drawer and I use this for storing my pencil case and school books when they're not in my bag. I have a plain coloured duvet cover and I only sleep on one pillow as I think two is excessive. On top of my chest of drawers I keep my hairbrush and my glasses case. I like things to be in order.

Apart from the three-toed sloth I have one other poster. It's a framed ABC Railway Timetable from the 1950s. I like timetables, especially train timetables, and I like trains too. I like to lie in bed and look at all the times and all the routes and destinations and think about all the trains leaving and approaching the stations and running perfectly on time.

These are the only posters I have, unlike Sarah whose walls are covered with band posters from magazines and photographs of her and her friends.

Sarah's room is the most untidy. I haven't been inside Sarah's room for years. Mum's the only one who braves it now. She tentatively steps inside once a month to empty Sarah's wastepaper basket and change the sheets on the bed. I don't think any of us have seen Sarah's carpet since she was twelve. It's covered with clothes, make-up, DVDs, school books, electric hairstyling equipment, bags and shoes. I only know this because I sometimes catch a glimpse of the room when Sarah opens the door.

Mum does force her to hoover every now and then. I

think Sarah pushes the mess to the edges of the room and hoovers the middle square of carpet. Recently Mum seems to have given up. *We'll have a big clear out when you go to university,* she says.

Mikey's room isn't half so bad. In fact, for a teenage boy he's pretty tidy.

Mum and Dad have the new bedroom over the kitchen. Sarah has the bedroom that Mum and Dad used to have and Mikey has the middle size bedroom.

The house is an average nineteen thirties semi with an arched porch and a bay window. Nothing exceptional.

After a while I hear the front door close. I go and see who's come in. Dad's sitting on the stairs taking his trainers off. He's wearing shorts. Dad always wears shorts, even in the winter. Sometimes he comes home with his whistle still round his neck.

He swivels round to look at me. 'Where's your mother?' he asks.

'She's not in,' I say.

'What's that smell?'

'Cake.'

He stands, sniffing the air. 'Sarah baking?'

I shake my head. 'Mikey.'

Dad frowns then, as if remembering something, he turns back to me. 'Good day at school?' he asks.

'Sure,' I say. 'Fine.'

My days at school usually fall into two categories. Tolerable or bad. I don't talk about school much to my parents.

The landline rings and Dad goes to answer. He lifts the phone off the cradle and stands next to it. Sometimes Dad does this. He forgets that phones aren't attached to a cord anymore and that you can move around with them.

'Where?' I hear him say. And then, 'She what?' He

looks puzzled. He listens for a moment. 'It's a mistake,' he says.

I creep further down the stairs.

I watch his expression change as whoever is on the phone continues to talk to him. 'Yes,' he says, and then, 'I see.' There's more talk at the other end of the line. 'Of course,' he says finally. 'I'll come now.'

He hangs up and stares at the phone.

'Who was that?' I say.

'Debenhams,' he says.

I'm not quite sure what he means as Debenhams is a department store and not a person.

'They want me to come and get her,' he says.

'Who?' I say.

Dad looks at me. 'Debenhams. They want me to come and get your mother. They caught her shoplifting.'

We both look at each other. For a moment I think one of us might laugh and I wonder which one of us it will be. The moment passes.

'They've made a mistake,' I say.

Dad shakes his head slowly, as if considering. 'I've got to go,' he says. He grabs his car keys and opens the door. He remembers that he's taken his trainers off. He picks them up and tries to put them on standing up for speed, hopping from one side of the hallway to the other. He leans against the wall. He looks confused.

'I'll come with you,' I say, darting past him and grabbing my shoes. I hate department stores and usually avoid them but this feels like an emergency.

'Perhaps that's a good idea,' Dad says, opening the front door. 'I'm not your mother's favourite person right now.' He shakes his head again. 'There must have been a mistake.'

2

It's a ten minute drive into the town centre, including parking, although the rush hour traffic slows us down a little. We live on the edge of an average size town. It takes approximately thirty -five minutes to travel on the train into London and lots of people commute to work. We have all the usual things in our town, a swimming pool, an ice rink, a cinema, a large park with an old country house that's used for weddings. We also have a museum with a stuffed Russian bear in it. Dad used to take Mikey and me to the museum on Saturday mornings whilst Mum went shopping. I liked the bear and Mikey liked the bees. There's a glass hive in the museum called a 'Living Honeybee Observation Hive' where you can watch all the bees going about their bee business and try and find the queen who is marked with a red dot.

Mikey has always liked bees. He knows lots of bee facts, like bees in flight beat their wings around 200 times a second, that they have an excellent sense of smell, and that the worker bees do a funny waggle dance to tell each other when they've found a good flower.

I sit next to Dad in the front seat of the car. 'Are you and Mum having a financial crisis?' I ask. 'Are you in debt? Why does Mum need to steal?'

'No, no, and I don't know,' Dad says staring straight ahead of him. He looks very worried.

We drive around to the back of the store.

'I'm sure it will be all right for me to park here,' Dad

says driving under a tunnel and parking next to a row of large bins. Dad hates paying for parking.

We enter through the back entrance on the ground floor by 'Men's Sleepwear'. It's near closing time and the shop is quiet, just a few stragglers finalising their purchases, and one or two members of staff tidying the rails.

'What do we do now?' Dad asks.

We walk to the front of the store, towards the cosmetics. A woman wearing pink lipstick is counting cash behind a desk.

'Excuse me,' I say. 'Can you call security for us?'

The woman looks from me to Dad. 'Have you found an unidentifiable package?' she asks.

'No,' I say. 'They've got my Mum.'

Dad nods in agreement.

The woman looks suspiciously at us. She slowly shuts the cash register, locks it, then pockets the key. She goes over to the perfumes where there's a phone fixed to a supporting pillar. She scans a printed list of numbers that's blu-tacked to the wall next to the phone. Glancing at us to make sure we're still here, she picks up the phone and dials.

'Barry, it's Julie from Beauty. There's people down here asking for security.' She covers the receiver. 'What did you say your name was?' she calls to us.

'Coulson,' Dad says.

'Cool-son,' Julie says returning to the phone. 'Sure.' She hangs up.

'He's coming to get you.' Julie returns to the cosmetics counter. 'You can wait by the escalator.'

When we get to the escalator Barry's already waiting for us. I'm not sure how he got there so quickly. He's wearing black jeans and a navy T-shirt. He must work undercover. The only visible sign he's a security officer is the flashing walkie talkie he holds in his hand.

He nods to us. 'Come with me,' he says, stepping onto the escalator. I jump on behind him. I hate escalators. They make me feel wobbly, especially when getting on and off.

We follow Barry up the escalator and then past various concessions of women's clothing. Barry opens a door for us that leads to a long corridor. A tall, slim teenage boy is pushing a rail of clothes with red tags marked SALE. The rail has a piece of paper sellotaped to it that someone has printed from a printer where the black ink is running out. It reads: BOGOF.

Barry turns to us. 'Has this happened before?'

Dad shakes his head. 'The first time.'

'Guess there's a first time for everything,' Barry says.

We reach the end of the corridor. We pass a locker area. I glance past an open door and see a large room filled with metal tables. There are six or seven chairs around each table and piles of magazines in the middle. A member of staff sits at one of the tables eating sandwiches wrapped in tin-foil and staring at his mobile phone. He glances up at us as we pass. I guess that this must be the 'eating your lunch' area. Perhaps the man didn't have time to eat his sandwiches at lunch time.

I like sandwiches a lot. Cheese and pickle are my favourite.

We follow Barry down some steps. He opens a door to a small room. The first thing I notice is that one of the walls is filled with TV screens. The screens are all showing black and white pictures of different areas of the shop. There's a desk in front of the TVs and two empty chairs. It reminds me of when you watch those traffic programs and you see the people who watch the screens all day from the cameras on all the different roads. Only they're watching for accidents, congestion and for people breaking the speed limit, not shoplifters.

The second thing I notice is Mum. She's sitting on a chair. One of her hands has been handcuffed to a rail. There's a pile of dresses on her lap that she's holding tightly onto with the other hand.

There's another man standing next to Mum. He has the same walkie talkie as Barry, only in a holder on his belt. He's taller than Barry, fatter too.

'Is that really necessary?' Dad asks, referring to the handcuffs.

'It was for her own protection,' Barry replies. 'And ours.'

'I thought it wouldn't be long before *you* turned up,' Mum says to Dad, reminding me of a princess in a satirical fairy story who refuses to be rescued by the prince.

'Hi, Mum,' I say.

'We have to get out of here.' She whispers to me as if no one else can hear. 'It isn't safe.'

Everyone stares at Mum, or rather at the person sitting in the chair handcuffed to the rail. I'm not sure what they've done with her, but the woman sitting on the chair handcuffed to the rail isn't my mum. Sure, the outer shell is there but the rest of her has gone. My mum doesn't shoplift or say things that only a crazy person would say. My mum makes sure we've got clean clothes and lunch, or at least lunch money. She pays the bills and does the food shopping and hoovers every Sunday morning while listening to Radio 4.

'Usually in these circumstances we'd hand her over to the police but...' Barry glances at the second security guard. 'It was clear to us, when we picked her up, that she wasn't quite - in the right state of mind.'

Dad stares at Mum who looks unfazed. 'Call the police?' he says. 'Surely you can see there must be some sort of mistake here. My wife isn't a teenager, for goodness sake. She doesn't *steal*.'

Mum looks from Dad to the security guards. 'I was told to do it,' she says. 'All the signs were there. They know everything. They were watching. They're *all* watching.'

'With all due respect, Mr Coulson, a great many shoplifters are middle-aged women.'

'Not this one,' Dad says. 'She's a civil servant.'

Barry shrugs. 'It takes all sorts.'

Mum makes no reaction at all to the 'middle-aged' comment which confirms to me her unusual state of mind.

The second security guard steps forward. 'She hasn't made any sense since she's been here. Does she have a history of mental illness?'

Dad shakes his head. 'No.'

This is a small lie and I am not comfortable with lies but I realise they are sometimes necessary so I stay quiet.

The two security guards exchange glances. 'Is she on her period?' Security Man Two asks.

Dad looks to me and I make a gesture as if to say, *How would I know*?

'I don't know,' Dad says.

'Shouldn't you?' Barry asks.

'Dad's sleeping on the sofa,' I say helpfully.

Dad rubs his head in that way he does when he's getting stressed.

Barry ignores me. 'Is she going through the change?'

he asks, nodding towards Mum who's staring at her handcuffed hand as if she hadn't notice it before.

'I don't think so,' Dad says. 'I haven't noticed any change.'

Barry frowns.

Mum tries to get up causing the handcuffs to knock against the rail. 'I need to go now,' she says. 'We've all been here long enough. Got to keep moving. It confuses them.'

'We're happy to let her go, if you'll take her?' Barry asks us, as if we might refuse. 'We'll keep an eye out for her - in the store. If it happens again...'

'It won't happen again,' Dad says. 'She must not be feeling well. You're right - she isn't herself.'

Security Man Two undoes Mum's handcuffs. She stands there rubbing her wrist, still holding the clothes.

'We'll need those.' Barry reaches out for the clothes but Mum moves away, clutching them to her.

'Maybe you should give them the clothes, Mum,' I say, like I'm talking to a child. 'Then we can leave. Mikey's made fairy cakes.'

Mum looks from me to Barry and then reluctantly hands the clothes over.

'That's it,' Dad says, playing along. 'We'll come shopping another time.'

'There may not be another time,' Mum says.

We follow Barry as he leads us back up the steps, down the escalator, and out of the store. He has to find someone to let us out as they've locked up already. Julie from Beauty has disappeared.

'Good luck.' Barry says to us, as if we might need it.

When we get to the car there's a delivery lorry blocking us in. We have to wait twenty minutes before the driver's finished unloading.

The three of us wait in the car. Mum gets in the back as if we're a taxi. We can see inside the loading area. The delivery man is standing around with a couple of staff members drinking a cup of tea.

Mum's the only one who speaks. 'I knew they'd try and pull a stunt like this,' she says, to no one in particular.

Eventually we're able to leave. The delivery driver glances at us and shakes his head as he gets into his cab.

'She'll be fine. Just fine,' Dad whispers to me once we're driving away. I think this is an attempt to reassure me. 'This sort of thing used to happen to my aunt Dorothy,' he says, gripping the wheel.

'What happened to her?' I ask.

Dad hesitates. 'She was fine, just fine.'

Mum sits quietly in the back not saying anything.

I reach for my phone and google *BOGOF*. It stands for Buy One Get One Free. Then I google *Is madness hereditary?* If it is, I've got no chance, especially if it's on both sides.

'Do they have sprinkles?' Mum says suddenly, breaking the silence.

'What?' Dad says.

'The fairy cakes. Do they have sprinkles?'

When we get home Dad has to explain to Sarah and Mikey that Mum isn't feeling well. Mum sits at the kitchen table eating her fairy cake. She nibbles it slowly, savouring it. She's enjoying the sprinkles.

For reasons that no one can work out, Mum decides she doesn't want to sleep in the bedroom. Mikey and I try to make the sofa as comfortable as we can for her. Dad takes the frog duvet upstairs. 'It's better down here,' Mum says. 'They watch from the telegraph pole, you know.'

Before bed, I go into the kitchen to get a glass of water and find Dad looking through the cutlery drawers. He's rummaging around as if he's lost something. He has the knife block tucked under his arm. 'I think I'll take these up with me tonight,' he says, referring to the knife block and the other sharp objects he's recovered from the back of the drawer; a tin opener, a vegetable peeler and a pair of scissors.

'Okay,' I say, as if this is perfectly normal.

Dad's mobile next to Mikey's baking books on the kitchen table starts beeping. He glances guiltily at his phone and I wonder if it's Kaylee. Do they text? I guess they must do.

Dad puts down the knife block, pockets his phone, then picks up the block again. 'Night then,' he says, walking off with all the sharp objects.

'Night,' I say.

I WAKE IN the night to the smell of burning. I'm very sensitive to smells. When I go downstairs to investigate the smell, there is a fire in the living room.

It's only a small fire but even so, it's disturbing. Mum's standing in the middle of the room in her pyjamas. She's pulling photographs out of an album, cutting them in half with a pair of tiny nail scissors and throwing the pieces into the large saucepan she usually uses for making winter stew. She's made a fire inside the saucepan. The flames are quite high and there's a lot of smoke. Mum has a box of matches poking out of the top pocket of her pyjamas. She's lit several candles and placed them around the room. The fire, the candles and the way Mum is methodically cutting up the photographs and throwing them onto the flames is very creepy. She stops to stir the ash in the bottom of the pan with a soup ladle. Her face, lit by the flames, is calm, serene. She looks like she's performing some sort of weird ritual.

'Mum!' I say, waving away the smoke from my face.

She turns to look at me. 'No need for any of these anymore,' she says, throwing a whole photograph onto the flames.

For a moment I'm not sure if I'm more distressed about the fire in our living room or that Mum's burning all our photographs. I hope Dad's backed them up. I'm not even sure if the ones from when Sarah and Mikey were little are digital.

I hear footsteps on the stairs. Mikey appears behind me.

'Shit,' he says.

'Call the fire brigade,' I say, remembering my emergency services education at primary school.

Mikey leaves the room and goes to find a phone.

I guide Mum slowly away from the fire.

I can hear Mikey talking in the hallway, giving out our address.

There is a scattering of cut photographs on the carpet that have missed the saucepan. I look at the pieces of our life on the living room floor, at all the fragments of my family. There's Sarah and me in front of a monkey at the zoo, Mikey and me outside a castle on holiday in Wales, and a very old one of Mum and Dad on a boat with Sarah strapped to Dad's chest. I recognise all the photographs. I used to like looking through the albums.

Mikey comes back into the living room. Sarah's with him. 'They're on their way,' Mikey says.

'Oh my god!' Sarah says.

'I'll get water,' Mikey says.

Mikey returns with a small plastic bucket filled with water. It's the special bucket Mum uses for hand-washing delicate clothes. Mum bought it from Lakeland. It's small enough to stand in a sink.

Mikey throws the child-size bucket of water over the saucepan. Mikey, Mum and I watch and see what happens. Sarah runs upstairs.

The flames sizzle and die. The fire is out.

Dad appears in the doorway coughing and batting at the air. 'Holy crap,' he says.

Mum's now sitting calmly on the sofa watching us. Dad glances at her then back at the saucepan.

'Mum was burning our photographs,' I say. 'Don't worry we've called the fire brigade.'

'Have you?' Dad says.

'Yes,' I say, feeling pleased with mine and Mikey's team effort.

Sarah returns wearing her favourite silk dressing gown. She's put her hair up. She takes a picture on her phone of the saucepan full of water, ash and charred photographs. 'I have to Instagram this,' she says.

I watch the fire engine arriving from the living room window. We've opened all the windows in an attempt to get rid of the smoke. The fire engine blocks the road. Two men jump out. They move quickly despite their heavy fire-fighting clothes. The outside security light comes on. I can see that there is at least one more man inside the vehicle. Where are the fire women? I think.

Sarah goes to let them in.

The two men, one youngish, one older, quickly run into the living room.

'Never walk away from scented candles,' the younger one says, glancing at the lit candles.

'It wasn't the candles.' I say. 'It was Mum, burning memories in a saucepan.'

The older one frowns. 'Use the recycling,' he says. 'A safer means of disposal.'

'Nothing's safe,' Mum says.

The older man tuts and shakes his head. 'You were lucky,' he says, surveying the damage. Now, with the living room light on, we can see what the smoke has done to the walls, ceiling and furniture. 'Is anyone hurt?' he says. 'Anyone having trouble breathing?'

We all shake our heads.

'I'm sorry,' Dad says to the firemen. 'This has never happened to us before.'

Dad seems to be apologising for a lot of things that have never happened before.

We all look at the black walls and the saucepan in the centre of the living room floor. The fireman lifts the saucepan with his gloved hand. There's a burnt patch underneath, a circle of singed carpet that smells really bad.

'Maybe we can put a rug over it,' Mikey suggests.

The younger fireman is staring at Sarah's legs.

The older one replaces the saucepan and looks at Dad. 'What alerted you to the fire,' he asks. 'Where's your smoke alarm? Do you have pets?'

'It was Lou,' Mikey says. 'She woke up first.'

'The smoke alarm's in the hallway,' I say. 'I think it must be broken. We've got an escaped hamster. He lives behind the fridge.'

The older fireman gives me a funny look.

We all go into the hallway and stare at the smoke alarm fixed to the ceiling.

Dad looks embarrassed. 'I've been meaning to buy fresh batteries.'

'I have to remind him to buy everything,' Mum says, suddenly appearing behind us. 'He always forgets the onions. You can't do anything without onions.'

'We have batteries,' I say. 'I've seen them in the drawer.'

I go to fetch the batteries from the kitchen. The drawer, for some reason, is already open. It must have been Mum when she was looking for matches. Dad should have thought about the matches, and nail scissors.

I bring the batteries into the hallway.

'Do you have a step-ladder?' The young fireman asks.

Mikey opens the door to the under-stairs cupboard. 'There's one in here,' he says.

'We'll do it for you now,' the older fireman says, giving Dad a look that clearly says: *if you can't be bothered to ensure the safety of your family, we will.*

The younger fireman takes the ladder from Mikey. I hand him the batteries. He climbs up and unscrews the alarm.

'Be careful,' Sarah says, as if it might be the most dangerous thing he's ever done.

He turns and grins at her. Sarah shyly returns his smile whilst tugging at the neck of her dressing gown to reveal a little more cleavage.

The doorbell rings and I think that it's probably the other man from the fire engine, come to see what's going on, but it isn't. It's Mrs De Souza from next door. She's wearing a large coat and slippers. She's gripping the coat tightly to her which makes me think that she probably isn't wearing anything underneath.

'What's going on?' she says as Dad opens the front door. 'Is everyone all right?' She sniffs the air and coughs.

'Are we blocking you in?' the older fireman asks.

Mrs De Souza shakes her head. 'I don't have to go

anywhere right now. It's three o'clock in the morning.' She looks up at the young fireman inserting the battery into the alarm.

'Our fire alarm was broken,' I say.

'Oh,' Mrs De Souza says, inviting herself in. 'I didn't know you could call them out for that.'

'You can't,' the older fireman says quickly.

'There was a fire in the living room,' Mikey says.

'Goodness.' Mrs De Souza covers her nose and mouth with the sleeve of her coat and peers into the living room, anxious to see the result.

Mum follows Mrs De Souza and grips her arm. 'Do you have a shredder?' she asks.

'A shredder?' Mrs De Souza looks at Mum, confused. Mum looks like she hasn't brushed her hair for week. There's a smudge of ash on her cheek.

'I think Geoff has a shredder. In the office.'

Mum lets go of Mrs De Souza and shuffles into the living room. She begins to gather up the remaining photographs from the floor. She tucks several albums under her arm. 'I'll come with you,' she says to Mrs De Souza. 'It isn't safe here anyway.'

Dad tries to gently manoeuvre Mum over to the sofa. 'Why don't you visit in the morning,' he suggests. 'Or perhaps Mrs De Souza can drop the shredder round.'

Mrs De Souza looks to me and Mikey. Mikey makes circles with his index finger next to his ear, trying to indicate that Mum's gone mad. Mrs De Souza doesn't seem to get it.

'Mum isn't feeling well,' I say.

Mr De Souza nods. She backs out of the living room, nearly colliding with the fireman in the hallway who's folding the stepladder and flirting with Sarah.

Mrs De Souza opens the front door, still clutching her coat with her free hand. 'I should go,' she says. 'I'm glad everything's okay.' She glances at Mum. 'It isn't often we have a fire engine in the street.' She steps out into the porch. She can't get away fast enough.

Once the firemen have decided there is nothing else they can do for us, they leave too. I'm pretty sure the younger one gave Sarah his number.

After they've gone we all go back into the living room. Dad picks up the saucepan and stares at the burnt patch of carpet.

Mum gets back into her sofa bed.

'Are you going to sleep in here?' I ask her. 'It's all smoky.'

'Yes,' she says. 'I am. And I'd appreciate a little privacy. We can't be too careful.'

'Come on,' Dad says to us, indicating we should go back to bed. 'The worst of it's gone. We'll leave the windows open for her. I'll pop back down later and make sure she's all right.'

'She *was* all right,' Sarah hisses at him before turning and marching up the stairs.

'What are we going to do?' I ask.

Dad sighs. 'I guess we could put a rug over the burnt patch. For a few days anyway. I'll repaint the walls and ceiling.'

Mikey stares at the smoke stains. 'We could claim the paint on the insurance. It would help if you could get a certificate - from Mum's doctor.'

'No,' I say to them. 'I mean - what are we going to do about Mum?'

'Oh,' Dad says. 'I don't know.'

'Are you going to leave Kaylee now?' I ask.

Dad shakes his head.

Mikey turns away. 'I guess I'll go back to bed then.'

THE FOLLOWING MORNING the living room door is shut. Mum must still be sleeping. I go into the kitchen. There's no milk in the fridge. This is very unusual. We rarely run out of anything in our house as Mum is usually quite organised. I look in the bread bin and discover there isn't any bread, only a plate with the fairy cakes on it. I find a bowl and take out a box of cereal. It's the cereal Dad likes. The posh one that looks like squirrel food. The one where, if you're lucky, you can win a fantastic prize just by opening your cereal box. The prize is always something like a camper van, or an acre of your own woodland. Usually you can choose to take the cash instead. *Who wouldn't take the cash?* Dad always says. And, *Where would we park a camper van?*

I find a carton of long life apple juice in the cupboard and pour it over my cereal. It actually tastes quite nice, although I'm still upset by the lack of milk. I hope it doesn't become a regular occurrence but I know I should prepare myself for the worst. After all, in the last three days my dad has admitted he's having an affair with an eighteen-year-old and is leaving us. Then Mum is caught shop-lifting in Debenhams and turns into someone who isn't my mum. Then there's a fire in our living room because the person who isn't our mum decides she has to burn all our memories. Now we're out of milk.

This sort of thing would never happen with Annabel and Neil.

I have this theory that I was swapped at birth and the child who belongs to my parents is living with Annabel and Neil whilst I have to live here. I've always thought this.

Of course I know it can't really be true because I've seen my birth certificate, and I have Dad's nose. Still, I think about Annabel and Neil a lot. It's kind of like a parallel universe, a universe where I was born to the right parents instead of the wrong ones.

Annabel and Neil are architects. They're a husband and wife team with their own practice, quite well known within their field. They weren't planning on having any children because firstly, they feel the world is over populated and there aren't enough resources to go around as it is and, secondly, their careers are very important to them. Annabel became pregnant by accident because she forgot to take her pill one morning and that's how I came to be.

Of course as soon as Annabel found out she was pregnant she told Neil and they were both really happy. I'm an only child and, although Annabel and Neil never smothered me with their affection, I always have their undivided attention. They discovered very early on how bright I was and they decided to home school me, knowing it was only way I would be able to fully express myself and learn at a speed that was best for me. I spent a lot of time around adults, Annabel and Neil's successful friends: other architects, structural engineers, property lawyers, surgeons, artists and musicians. This kind of upbringing, Annabel and Neil thought, meeting so many interesting people and being surrounded mostly by adults would ensure I grew up to be a fully rounded human being who would go on to do something interesting with her life and who would never be exposed to peer pressure or other teenagers with their many psychological problems.

I remained an only child. Annabel and Neil never wanted another baby as they were so happy with me and I never asked for a sibling. Not once. Annabel made sure she took her pill every day and there was never another mishap.

We live in a house on the edge of a loch in Scotland. I've never been to a loch in Scotland but I've always wanted to go and I know that's where Annabel and Neil built their house and that that's where we live. It's a very impressive house. Annabel and Neil designed it themselves and were involved in every decision relating to its construction. It was their baby before I was their baby. In fact, it was finished only two years before I was born.

The house has amazing views over the water which is always calm and still. We have a boat and we sometimes go out on the loch. We like to go trout fishing. Neil built this amazing model railway in our garden for us because Neil likes trains as much as I do. It's one of his hobbies, along with drawing old churches. When I was little Annabel and Neil took me on the Jacobite steam train. Neil and I often go together to Loch Morar and watch the trains come into the station.

Annabel and Neil have to travel a lot for work. They have an office at the house and we often have people to stay but sometimes they have to travel in order to see their clients. I've seen many European cities: Barcelona, Vienna, Prague, Paris and Florence. Annabel and Neil always take me with them when they travel.

Dad walks into the kitchen.

'I think we should take your mother to the doctor,' he says.

I nod in agreement. This sounds like a sensible idea.

Dad looks in the fridge. 'There's no milk.'

'There's apple juice,' I say.

'We'll pick up some milk on the way back.'

'Is Mum still asleep?'

'She's in the shower. I think I've managed to persuade her to go the surgery. She told me we'd be followed.'

'Shall I come with you?'

'I think *one* of you should. Mikey's up I think.'

'I'll come,' I say, sliding off my chair.

'All right,' Dad says. 'I'll phone the doctors, see if I can get an emergency appointment.' He disappears into the hallway.

Both Dad and I know Sarah won't go with him. Not only is she mad at Dad but she doesn't get out of bed before 1.00pm at weekends and it's only nine-thirty. I don't know how she can stay in bed for so long. I get hungry. I think she must stay up late talking to people online. We had a load of stuff posted to our address once, presents for Sarah; designer handbags, perfume, bikinis, and a framed photograph of a horse. Sarah admitted she'd been speaking to some rich forty-year old man in Texas who lived on a ranch and he'd posted her all these presents from the States. Dad made her block him on Facebook, destroying her cowgirl dreams.

Dad returns looking defeated. 'They haven't got any appointments. I spoke to the doctor. He said there isn't much they can do from the surgery. He recommended we take her straight to the hospital. He said we should pack her an overnight bag - just in case.'

'Oh,' I say. This does not sound good.

AN HOUR LATER we arrive at the hospital with Mum. We find somewhere to park. Dad reluctantly pays. We leave the vast multi-storey car park and follow the signs to

A&E. We walk past a thin lady in a red dressing-gown with her leg in a plastic cast. She asks us if we've seen her wheelbarrow and we tell her we haven't.

When we reach A&E, there's a few people standing outside the doors smoking. We walk in and take Mum straight up to the desk. We try to explain about the shoplifting and the fire in the saucepan and the strange things that Mum's been saying. The lady behind the desk gives us a form to fill in then tells us to take a seat.

Mum sits patiently. Dad asks her if she wants a magazine. She says she doesn't. I look around the waiting room and try to figure out why everyone is here. With some people it's obvious, with others it isn't.

There's an old lady with a bruised eye. She's sitting on her own and I feel sorry for her. Either she fell over or she was mugged. I hope she wasn't mugged. There are only two children in the waiting area. There's a girl, about seven or eight, wearing headphones, sitting next to her parents with a bandage over her hand. Then there's a small boy with a rash. The boy is waiting with his mum and playing a game on an iPad. He keeps letting go of the iPad with one hand to scratch his tummy. 'Don't scratch,' his mum says. 'Hold it with both hands.' I imagine that the girl with the bandage on her hand has been bitten by a guinea pig and that the boy with the rash has eaten too many tomatoes because his rash look likes the rash my friend Sam gets when he eats too many tomatoes. Nightshades are one of the food groups he can eat only in moderation.

'Won't be long now,' Dad says to us. 'I've seen it much busier than this.'

Dad occasionally has to come to A&E with pupils who have P.E. related injuries.

'I'm prepared to tell them everything I know,' Mum says.

When Mum is finally seen she goes into a room with the doctor. Dad and I wait in another room. We sit on blue chairs. I read the posters on the wall. *Breast milk is best. When you see this poster, wash your hands. Do you need the flu jab? Coughs and Sneezes Spread Diseases.* Then the doctor wants to see Dad and me alone.

'We'd like to keep her in,' she says. The doctor is a Welsh woman with long red hair and glasses. We're in another small room with a bed and three chairs.

'Will she ever be normal again?' I ask.

The doctor smiles at me. 'I should think so,' she says.

'What's wrong with her?' Dad asks.

'We believe she's having a short psychotic episode.'

'How long will this - episode - last?'

The doctor shrugs. 'Could be a few days. Could be a few weeks... We need to keep a close eye on her, help her to get better. We have a new mental health unit here at the hospital so she won't need to be transferred.'

Dad looks stressed.

'Do other people get this?' I ask.

The doctor smiles again. 'Of course. It's much more common than you might think. It's called Brief Psychotic Disorder, if you want to look it up. I must ask - can you think of any reason why this might be happening to your Mum now?'

Dad shakes his head.

'It's usually brought about by some kind of stress, or traumatic event,' she says helpfully.

'Mum and Dad are having a trial separation,' I say.

'Ah,' the doctor nods encouragingly.

'With a view to permanent. Dad's in love with an

eighteen-year old. She's called Kaylee Deal. She's in the Sixth Form.'

The doctor looks alarmed.

Dad laughs nervously as if I've made a joke. He clears his throat when he realises we're both watching him. 'Things have been a *little* tense at home,' he says.

The doctor peers at Dad over the top of her glasses. 'I see.'

'Mum decided to burn all our photographs,' I say. 'Which could be interpreted as a form of catharsis.'

The doctor looks surprised. 'Did she tell you this?'

'No,' I say. 'I formed my own conclusion.'

I know about catharsis, which is what the Ancient Greeks used to say happened when they watched a tragic play. It means a kind of cleansing that takes place after a brutal act.

The doctor looks to Dad who shrugs and makes a face as if to say. *Yes, I know she's my child but I take no responsibility for what she says or thinks.*

'Right, well…' The doctor stands. 'If you follow me I'll take you to her so you can see where she is. You can come back during visiting hours.'

Dad and I follow the doctor along various corridors then up two floors in the lift, then more corridors until we come to the Psychiatric Ward. I know it's the Psychiatric Ward because there's a large sign over the door.

'She's just through there. Second bed by the window. Ask at the desk if you need anything.' The doctor disappears, leaving us alone.

Mum's sitting up in bed, fully clothed, doing a crossword puzzle in a newspaper. 'The clues are here,' she says.

'We have to go now,' Dad tells her. 'We'll come back soon and see how you're getting on. Give us a call if you need anything.'

Mum looks up at us. 'I've hidden my phone,' she says. 'They won't find me in here.'

'Right,' Dad nods.

'Bye Mum,' I say, not entirely happy about leaving her so soon.

Mum smiles at me. 'Don't forget to do your homework.'

We leave Mum in the Psychiatric Ward and go back to the car to pay for the parking. We have to wait in a queue to insert our ticket into the machine that tells us how long we've been at the hospital and how much we have to pay. Dad looks cross.

Neither Dad or I say anything on the way home. It feels like we've left a dog at the kennels. We know it will be safe but, still, we feel guilty. We don't have a dog as Mum says it wouldn't be fair because there's no one home during the day. Annabel and Neil have a dog, a border collie called Renzo.

We take Renzo on long walks around the loch and he sometimes comes in the boat with us when we go trout fishing. Renzo's a very special dog, the sort of dog that would rescue you if you fell into a river, or alert you to danger if he found an intruder in the house. Luckily he's never had to do either of these things as I'm quite sensible around water and Annabel and Neil have an Xpander security system which detects movement using infra-red sensors.

I'm really not happy to be leaving Mum but I'm pleased to be away from the hospital. I don't like hospitals very much as they remind me of dying.

I'm very uncomfortable with the fact that I will die. I often wonder what the point of living is, if we then have to die. No one seems to be able to answer this question for me. I hope that by the time I'm old, I will have figured this out. I think of death like an annoying fruit fly you keep catching glimpses of in the kitchen but you can never seem to squash. You can forget about it most of the time, but then it appears again, just as you're about to take a bite of your sandwich.

When I was very little and I found out about dying, I became quite distressed. I used to cry and there was nothing Mum could do to console me. It used to worry her. Neither Sarah or Mikey have ever gotten quite so hysterical about their own mortality. In the end, to pacify me, Mum told me that by the time I was old they would have invented a pill to take that would mean everyone would live forever. I believed her for quite a long time. I now realise she lied.

When I went to nursery school we were read Bible stories and I asked Mum and Dad a lot of questions about heaven. Mum and Dad aren't religious and, although Mum was happy to give me false hope when it came to scientific progress, she was not willing to do so when it came to my questions about heaven and where people go when they die.

'Nowhere?' I said. *'They go nowhere?'*

'Nowhere, Lou. There's nothing after, I'm afraid. That's why we've got to make the best of this world.'

'Nothing?' I would say.

Mum would shake her head and carry on with whatever she was doing. I can see her, standing by the kitchen window, scrubbing potatoes. She looks very tall because I was much smaller then. I couldn't believe there was nothing, and even though I knew I'd never have to worry about dying because of the magic pill that was going to be invented, it still troubled me. *Nothing?*

I'm the only person I know who's been having an existential crisis since they were four years old.

I know this because I googled *What is the point of living?* and found out that people who think too much about this sort of thing are having an existential crisis.

Then I read that children who have these thoughts are more likely to be highly intellectual, gifted, or talented in some way, and that cheered me up a lot for a short amount of time.

I wonder what anyone did before the internet. When I think of a time before the internet, I imagine people wandering around in a state of confusion, or perhaps using libraries.

When we arrive home, there's an electric shredder on the doorstep. Dad picks it up then leaves it inside the hallway. The house smells like cake again. Mikey's in the kitchen wearing an apron of Mum's. There are two cakes in the oven.

'Two cakes?' I say.

'It's one cake,' Mikey says. 'Victoria sponge. I'm baking the two halves. The filling goes in the middle.'

Dad looks at the bowl of cream Mikey's whipping up. 'Did you go to the shop?' he asks, realising that we just drove straight past it.

Mikey nods. 'I got bread and milk, and a few ingredients. I used the ten pound note from behind the utensil jar.'

Dad looks at the packet of sliced bread that Mikey's left out on the counter top. 'I didn't know there was a ten pound note behind the utensil jar,' he says.

'Mum always keeps one there,' Mikey says. 'It will need replacing. It's there for emergencies.'

Dad looks as though he's going to say that Victoria sponge isn't an emergency but he changes his mind and sighs. He opens his wallet and replaces the note, tucking it behind the jar.

He opens the bread and takes out a few slices. 'I'm making a cheese and pickle sandwich,' he says. 'Does anyone want one?'

'I do.' I say. Cheese and pickle sandwiches are my favourite.

'Me too,' Mikey says.

'Where's Sarah?' Dad asks. 'Is she up?'

Mikey nods. 'She's in the living room watching *My Big Fat Gypsy Wedding* and eating Honey Nut Loops.'

'That wouldn't go well with cheese and pickle,' I say. 'And it's Honey Loops now. They dropped the nut.'

'I'll just make them for us then,' Dad says.

Dad finishes making us the sandwiches and we sit at the kitchen table eating and not saying anything to each other whilst the two cakes rise in the oven.

After lunch I decide to catch the bus into town. I do what I always do when things are a little difficult at home, or school. I go to the station to watch the trains.

I buy the cheapest ticket available, a child's ticket to the next station. I walk up the steps and onto the platform. There are only two platforms. I wait on the one where the trains go to London Liverpool Street. There's a train every fifteen minutes at this time of the day. During the week, at rush hour, they come every ten minutes.

I walk along the platform to get away from all the people who are standing close to the top of the steps. I sit down on a bench to wait for the next train. There's a man sitting at the other end of the bench. I've seen him before. He seems to spend a lot of time at the station like I do. Usually, he stands at the end of the platform.

The man looks like someone's granddad. He's wearing an old wax-cotton jacket and a brown hat with a feather in it. He's writing something in a small note-pad with an even smaller pen.

An announcement is made that the next train will be arriving on platform two, the platform I'm on. All the people begin to pick up their bags and get themselves ready for the train's arrival.

I'm never sure, when I come to watch the trains, which moment I like best. Whether it's the moment just before the train arrives, the moment you see the train in the distance and even though you know exactly what's coming, you still feel the excitement in your tummy at the train's inevitable arrival.

Then there's the other moment. The moment when the train *does* arrive. I love that moment too. I love it so much it often makes me want to laugh when it happens. I don't know why. It's like you've been waiting and waiting and you're so excited but scared too and then, when the train does arrive, it's so wonderful there's nothing else to do but laugh.

The train arrives and I swallow a small giggle which comes out as a kind of strange hiccup. The man at the other end of the bench in the hat glances at me then quickly looks away again. He crosses something off in his tiny note-pad.

Everyone on the platform gets onto the train, except for me and the man on my bench.

He doesn't get on the next train either. I wonder if

he's waiting for someone, or if he's like me, just here for the trains.

We sit together on our bench and I feel, even though we haven't spoken to each other, that we have bonded just by sitting on the same bench together for such a long time. 'Are you waiting?' I ask.

He glances at me. 'We're all waiting,' he says. He looks quickly away as two women wheeling suitcases pass us on the platform.

People nowadays can't talk to children they don't know, because if they do it will be assumed they are paedophiles. I like talking to adults because I can learn things from them and I feel pretty safe on the platform with all the other people around. Besides, I'm not a particularly attractive child.

I try again. 'Are you here for the trains?'

'That's right.'

'I am too,'

He looks at me again, this time with interest. 'Are you?'

I nod.

'There's not many of us now,' he says. 'You're the new generation.'

I nod again, trying to give the impression I know what he's talking about.

'You don't use a dictaphone?' he says.

'No,' I say. 'I'm not that advanced. I just like the trains. Timetables too.'

'Ah,' he says. 'You're not much of a spotter, are you? More of a watcher.'

'I like to watch,' I say. 'And I love timetables.'

'They don't print timetables so much now. It's all digital.' He pauses, perhaps to think about timetables. 'It's engines I like,' he says. 'I use a dictaphone sometimes. Not today though. It isn't worth it. Not here. I had an Ian Allen when I was a boy. It was much easier then. I don't suppose you remember those?'

I shake my head. 'I have an ABC Timetable, on my bedroom wall.'

He looks pleased. 'Ah, the old ABC.'

There's an announcement on the other platform. We can hear the sound of the approaching train.

'You wait,' the man says. 'Three eight eight, one two nine, coming straight through.'

The train rushes past us without stopping. I can't help but smile and I notice the man does too. He holds onto his hat.

'I haven't seen you before,' the man says, once the train has passed.

'I can't come often,' I say. 'I have to go to school, and my family don't understand. They can't see the point of watching trains.'

'What's the point of anything?' the man says.

The platform begins to fill up again. It's windy and a newspaper is being blown along the platform.

'I have to go now,' I say. 'I have to be home for dinner, and my mum's in hospital.'

'I hope she gets better soon,' the man says. 'I'm Ray, by the way,' he says, holding out his hand.

'Lou,' I say. We solemnly shake. We have bonded over more than just sharing the same bench. We are train buddies.

'Perhaps I'll see you again,' I say, getting up from the bench.

'Perhaps,' Ray says, tipping his hat.

On Monday at school I sit and eat my lunch with Sam. I have soft cheese sandwiches and a tangerine because Tuesday is a good day for orange foods. Sam has little pieces of pepper, cucumber, carrot, and celery chopped up and in very small containers. Sam likes to keep his food colours apart and eat them separately. He says it's important to eat foods of all different colours because it's the only way our cells can glow.

Sam and I like to eat lunch together because it's safe; we can talk about whatever we want without seeming weird, which is generally what other people think we are. We don't walk around together much in the corridor, or outside the buildings, because this would expose us to ridicule and make us a target. If we did this we would be shouted at, called derogatory names, and it would be assumed we were more than friends because, in school, members of the opposite sex don't just hang out with each other. This actually entirely defeats the point of 'mixed education'.

My conclusion on the matter of mixed education is that most teenagers are spiteful and mean and are, of course, exposed to 'peer pressure', which is the stupid term they use for saying that one person will always want to be like another person so they can feel they belong somewhere in life. The problem is that we belong nowhere in life. We are just a random cluster of cells inhabiting a very small space on a spinning blue planet lost somewhere in a very large and dark universe. My theory is that teenage girls and teenage boys are mean in different ways. Therefore, being exposed to one less type of meanness can only be a good thing. Unfortunately, my parents didn't see it this way and are in favour of 'mixed education'.

Sam and I are both of the same opinion that our time at

secondary school is a prison sentence. If we do not serve the sentence ourselves, our parents will have to serve it for us, which isn't really fair on them because they have already served it. Our teachers are always telling us if we skip school our parents will be sent to prison and that we will never get good jobs. Getting a good job means we can have somewhere nice to live; maybe a car, holidays, a big TV. Then we will be just like everyone else and feel that we belong somewhere in the universe, even though we don't belong anywhere because there is nowhere to belong.

The tables in the school hall, where Sam and I are sitting, are large as two tables are always pushed together. Today Sam and I are sitting alone but, because of the size of the tables, we are often joined by other uncool kids from different classes, and sometimes even different years, who are looking for somewhere safe to eat their lunches.

'Uh, oh,' Sam puts down the piece of carrot he was thoughtfully chewing.

'What?' I say.

'Behind you.'

Before I have a chance to turn around, our table is approached by two girls from our year, Cherry Wiles and Bryony Silver.

They stop in front of our table and peer suspiciously down at us as though we are an inferior species. Prey, but not quite edible.

'Lianne Parks wants a word with you,' Cherry says. 'She's outside.'

'Yeah,' Bryony says. 'She's gonna beat you up and if you don't come now she's gonna get you after school so you might as well come out now.'

Sam lowers his eyes to his lunch. There is nothing he

can do to save me. He is like a captured pirate out at sea who must watch a friend walk the plank before him.

'All right,' I say. A line comes to me from somewhere. *Resistance is futile.*

The girls move away from the table as I slowly gather my things together, the carefully folded tin foil my sandwich was wrapped in and my tangerine peel.

It would be pointless to ask why I'm about to be beaten up. It would only make it worse. I am not one of them and that is enough.

I walk to the conveniently provided bins and deposit the tin foil and peel. The girls are already walking towards the doors, out of the school hall and into the playground. Bryony looks over her shoulder to make sure I'm still there and that I'm following. They wouldn't want to walk too close to me in case someone were to associate someone like me with someone like them.

Outside by the picnic tables, a crowd has formed. Not enough so as to attract attention from any teacher (they are pretty elusive at lunch times anyway), but enough to let me know that they are waiting for me and that this will be a big moment for Lianne Parks. I shall be her latest conquest; a sacrifice to the angels of popularity who ensure she is both feared and revered in the magical world of Westland Comprehensive.

Lianne approaches, surrounded by her maiden warriors. What will be her line of attack, I wonder?

'Your dad's a fucking pervert,' she says.

'Yeah,' Bryony helpfully echoes. 'And you're a freak.'

Cherry leans in towards me. 'You've been saying stuff about us.'

This is completely untrue but to say so would only

provoke them so instead I remain mute, always the best line of defence.

I take my glasses off and put them on one of the picnic tables behind me.

'Get her before she gets away,' one of the boys calls out from behind Lianne.

'Shut the fuck up, Seb,' Lianne says. Seb does as he's told and shrinks away into the brickwork of the nearby block that contains the P.E. changing rooms.

Then it begins. Lianne punches, she kicks, she slaps. Even though I knew what was coming I am still so surprised that it doesn't even hurt. I make no attempt to fight back as that will only prolong the execution of Lianne's sharp little punches that seem to be stabbing at me from all directions. All I can see is a flurry of fists.

Suddenly she stops. She stares at me for a second then, satisfied, she quickly walks away whilst I stagger backwards into the table, groping for my glasses.

The crowd, sniggering and, to be honest, looking a little let down that there wasn't more violence or blood, quickly disperse.

I put my glasses on and straighten my tie. I cross the playground and go into the Humanities block, thinking that the toilets by the music rooms are probably the closest and are likely to be the least busy.

It feels like my whole body is throbbing. My eye feels weird and I wonder if I will be permanently blinded. I realise, as I push through the doors and into the building, that I am shaking.

I pass two prefects from Year Ten in the corridor. They are busy doing their make-up in a small mirror they have blu-tacked to the inside of a top locker. I keep my head down and they ignore me as I walk past.

The toilets are deserted. I stand in front of the row of smeared mirrors. I'm surprised that I don't actually look too bad.

I dare to move a little closer to the mirror. My face is red and my left eye is puffy. I look down at my legs. I have a pain in my shin; probably my legs are going be pretty bruised but luckily no one will see anything through my black tights.

I smile at myself in the mirror. An odd thing to do, but sometimes what else is there to do other than to reassure yourself that whatever has happened you are still there. Still you.

This isn't the first time this kind of thing has happened to me but it hasn't happened for a while. I try to stick to the no eye contact rule. I never say anything in class. Still, once in a while, someone like Lianne Parks will be having a bad day and today it happened to be my turn to make her feel better about herself.

Dad sleeping with a sixth form student is also clearly not helping my quest for invisibility.

I take off my glasses and splash a little cold water on my face. A girl walks in and stares at me. She dives into a cubicle, slamming the door behind her. I dab my eye with a paper towel and blink two or three times. I replace my glasses and take one last look in the mirror. I am confident no one will notice anything different about me. To tell a teacher is completely out of the question. Lianne has friends, lots of friends. My days at school would become a living hell if I grassed her up. I've seen it happen to others. I would be worn down, stamped out like a bug. One day I just wouldn't be in school anymore.

The bell rings and I dash out of the door. I have to collect my science textbook from my locker before chemistry.

History is my final lesson of the day. It's in one of the 'huts' as everyone calls them. Two prefab huts, quickly erected, were built on the edge of the school playing field as extra classrooms. They are always freezing cold in the winter and the teachers don't like teaching in them because there are no interactive whiteboards and their laptops never work.

I still don't feel very good after what happened to me at lunch time. I know I should have gone to the medical room about my eye but they would only have asked me awkward questions. I try to concentrate on the lesson as best I can.

This afternoon we are doing 1066 and the Battle of Hastings, a large and bloody battle that took place between the Normans who came from France to conquer England from the Anglo Saxons in 1066. Once the new King had conquered England, he divided up the land between his favourite soldiers. Nowadays most of the land in England is still owned by these same families which means they have owned their houses and their land, and the little crests they were given to show they were important, for over a thousand years. A thousand years! If you are in some way related to one of these Norman families and have a Norman surname you are eight hundred times more likely to go to university at Oxford or Cambridge, or so our teacher tells us.

This is quite interesting for a while but then our teacher shows us some old maps with little Viking boats that look like tiny insects with many legs heading towards England and I find I am no longer concentrating. I guess I am still feeling a little shaken. This has not been a good day. All I want to do is go home but when I go home Mum won't be there, probably no one will be there. Dad will still be at work, Sarah will be out with her friends. Mikey might be there. Mikey doesn't like school much either although all the teachers like him so he has an easier time than me. He doesn't get teased by the girls because they ask him what they should do with their hair, and he doesn't get teased by the boys because they haven't worked out yet that he's gay and so they admire him for being so popular with the girls.

I look out of the window and across the school field. My eye still hurts. I think how nice it would be to be free, to get up and walk out the door, across the field, and go somewhere, anywhere that isn't school. I watch a group of birds flying over the field. They make a V shape in the air. I think I would like to be free like one of those birds. I would like to be flying in the air rather than sitting in a cold classroom learning about the Vikings and their tiny insect boats.

I imagine I am one of the birds flying in the V with the other birds, our wings all beating in harmony with each other. Birds know how to use the air, they like to get a free ride as much as anyone. I imagine I'm soaring, using the force of the air generated by the other birds to pull me along. I feel the air rush through my feathery wings. If I look to the side, I can see the other birds enjoying the air. I can see the clouds. If I look down I can see the fields and the houses and all the crazy human beings going about their crazy lives. I can see the prefab hut next to the school playing field where my human self is looking out of the window, trapped in a boring history lesson. I soar above the clouds. I can see the edge of my little bird belly. My little bird stick legs are tucked underneath me. I am flying. I am free.

'Louise Coulson, would you mind concentrating on what is going on *inside* the classroom.'

I blush and look down at my exercise book. I realise I

must have been staring very intently out of the window. It is irritating to me, that at nearly fourteen years old, and as a semi-free human being, I can still be told off for staring out of a window. If you tell teenagers off like they are children, they begin to behave like children. This is why secondary schools are able to exist and why kids go so crazy in them.

Mr Olds continues pointing at his maps and then we have to write some stuff down that we have learnt. Mostly we write facts; names, dates. These are facts I know I will forget as soon as I leave this classroom because this is what always happens to me. I have been told other facts in other classrooms today and I will forget these too. I will forget all the facts because I am not interested in them, and because they are all random and dislocated in my head with nothing to stick them together, and also because I have been told these facts rather than had the opportunity to discover them for myself.

This is why Annabel and Neil home school me. They understand the limitations and the pointlessness of compulsory secondary education. Although we always have to cover the basics we only cover one subject a day, usually in the morning. I am encouraged, in the afternoons, to pursue my own interests.

Neil teaches me Maths, Science, Art and Geography, and Annabel teaches me English and History, although of course, in a way, they both teach me everything as they are both there and we discuss things together in the evenings at our large reclaimed teak table in front of our large glass windows that overlook the loch.

The bell rings. I am very glad this day is over.

As we leave the classroom, Mr Olds is already wiping the facts about the Vikings off the board.

I WAKE IN the night and decide it must be because I'm worried about Mum, or perhaps because I am still feeling a little out of sorts after being beaten up at school today. Then I hear a scuffling noise coming from the landing and I realise it's Hammy who's woken me.

Hammy is Sarah's hamster. Dad bought him for her last year after she went up a set in maths. This year she's gone back down a set. Hammy is a very unoriginal name for a hamster but unsurprising because Sarah has a very unoriginal mind. Sarah was supposed to keep Hammy in her bedroom but he made too much noise at night. Sarah complained that he chewed loudly and that he exercised on his wheel when she was trying to sleep. Dad said he'd try WD40 on the wheel but Mum said Hammy might lick it and die from the poisonous substance. In the end the cage went downstairs to the living room, only then Hammy escaped.

Hammy's cage is round and has two funny tubes sticking out of it like antlers. At the top of these tubes are Hammy's bedrooms, two round containers with clear plastic removable roofs. One night Hammy managed to push off one of these roofs. Dad says Sarah must not have screwed it on properly. Sarah says she did, and that Hammy must have worked out how to unscrew it. Perhaps that's what all the wheel work was about. Hammy was building himself up, planning his escape via the unscrewing of the roof of bedroom one.

After that Hammy lived behind the fridge freezer for a while. I think he probably still does, or at least some of the time. The rest of the time he scurries around the house, mostly at night. We've tried lots of things to coax him back into his cage. The first few nights we left a trail of hamster food from the freezer to the middle of the kitchen floor, where we left his cage with the door open.

Hammy ate the food, then went off again.

Now we leave his cage where it was, in the living room. Sarah still tops up his food and water and Hammy goes back in the night, stuffs his cheeks with as much food as he can carry then returns to his current hide-out. He's never been caught.

As much as we'd all like Hammy safely back in his cage, like a prisoner that escapes from a high security US prison by exiting through the heating system and who is then hunted across America, you can't help but admire his tenacity and secretly cheer him on until he's shot dead somewhere near the Canadian border and then you feel immediately relieved. I feel a little like that about Hammy. I admire his resourcefulness and, unlike a prisoner convicted of first degree murder, Hammy hasn't really ever done anything wrong and isn't a danger to society. Although, Hammy does leave his droppings all over the house, and he once chewed up Dad's *Independent on Sunday* after Dad left it on the living room floor one night. *Never mind,* Dad said. *It was only the Arts section.*

I creep out of bed and onto the landing.

'Hammy,' I whisper.

The scuffling sound immediately stops and, as much as I would like to be the one to re-capture Hammy and earn a much needed brownie point with Mum and Dad, or just Dad, as Mum has other things on her mind right now, I decide it isn't worth the effort. I would have to put the landing light on and risk waking someone. Also, Hammy has never bitten me but I wouldn't put it past him. Needs must, and Hammy clearly enjoys being a free agent.

I climb back under my duvet and decide that, seeing as the sheets haven't been washed for a while, tomorrow night I will at least wear fresh pyjamas. There is nothing like fresh pyjamas to cheer one up and to help one to face the world.

3

ON Wednesday there's a new girl in our class at registration. I have never seen the point of registration. It's the time first thing in the morning, and then again after lunch, when we meet in our tutor groups, in our registration classroom, so our Form Tutor can take the register. I don't see the point of it because the register is taken in all of our classes anyway and mostly, during registration, we sit around in groups and talk. It's supposed to be the time when our Form Tutor tells us 'important information', about changes to our timetables or charity cake sales or school sporting events, or other uninteresting things.

The new girl stands next to our Form Tutor, Mr Wexhall, who teaches music. This is why we have our registration in one of the music rooms and why there is a piano in the corner.

Mr Wexhall coughs loudly. 'Everyone. This is Faith Cattle.'

No one takes any notice of him as no one wishes to appear too interested in case they have to make a space for this new girl at their table, although someone calls out 'moo!' in relation to the new girl's surname which Mr Wexhall decides to ignore.

The new girl doesn't respond either. In fact, she looks bored, not nervous as you might expect a new person starting a new school in their third year, and a quarter of the way through the term to look.

She studies her fingernails which are painted black. We aren't allowed to wear nail polish. Obviously, no one has told her this. Some of the girls do wear nail polish but usually only in muted colours so they are less likely to attract attention.

I notice she is wearing quite a lot of very dark eye make-up. She has her hair twisted up into two knots, one on either side of her head. The knots are large which must mean she has lots of hair. Her hair is also very black. She is tall and heavily built. Not overweight exactly, just taller and bigger than some of the girls, especially me as I am small for my age.

Mr Wexhall looks desperately around the room for somewhere to place this new girl with the dark make-up. Friendship groups were formed a long time ago and all the tables are crowded, apart from mine because I sit at the reject table, a sort of no-table for people with no friendship group and nowhere else to go. I usually sit at this table with Sam. Sometimes another geeky kid with bad acne whom everyone calls Zero sits with us at our table. Zero's only ambition is to be a computer hacker. His intention is one day to bring the world's financial system to a standstill for one hour. Perhaps not a very admirable ambition, but an ambition nevertheless. Zero believes he will have the knowledge and resources to be able to do this around the year 2020. Everyone calls him Zero because, in our first year, our maths teacher, Mr Abraham, put a very long maths problem up on the board and gave us half an hour to work it out without calculators. After three minutes Zero put up his hand and said, *the answer is zero,* and Mr Abraham looked at him and said, *How did you do that?*

Sometimes a girl with a lisp called Amanda, who grew

up in Hong Kong, also sits with us at our reject table. There was a girl called Sally-Anne that sat with us for a while but never spoke. Lots of people used to tease her because everyone knew her family were poor. She always wore white socks that had turned grey with too many washes and her Mum used to cut her hair all wonky. One day she left school and we found out that Sally-Anne's mum had met a plumber and they'd moved to Shropshire.

At the moment Mr Wexhall is searching the room I unfortunately look up and accidentally catch his eye. It is also unfortunate that there is a spare chair next to me.

Mr Wexhall beams at me. 'Why don't you sit there,' he says to the new girl, Faith. 'Next to Louise.'

Faith lifts her eyes from her nails.

'Louise can show you around, can't you Louise?'

I can't quite bring myself to nod.

Mr Wexhall is clearly pleased with himself. 'Yes,' he says. 'Louise can be your buddy for this week. She'll see you find your way to all your classes on time.'

I think to myself that I am the worst person to show anyone around as I am always getting lost myself. I have a terrible sense of direction, and I'm not sure how I feel about being anyone's 'buddy'. I sometimes find it difficult to talk to people because I feel as though I have to pretend to be someone I am not. This is because usually in conversation you have to make 'small talk' and I am not very good at making 'small talk'. After having conversations with people I feel very exhausted at all the pretending I have to do and at having to listen very hard to what they are saying so that I can sound like them. I have to do this a lot at school which is why when I get home I like to be very quiet and spend a lot of time alone in my room watching nature documentaries.

I reluctantly move my books to make a space and Faith slides in next to me. Mr Wexhall returns to his desk and his laptop to continue with whatever it was he was doing. Some people say he could have been a famous musician, only he fell in love with a woman who is now his wife and when they had children she told him he couldn't go on traveling the world with his trombone, and that he would have to get a proper job. Or maybe that's just a story.

Once Faith has sat down the class loses interest and the noise levels in the room return to normal.

Faith begins to copy the timetable Mr Wexhall has given her into the back of her homework diary. She takes a green highlighter from her pencil case and begins filling in the six squares for each class of each day, all in green.

This makes me feel quite strange because, in my mind anyway, different subjects are associated with different colours. Just like numbers and letters and days of the week also have their own colours.

Art is the only green subject. English is yellow. Maths is red. Science is blue, food technology is brown, P.E. is pink and so on. I have special coloured pens, and I have filled my own timetable in using the correct colour for each subject. I have also underlined each day of the week in its own colour. Monday is red, Tuesday is orange, Wednesday is yellow, Thursday is green, and Friday is blue.

Faith writing all her lessons in her homework diary in green is making me feel quite dizzy.

'Would you like to borrow my coloured pens?' I ask her. 'So you can write the subjects in their correct colours?'

Faith stops and looks at me for a moment. 'The green is good,' she says, resuming writing her subjects in green.

Mr Wexhall calls the register. When he calls Faith's name she looks up from her homework diary and says, 'Over here', instead of just 'here', which makes some of the others laugh. I don't think it was Faith's intention to be funny. She looked kind of bewildered. Perhaps she was just absorbed in the task of filling in her timetable.

When she's finished she puts the green highlighter back in her pencil case.

The bell rings and we gather up our books. 'Do you need me to show to your class?' I ask her. She shakes her head. 'I've got it,' she says, not in a way that is unfriendly, just in a way that indicates she knows where she's going.

We all file out of the classroom. Faith pauses by the door. 'I might catch up with you at break time,' she says. 'I need to know where I can get a croissant.'

'Sure,' I say, aware that Mr Wexhall might still be watching or listening to us and trying to give the impression that I am fulfilling my role as 'buddy'. 'I think they sell pastries in the canteen.'

Faith nods. 'I should be able to figure it out then.'

'They do almond or plain,' Sam says helpfully. 'But you have to get there early.'

'Sure.' Faith says, peering down at Sam through her heavily made-up eyes.

'Maybe I should give you my number,' I say. 'In case you need to ask me something.' I don't usually give people my mobile phone number but I feel I should be taking my 'buddy' role as seriously as I can. I have been given a responsibility and, even though I didn't want it, I always try to carry out my responsibilities.

'Okay,' Faith says, pulling out her green highlighter from her blazer pocket.

'Do you have any paper?' I ask.

Faith rolls up her sleeve. 'Write it here,' she says, offering me her arm.

'Um, maybe I can just tell you,' I say, taking a step back.

'Go for it,' Faith says.

I tell Faith my number and she writes it on her arm.

'Thanks,' she says, putting the highlighter back in her pocket. She turns and walks away, heading slowly out of the room and along the corridor.

A couple of the girls behind us giggle. Maybe because Faith has a large hole in the back of her tights.

IT'S SATURDAY MORNING and Neil and I are out on the loch. Our small motor boat glides quietly through the still water, moving across the reflections of the hills. It's early and the sun is still low. Above us is a great expanse of cloudless sky. Neil and I have bought our fishing rods, a box of bait, and Marmite sandwiches in case we get hungry. I like Marmite sandwiches almost as much as cheese and pickle. We fish more for the pleasure of being out on the water than for catching anything. We only keep a fish if we know it is in good supply, and if we are planning to eat it, as we both know that over seventy percent of the world's fish stocks are in decline.

We reach a spot that we like and turn the engine off. It's so quiet it feels as though we are the only human beings on the planet or that we have stumbled through a portal and into a pre-historic age.

The doorbell rings, breaking the silence of my morning on the loch. After a moment it rings again, and then again. Clearly no one else is going to get it. I reluctantly get out of bed.

I will return to the loch later.

Standing on the doorstep is a girl dressed in jeans, trainers and a purple wind-cheater jacket, even though it isn't that windy. She has her hair in a pony tail and she is wearing one of those stretchy black headbands to keep it in place. She's tall and quite pretty, in a sporty kind of way.

'Hi,' she says.

'Hi,' I say, wondering if I should know who she is.

'You're Lou,' she says.

'Yes,' I say.

We continue to stare at each other. She looks familiar.

'Is Eric in?' she asks.

For a moment I wonder who she's talking about.

Dad. Of course.

I realise that the girl on the doorstep must be Kaylee. I wasn't sure what I expected her to look like, but I know that I didn't expect her to look like this. She looks normal. Not at all hairy.

'I think so,' I say. 'Do you want to come in? I'll go and find him.' I suddenly feel self-conscious, standing on the door mat in my pyjamas.

Kaylee smiles and steps inside. She glances quickly around and it's clear she hasn't been here before, which is something at least.

'I'm sorry it's early,' she says. 'I was passing and...'

'It's okay,' I say. 'It's not *that* early.'

She smiles gratefully at me. I don't understand why I am being so nice to this person who has broken my family and who may, depending on Mum's psychiatric evaluation, be the reason Mum decided to steal clothes from Debenhams and burn our photographs in a saucepan.

She doesn't look like a person who could cause so

much trouble, but I feel I should not be so nice to her. I should be loyal to my mum.

I shut the front door then look at her in what I hope is more of a cold and withering sort of way, difficult to achieve when I am so much smaller than her and wearing pyjamas with rabbits on.

'Have you got something in your eye?' she asks, peering at me.

'No,' I say, blushing and looking down at my bare feet. Clearly I need to work on my cold and withering looks.

I turn towards the stairs and shout 'Dad!' in a loud voice but not too loud as I don't want to wake Sarah and Mikey.

Dad appears at the top of the stairs. He's dressed but his hair is damp and he's got a small towel slung over his shoulders. He's probably just had a shower.

Kaylee smiles like it's the cutest thing she's ever seen.

Dad looks from me to Kaylee. 'Everything okay?'

Unsure of who he's speaking to we both nod.

Dad comes down the stairs and leads Kaylee towards the kitchen. 'Come through,' he says, smiling at her. I get the feeling he might have hugged or kissed her or something if I wasn't standing in the way.

'Thanks,' Kaylee says. 'I hope you don't mind...'

They go into he kitchen and shut the door behind them. They seem to have forgotten about me. I can hear them talking but I can't hear what they're saying. I've never been a very good eavesdropper. Then I hear Dad fill the kettle which makes it even more impossible.

The doorbell rings again and I guess they haven't heard as they are too busy talking with the kettle boiling and the door being shut so I go back to see who it is.

Through the small rectangle of glass I can make out the pixelated shape of a person wearing pink.

I open the door.

'Lou, how are you dear? Give us a hand with this will you? Weighs a ton.'

It's my nan. She thrusts a small suitcase into my hands and steps past me into the hallway. She's wearing a bright pink cardigan. It's very pink. 'Hi, Nan.' I struggle with the suitcase, leaning against the front door to shut it as Nan stands in the hallway watching me.

'Still in your jim-jams, Lou? It's nearly nine o'clock.'

'Sarah and Mikey's aren't up yet,' is the only thing I can think to say in my defence.

Realising I am still holding the suitcase, Nan says. 'Put that down over there, Lou. By the stairs. Where's your Dad then? I couldn't get him on the phone at all yesterday evening, it just kept ringing and ringing. I kept getting the answer-phone.'

An image from yesterday evening returns to me. Dad, sitting on the sofa watching *Match of the Day* with the phone next to him on the coffee table. *Don't anyone get that. It's your nan.*

'He's in the kitchen,' I say.

Nan looks at me sympathetically. 'How are you all holding up?' she says. 'A terrible thing... My sister, Dorothy, went away once in fifty-seven. She thought the postman was a Russian spy.'

'We're all right,' I say.

'That's the spirit,' Nan says.

I look to the kitchen door. The voices have stopped. Dad must have heard Nan talking. I wonder how he's going to explain Kaylee.

'She stole from Debenhams,' I say, trying to continue the conversation to avoid Nan going into the kitchen.

Nan frowns. 'There are some things, Louise, that are

best not spoken about out loud. Silence is discretion. Keep it under your hat, they used to say. Of course it's okay when it's *family* but some things, well, they're best not mentioned.'

I nod.

'Why is this shut? Is your father burning toast again?'

Before waiting for an answer, Nan pushes the kitchen door open. Dad quickly turns around. There's no sign of Kaylee. There are two mugs of instant coffee on the kitchen table. One is in a mug with chickens on, the other's in a mug that says *I'd Rather be Water Skiing*.

'Hello, Mum,' Dad says.

Nan stares at the two mugs of coffee. 'Are you drinking coffee now, Lou?'

'Sure,' I say, coldly, staring at Dad, who looks at the floor. I wonder for a moment if Kaylee is hiding under the kitchen table. Then I notice the back door is ajar.

Nan puts her handbag on the kitchen table. 'I'll have one then,' she says. 'Not instant. I can't abide instant. It gives me a headache. Thought I'd pop in. See how you're all coping. I'm sure she'll be right as rain in a few days. We all need a rest sometimes.'

Dad keeps glancing towards the back door. He goes over to the sink and fills the kettle again. 'You didn't tell us you were coming over,' he says.

'You didn't ask,' Nan says. 'If you'd answer the phone once in a while, Eric, then I might have been able to tell you, mightn't I?'

'You could have left a message,' Dad says huffily.

'I can't stand those answer things. Anyway, I thought you might need some help. Doreen said she'll come in and feed Clive.'

Clive is Nan's cat. She got him after my granddad died,

although my granddad wasn't called Clive, he was called Frank. My granddad used to grow vegetables. He also used to bounce me on his knee when I was little, and eat all the ginger nut biscuits from the biscuit tin.

Dad turns and stares at Nan who has sat down at the table and is in the process of slipping off her shoes. She pulls a pair of slippers out of her handbag. I'm always amazed at the number of useful things Nan keeps in such a small handbag.

'You're staying?' Dad says, looking worried.

'Just for a few nights. Until you're all back on track.'

Dad looks towards the back door again. 'Lou, would you, please... Go and check, you know, on that... In the garage?'

We look at each other; Dad almost pleading, me trying to convey how unimpressed I am with this idea.

'Fine,' I say.

I put on an old pair of trainers that Dad has left by the back door. They are much too big and I feel like I'm wearing flipper feet. I leave Dad and Nan in the kitchen. I take my flipper feet outside and flip-flop along the gravel passageway between the outside wall of the kitchen and our neighbour's fence until I reach the garage door.

Inside the garage Kaylee is waiting patiently amongst the storage boxes and old furniture. She leans against Dad's exercise bike.

'Oh, hi,' she says, as if it's perfectly natural that I should find my dad's teenage girlfriend hiding in our garage. 'I can't seem to figure out how the doors work.'

'Oh, right,' I say, moving towards the doors. 'They're electric.' Kaylee watches me carefully to see which button I press. In case, I think, she is ever trapped in our garage again.

The garage doors rise slowly. Kaylee looks as though she might duck under and make a quick get-away.

'It's best to wait,' I say. 'Until they reach the top. Could be dangerous.'

Kaylee nods. She takes a step back. 'I know this must seem weird to you, Lou, but your dad and I... We're really very happy.'

I'm not sure what to say to this so I pretend to be concentrating on the moving doors and the strip of driveway that's growing ever larger.

'Age is irrelevant to love,' she says.

'Sure,' I say, not wanting to pursue this conversation.

Kaylee smiles at me. 'Thanks for understanding,' she says. 'Not everyone does.'

I am not too comfortable with this assumption, but before I can say anything the garage doors stop moving and Kaylee steps out onto the driveway. 'Well, see you, Lou. I have to run. I've got a swim class.'

I look at her and I get the feeling she is telling the truth. She doesn't look like the sort of person who would lie. 'Right,' I say, shifting uneasily from foot to foot in the giant floppy trainers.

A Sainsbury's delivery van is pulling up outside Mrs De Souza's next door. I feel cold, and a little exposed in my cotton pyjamas, even though they are my winter pyjamas.

Kaylee waves to me as she walks down the driveway. I wave awkwardly back, watching her shiny ponytail swing from side to side.

I return to the kitchen. Nan is sitting at the table flicking through a copy of *The Radio Times* whilst Dad drops thin rashers of bacon into the frying pan.

'I'm making us bacon sandwiches for breakfast,' Dad says, smiling at me in that slightly guilty and overly friendly way he has been smiling at all of us since he announced his affair. 'A treat,' he says, as though he's offering me a sweet after a trip to the dentist.

'Thanks,' I say, thinking, despite all this, that I wouldn't mind a bacon sandwich.

'Don't forget your coffee, Lou,' Nan says. 'It's growing cold.'

THAT AFTERNOON, WHEN Mikey and Sarah are up, we all go to visit Mum at the hospital. Nan doesn't come with us, declaring it might be 'too much', for Mum and that there isn't enough room in the car.

When we leave she's sitting on the sofa in her slippers with a box of Turkish Delight watching repeats of *Come Dine with Me*, a television show where strangers cook for each other in their houses then nose around the other contestants' bedrooms making fun of their belongings.

Sarah sits in the front of the car next to Dad but she still isn't speaking to him. She even refused a bacon sandwich when he offered.

I sit in the back and stare out of the window. It's a sunny day. Windy. 'A blustery day', Winnie the Pooh would say. The leaves are beginning to turn brown.

Autumn is my favourite time of year. Mum says she doesn't like autumn because things die, or go into hibernation. But I like autumn because it reminds me of jumping in piles of leaves when I was little and of wading through puddles in my wellies. I like collecting conkers and acorns from beneath the trees in the park and I like to see the brown, crispy leaves dancing along the pavements and, anyway, things sometimes have to die a little in order to be reborn again.

Autumn by the loch is very beautiful. The trees are all different colours, reds, oranges, and yellows. We get purple heather too. The reflections in the water look like a rusty patchwork quilt. Sometimes, in the mornings, there's a mist covering the water and the loch seems like a magical fairy-tale land. We get red deer too. They come close to the house. In the mating season the stags fight over the female deer by locking their antlers together and pushing each other backwards and forwards like boxers in a ring.

We park on a housing estate near to the hospital in order to avoid parking charges. It actually isn't that close and we have to walk along a grass verge at the side of the main road to reach the entrance of the hospital. We follow Dad like ducklings, all walking a little apart from each other so no one can mistake us for a family.

Outside the main building there's a small roundabout. On the roundabout there's a display of modern art. Giant curved stick-like sculptures in bright primary colours have taken over the roundabout. They're tall and, I think, menacing. Not very relaxing. If I were staying in the hospital, every time I looked out of a window I would think that giant alien stick insects had invaded the earth.

When we find Mum's ward one of the nurses puts a hand on Dad's arm. 'I think it may be better if the children see her alone.'

'Why?' Dad says. 'I'm her husband.'

'Only technically,' the nurse says. 'Why don't you go and wait in the corridor. There's a vending machine. They stocked up the mint Aeros only this morning.'

'All right,' Dad says, seeming to like the mint Aero idea.

When we find Mum, she's sitting up in bed with a little

table over her legs. She's colouring in something in a colouring book. There's an assortment of coloured pencils on the table, along with a spiral of shavings.

We all shuffle around the bed.

'It's part of my programme,' Mum says. 'I'm doing a jungle scene. I need more greens. The greens keep disappearing. Mary in bed five hides them under her pillow.'

I look at Mum but it isn't Mum. It's just as before, the outer form is the same but the rest of her isn't quite there. I wish that I was younger, that I could get up onto the bed and curl up with her whilst she colours, snuggle against her jumper like the way I used to when I was little.

Of course I can't do this because I am thirteen and a half. And anyway, she isn't wearing a jumper. Hospitals are too hot for jumpers.

Sarah is flicking through a fashion magazine someone has left on the end of Mum's bed.

'Help yourself,' Mum says. 'It isn't mine.'

'Are you feeling better?' Mikey asks.

'They don't let you have the pencils,' Mum says. 'Until you reach stage two. Stage three and I'll be allowed a phone charger.'

'Nan's staying over,' I say.

'That's nice,' Mum says. She's busy selecting a red for a parrot.

Sarah is leaning against the edge of the bed, still looking at the magazine. A displacement activity, so she doesn't have to feel upset, I decide. 'There's a voucher here,' she says. 'Twenty percent off Topshop. I can't believe no one's cut this out. Do you have any scissors?'

'Scissors are definitely stage four,' Mum says.

'Tear it out' Mikey suggests. 'Is it Topshop man or woman?'

Sarah glares at Mikey. 'Women only,' she says, ripping the page out in one quick movement.

We don't get to spend very long with Mum because they start to serve lunch. 'You always get a pudding,' Mum says. 'Tinned custard. Like when you were at school.'

None of us are quite sure how to say goodbye to Mum. Mikey hugs her first. Then Sarah, and then me. We form a hugging queue.

Mum looks exhausted after all the hugging. When we leave the ward I glance back at Mum. She's already selected a blue and is beginning to colour another parrot.

4

SAM and I don't see the new girl, Faith, at break time or lunch time on Monday. She's in a few of our classes but we don't speak. I figure that if she needed to ask me something she would ask. Maybe she is a person with a good sense of direction who doesn't need a 'buddy'. She must have found her croissant.

I don't see her again until the following morning in registration.

Today, she has a black flower in her hair and purple gloss on her lips. I never wear lipstick for several reasons. Firstly, it looks weird on me, like I am playing at dressing-up and have snuck into my mum's bedroom to borrow from her make-up bag, secondly, because I get dry lips and lipstick makes them more dry. I like to use a shea butter lip balm on my lips because, according to the pot, it is natural and chemical free. I also don't wear lipstick because once, when I was waiting for Mum in the hairdressers, I read something in a magazine about how much lipstick the average woman eats without realising it every year and it made me feel a bit sick.

'Hi,' I say, as Faith sits down next to me.

'Yo,' she says, in a casual kind of way. I notice all of the other girls have avoided Faith so far. This may be partly because she's new, but I also think it has something to do with the fact that she is a little intimidating. She seems very sure of herself, although my mum once told me the people who seem most sure of themselves are really the least sure of themselves.

Before I get a chance to say anything else Mr Wexhall stands. 'Assembly!' he says.

Everyone groans, and then there is a shuffling of books and a scraping of chairs as we leave the room.

We are supposed to walk to assembly quietly, in an orderly fashion, but this rarely happens until we get close to the hall where Mr Wexhall makes us stand in single file as this is the way we have to enter the hall.

Assembly is usually taken by a senior staff member, sometimes two as perhaps, when standing in front of three hundred teenagers, there is safety in numbers.

Today Mr Dodd is standing alone on the stage behind his lectern, although I notice Mrs Freeman, our history teacher, is standing at the back of the hall, ready to swipe any mobile phones that might be being looked at during assembly.

If your mobile phone is confiscated, it's extremely annoying as you have to wait until the end of the day to get it back. You have to go to the front office and queue up with all the other kids whose electronic devices have been confiscated throughout the day. Then you have to wait whilst someone finds the key to the safe and there they all are, the sad, banished phones, and iPads, that have been 'doing time' in the safe since they were rudely and unnecessarily stolen.

Mr Dodd announces that today's assembly will be 'inspirational'. He tells us that we are about to hear from students in the upper years who have 'achieved'. They will tell us about their unique interest and their achievements he says. He then hastily adds that all the achievements were made without any detriment to each student's studies in school.

First a sixth form student steps up onto the stage and plays us something on his guitar. He is pretty good and everyone claps. Mr Dodd then asks him a few questions about the band he is a member of and where they are performing.

Then a girl who makes small pottery animals and sells them on eBay steps up and Mr Dodd asks her about the business skills she must have acquired. The girl is in Year Ten and very quiet. She holds up a handful of tiny pottery animals for us to look at but it's hard to see them because they are so small and so far away.

Then Mr Dodd announces a sixth form student, this time with a sporting rather than a musical achievement. It's Kaylee. She's wearing tight blue jeans with red Converse and a black T-shirt that says 'France' on it in large white writing. At our school sixth form students don't have to wear a uniform. They are so lucky.

Kaylee looks relaxed as she steps onto the stage. She's holding a medal of some sort. Her hair is in another shiny ponytail. I have the strange thought that I could be looking at my future step-mum.

Mr Dodd asks her some questions and she tells us how she won a medal in her first senior swim at the British Swimming Championships. Mr Dodd says that she must have trained very hard to win such medals and Kaylee says she goes to the big pool in town almost every day before school and sometimes after. Mr Dodd says Kaylee's friends must enjoy watching her swim in competitions and that her parents must be very supportive. Kaylee says that they are, but then she says she wouldn't have achieved anything at all without the support and encouragement she received from Eric.

Mr Dodd looks uncomfortable and tries to wrap up the

conversation by thanking Kaylee for inspiring us. A few kids in the hall are giggling as they realise who Eric is.

'She had sex with Mr Coulson,' a girl behind me whispers to her friend.

I feel that I have gone very red. I stare at my shoes and hope no one is looking at me.

I glance up at the stage. Kaylee looks happy and not at all bothered by the look on Mr Dodd's face or the whispers and stifled giggles.

After Kaylee steps down, Mr Dodd clears his throat and quickly changes the subject to something about mock exams. I know everyone is still thinking about Kaylee and my dad.

'Is he a teacher here?' Faith whispers to me.

'He's my dad,' I say.

Faith shrugs. 'Tough,' she says. I'm not sure if she means that this must be tough for me or tough for Kaylee, or my dad. I assume me.

We sit in silence and listen to the rest of the assembly, the boring stuff. All I can think about now is Kaylee and my dad; Kaylee attributing her success to my dad's 'support' and 'encouragement'. Do they really love each other? I wonder. Did my dad do a good thing in helping Kaylee? Did he spot her talent and encourage her to follow her dreams? Is my dad such a bad guy after all? Nothing is ever black and white, Nan always says.

WHEN I ARRIVE home from school, there's a man on a motorbike on our driveway. 'Hi,' he says, as I approach. He smiles sheepishly at me and I recognise him as one of the firemen who came round after our saucepan fire.

'Hi,' I say, walking past him.

I am still on the doorstep looking for my key when Sarah opens the front door and breezes past without acknowledging me. The fireman gives her a helmet and she climbs onto the back of the bike.

I watch as they speed off together into the distance. Well, they turn in the drive then ride off along the road, the bike making popping noises that don't sound at all healthy to me even though I know nothing about motorbikes.

I am surprised to find that everyone else is in. I catch a glimpse of Dad in the living room. He's looking at something on his laptop.

Mikey is in the kitchen making a Boston Cream Pie with Nan who is wearing one of Mum's aprons. I know they are making a Boston Cream Pie as they have Nigella's *How to be a Domestic Goddess* open on the kitchen table at the Boston Cream Pie page. Nan is clearly enjoying herself and appears to be supervising the making of the pie which looks to me more like a cake. I suspect that Mikey doesn't need supervising, but that he is enjoying someone taking an interest in his new hobby. Nan has never been a very good cook. She made me a cake for my sixth birthday. It was collapsed in the middle and the frosting had the consistency of breadcrumbs. Everyone ate a tiny piece and later that evening Mum scraped it into the bin then went and bought me a cake with a train on it from Marks & Spencer.

'Will you take this in to your dad,' Nan says, handing me a cup of tea. 'There's a good girl. He's home from work early because he isn't feeling well.'

I take the cup of tea and Nan returns to whisking something dark and chocolaty in a bowl. It quickly gets the better of her and she hands the whisk to Mikey.

Dad is sitting in the living room. He has his laptop on the coffee table and I can see he's on *Rightmove.*

I put his cup of tea down next to his laptop.

'Thanks, Lou.'

'Are you sick?' I ask.

Dad looks at me. He seems unsure how to respond to this simple question.

'Actually, no,' he says. He sighs heavily and reaches for his cup of tea. 'I suppose you'll find out sooner or later. I'm taking some time out from work. They thought it might be best.'

I wonder why it is that adults always speak in this way, never saying what they really mean or what has really happened. They like to try and create a puzzle that everyone else has to work out.

'Have you been sacked?'

'Not exactly,' Dad says. 'Suspended. And there's something else,' he says, unable to look at me. 'Not right now of course. With your mother - away. But soon. I'll probably be moving out.'

'I see,' I say, glancing at the laptop screen.

'It might be best not to mention any of this to your nan. Just for now.'

'Okay,' I say, a little reluctantly. There was a time when I might have been pleased to be sharing a special secret like this with my dad. That time has passed.

'She'll find out,' I say.

'Yes. But not yet, Lou.'

'All right,' I say.

Dad begins to scroll through the pages of houses and I leave him alone with his tea.

I GO UPSTAIRS and lie on my bed. I spend a lot of time laying on my bed thinking. Sometimes, if I'm feeling very overwhelmed, I sit on the floor. Today the bed is okay.

I stare at my ABC train timetable and try to forget that I will have to go to school tomorrow. Looking at the train times relaxes me and I think that I must go to the station again at the weekend and see if Ray is there with his flask and his notepad.

Another way I like to relax in the evenings is by watching Sir David Attenborough's documentaries. I have five box sets of Sir David Attenborough's documentaries. I enjoy learning about the natural world and I find his voice and the music very soothing. I like to watch the animals in their natural habitats, going about their business without destroying the world by building cities on forests or erecting cell phone towers, or sweeping up marine life in big nets from the ocean floor like a giant hoover.

Animals seem to just take what they need. They don't require metal and radiation in order to talk to one another and they don't need to wrap their food in packaging and carry it home in plastic bags that will take a thousand years to degrade.

There's so much plastic in the ocean now, it would be almost impossible to get the ocean back to the way it was before human beings started using plastic. It's also very harmful to animals. I recently read a story about a sperm whale found dead in the water next to a Greek island. When they opened up the whale's tummy they found it had accidentally eaten almost a hundred plastic bags. One of the bags was from a local take-away restaurant.

As I am laying on my bed feeling sad about everyone talking about my dad and Kaylee at school and whispering in assembly and Mum being in the Psychiatric Ward, I make a list in my head of all the things that make me happy to cheer myself up.

1. Trains pulling in and out of stations
2. Frosty spiders' webs
3. Eating tangerines, or apples that have been cut into segments
4. Fresh pyjamas
5. When it rains so hard that you can hardly see out of the window.

I sit up and reach for my laptop and select *Frozen Planet,* one of my favourites. I watch a female polar bear making a nest in the snow for the winter when all the other animals have gone south. She won't eat again until spring, Sir David Attenborough tells us. I wonder what it would feel like not to eat again until spring.

After a while Dad calls me downstairs for dinner. Sarah is out so it's just the four of us. Dad has made spaghetti Bolognese, although I know he took the sauce out of the freezer this morning because I saw it on the side, so we're really eating a dinner that Mum made. Sometimes, when she feels inspired Mum will make a batch of something and freeze it. This doesn't happen very often. I only have the Bolognese as I don't eat starch and protein together and Nan only has Bolognese because she thinks pasta is exotic.

After dinner I go up to my room to carry on watching *Frozen Planet* and Mikey goes up to his room to carry on watching *Brideshead Revisited,* which he has been watching for several weeks. Sometimes Mikey puts it on in the living room. There are two men who seem to go on a lot of picnics together. One of them has a teddy bear called Aloysius.

I realise, once I get to my room, that I would like a glass of water so I go back downstairs. It is very important to drink water. The human body is made up of fifty to seventy-five percent water. I am halfway down the stairs when I hear Nan and Dad talking in the kitchen. I know that eavesdropping is rude but sometimes it can be useful.

'He's used all the tins,' Dad says.

'You should encourage it,' Nan says. 'He's got skill. Even my mother couldn't get that kind of consistency.'

I realise they are talking about Mikey. I stand in the hallway listening.

'He never goes out,' Dad says. 'When I was his age, I was never in. There was always a game on down at the park. We'd use our jumpers for goalposts.'

'He isn't into all that rough and tumble,' Nan says.

'I can't even get him interested in the Hammers,' Dad says. 'It isn't healthy. Boys need exercise.'

'He must do it at school.'

I hover outside the kitchen door. Dad grunts. He knows Mikey only does the minimum requirement of P.E. at school, never the after school clubs. Mikey will always pick badminton or table tennis over football or rugby.

'You can't let talent go to waste, Eric,' Nan says. 'One day he'll meet a girl who'll be thrilled to bits he can separate an egg. Most men can't.'

'Separating an egg isn't useful,' Dad says, in a voice that suggests he's losing the argument. 'What's he going to do when he leaves school? How can anyone make money from cake?'

'It will be easier,' Nan says. 'When things have settled down with Gwen. I always said the two of you weren't suited.'

Gwen is my mum. She's never liked her name. She says her mum called her Gwen after an American movie actress. She saw a film when she was pregnant. She hadn't been able to think of a girl's name she liked and when the credits appeared, she told herself that she must pick a name from the credits and stick with it. She picked Gwen as she preferred it to the name of the actress who had the lead role.

I like to think I am named after Lou Salome, one of the first female psychoanalysts. I watched a program about her once. Unfortunately, this isn't the case. Mum told me she just liked the sound of our names together. I think she thought about how they would sound when she wrote out her Christmas cards.

Happy Christmas! Love From Eric, Gwen, Sarah, Michael, and Louise.

Nan has never liked my mum very much. Dad told me once she thought he was tying himself down too quickly when he met my mum. Also Nan thinks Mum has ideas above her station. I have often overheard her saying this to Dad, like when he told her about the kitchen extension, *There's nothing wrong with that kitchen. She's got ideas above her station,* and when he told her Mum was going for a promotion at work (which she got). *I've told you Eric, she's got ideas above her station. The children need her at home.*

Whenever Nan says this, all I can think of is stations. I like stations because I like trains. I like small old fashioned stations with old lights and old clocks that still look they did a hundred years ago. I like to walk over the bridge at these stations. Once I have walked over the bridge to the other platform, I like to walk back over to the first platform again. I especially like an old fashioned station in Goathland which is in Yorkshire. I visited this station with Mum and Dad and Sarah and Mikey on holiday one summer. We took a ride on a steam train. I was so excited I stood next to the window the entire time. You should never ever lean out of the window of a moving train. It is very dangerous. I did do this, but only when the train had stopped and when it was on a single track so I knew there could be no other trains coming in the other direction. I leaned out of the window a teeny tiny bit so I could look at the front of the train and along the platform only then the train let out a big puff of steam and I got a piece of grit in my eye. I had to sit down and blink a hundred and forty-six times before I managed to get it out. It was quite painful.

I like old-fashioned stations because I like to imagine all the people over all the years who have sat on the same bench with their suitcases waiting for the train. People waiting at stations with their luggage are always on their way somewhere. They are always on the point of leaving. This is a little like life. I have always thought of life as being a platform, or a waiting room. We try and find things that will fill the time until our train arrives.

I like large stations as well as small stations. My favourite large station is St Pancras International in London and I go and visit it sometimes. The last time Dad took me up to London we went to St Pancras International and I stood and watched the trains leaving and arriving. Dad was happy because when he takes Sarah to London she always wants to go shopping and have lunch somewhere expensive, whereas I just like to look at trains and eat sandwiches.

'If you'd only listened to me in the beginning,' Nan is saying to Dad. They are still talking and I am still eavesdropping.

'Don't start Mum,' Dad says wearily.

'At least they're not little anymore,' Nan says. 'It'll be easier for them to cope with the readjustment. Although Michael is sensitive. You mustn't forget Michael is sensitive. Middle children always are.'

At this point I decide to enter the kitchen for my glass of water.

'I'm just getting a glass of water,' I say as both Nan and Dad stop talking.

There's a scuffling sound from behind the fridge.

Nobody moves.

Nan frowns. 'Haven't you caught that rodent yet? You should put something down.'

Dad and I both look very disturbed by this idea. 'Don't be silly, Mum,' Dad says. 'It's Sarah's pet.'

The scuffling stops. I pour my glass of water.

Nan mutters something about traps and begins scrubbing the spaghetti saucepan.

I think that at least Nan knows about Mum and Dad getting a divorce, even if she doesn't know about Kaylee yet.

LATER THAT EVENING, Dad tells me Mum is coming home at the weekend. He's going to pick her up, he says. I decide this means Nan will be leaving us, but she says nothing about going home, although I know she takes the bus back to her flat every day to check on Clive.

Nan is sleeping on the sofa bed in the back room. The room is a sort of add-on off the living room, built before Mum and Dad bought the house. When we were little we called it the playroom. Now it's just the 'back room', although Mum has started to call it her 'snug'.

If Mum really is coming home that means Dad will probably be sleeping on the sofa in the living room again under the frog duvet. The house will be pretty full, what with me, Mikey, Sarah and Mum in our bedrooms, Dad in the living room, Nan in the back room, and Hammy behind the fridge.

I wonder if Mum will be Mum again when she comes home. I wonder if she will remember that she tried to steal clothes from Debenhams and that she burnt our photographs in a saucepan. I wonder if she will remember that Dad is having an affair with a girl who, only last year, was too young to legally drink alcohol.

The last time we saw Mum she was very focused on her colouring. It was as if they had given her a pill that had made her forget everything. I don't mind if she doesn't remember, I just want her to be Mum again because, even though I should really be living with Annabel and Neil, she is still the mum that was designated to me, and she does her best. She has always been a good mum. She has seen that we are clothed, fed, that we don't eat too many sweets that will rot our teeth, and that we have a good supply of Disney DVDs for rainy days. I want my mum back.

ON FRIDAY NIGHT Sarah has a sleepover. She has two friends to stay. She tells Dad that Mum said it would be fine for her friends to stay over. She says that she needs her friends to stay the night as they are getting up early in the morning to go shopping at Westfield Shopping Centre. Dad reluctantly agrees.

Sarah's room is big enough for one friend to stay over as she has a bed that pulls out from beneath her own bed, but she can't fit two friends in her room. This means they will sleep downstairs in the living room, one on each sofa, and one on the bed that lives underneath Sarah's that Dad will have to bring down.

Nan is going to sleep in Mum and Dad's bedroom as it will be too noisy for her to sleep in the back room with Sarah and her friends in the living room. Dad will sleep in Sarah's room because Sarah said she didn't want her bedroom smelling like an old person, which I thought was quite mean because Nan only smells of Pears soap.

The sleeping arrangements in this house are pretty complicated.

When I arrive home from school on Friday evening, Sarah is already there. This is probably because I walked home very slowly, cutting across the fields. Walking across the fields is a short cut to our school. There is a gate on the playing field that is usually left open. Mum doesn't always like us to use this cut-through as it makes our shoes muddy, especially at this time of year, so when I get home I scrub my shoes in the sink.

Sarah uses the cut-through as she is often late for school because she takes too long doing her hair and make-up whilst listening to KISS FM. Mikey never uses the cut-through as he doesn't like his shoes to be muddy.

Sarah and her friends enter the kitchen. They take out two frozen pizzas from the freezer. One of the girls has dyed blonde hair that hangs in two plaits. She's wearing a pink top that is either too short for her or designed to show off her belly button. The other girl has very long red hair, a nose piercing and is dressed all in black.

'Who's that?' The girl with the long red hair and nose piercing asks.

'My sister,' Sarah says, not looking at me and tearing the plastic wrapping off one of the pizzas.

'Does she live here?' the girl asks.

'Yeah,' Sarah says, moving towards the microwave. Apparently the oven is still beyond her capabilities.

I carefully put my shoes down on a sheet of old newspaper by the back door in order to let them dry. The girl with red hair is still looking at me.

'Does it have fish on it?' The girl with the plaits says to Sarah. 'I don't eat fish. I have a fish phobia.'

'It's pepperoni,' the girl with the nose piercing says, no longer interested in me.

I have never heard of a fish phobia before. Does it mean she is frightened of all fish, or only dead fish on pizzas? Can she not even look at a fish? What would happen if she visited an aquarium?

'Shall we do chips? Sarah says.

'Sure,' says the girl with the nose piercing.

Sarah loves junk food. She has very good skin which really isn't fair.

'I can't fit them in,' Sarah says, frowning at the microwave.

'Do them after?' the girl with the plaits suggests.

'Will the pizza still be hot? Sarah says.

All three of them stare at the box of chips and the pizzas and the microwave.

You'd think they were trying to crack the Enigma Code.

I leave them to figure it out and go upstairs to my room.

I HAVE TO stay in my room for most of the evening in order to avoid Sarah and her friends. Mikey does the same. I can hear the theme tune from *Brideshead Revisited* as I pass his door on my way to the bathroom. Dad is out, probably with Kaylee, and Nan has gone to her Spiritualist church.

As I pass Sarah's bedroom I can hear giggling and the beeping of hair straighteners. Sarah has left her door ajar.

'We did it three times in the back of his dad's car,' I hear the blonde girl with the plaits say as I pass.

Then I hear them take all their stuff downstairs to the living room. Usually when Sarah has friends to stay over they watch horror films so I imagine this is what they are doing. I don't like horror films much as I don't like anything that makes me jump. This is why I don't like balloons or emergency vehicles, or even telephones.

I do my maths homework so I don't have to do it over the weekend. I know this is a little strange, to be doing homework on a Friday night, but I like to get it out of the way. Mikey sometimes does his at the kitchen table in the hope that Mum or Dad will stop and ask him what he's doing and 'help' him, which basically means doing it for him. Mikey doesn't need anyone to do his homework for him because he is very clever, he just doesn't enjoy it and he likes an easy life. Sarah used to get Dad to help her with her homework, until she discovered she could copy her classmates' homework in registration. No one at school ever says no to Sarah.

After I have finished my homework I go into the kitchen, turn the lights on, and open the tin that contains Mikey's Boston Cream Pie. Already, since yesterday evening, half of it has been eaten. Mikey said we could help ourselves. Cake never lasts long in this house. I cut myself a slice, wrap it carefully in kitchen roll and take it upstairs to eat in bed whilst I watch another episode of *Frozen Planet*. I am very careful not to get crumbs in the bed. I hate crumbs in my bed.

I WAKE IN the night to screaming. It takes me a moment to register that I have woken to the sound of screaming, and then another moment to register that the screaming is coming from downstairs.

Fearing another saucepan fire, I get quickly out of bed and step onto the landing. All the other bedroom doors are closed. Quite clearly I am the lightest sleeper in the house.

I go downstairs. The screaming has turned into a kind of shrieking. It's coming from the living room. I pause by the door. I know Sarah will be very unhappy about me barging into the living room where she and her friends are sleeping, but I also know that I am good in a crisis. I remember the first aid I was taught in Brownies, whereas Sarah left Brownies after getting only one badge, the hostess badge, and even then she cheated as she didn't make the sandwiches, or do the washing up.

I push the door open. Someone has put a lamp on. The girl with plaits who doesn't have plaits anymore is standing on one of the sofas in a tiny leopard print nightdress with a pink trim. She's making funny squealing noises and hopping up and down.

The girl with the nose piercing is lying on the camp bed in a brown onesie that has bear ears. She looks groggy, and a little annoyed.

Sarah is sitting on the other sofa laughing.

'Shut up, Abigail,' the girl in the onesie with the nose piercing says.

'There was a fucking mouse!'

Sarah is clutching her stomach. She is laughing so hard she has tears in her eyes.

'It's not funny!' Abigail turns to took at me, probably because she's not getting sympathy from anyone else. 'There was a mouse. It was on my sleeping bag!' She points to the end of the sofa.

'Did it have a tail?' I ask her.

Still standing on the sofa she stops to think about this. 'No,' she says finally. 'It was cut off.'

This makes Sarah laugh even more.

'Jesus Christ,' the girl in the onesie says. 'Some people are trying to sleep here.'

Sarah manages to compose herself. 'It was Hammy,' she says.

I nod in agreement. 'Our hamster,' I say.

'My hamster,' Sarah corrects me.

Abigail looks from me to Sarah. 'What the fuck is a hamster doing on my sleeping bag?'

'He escaped,' I say. 'He lives mostly behind the fridge but he likes to roam the house at night.'

'Weird,' the girl in the onesie mutters. Her eyes are closed.

'Well, where the fuck did it go? I'm not sleeping in here with a hamster.'

'He's probably gone now,' Sarah yawns.

'He doesn't like loud noises,' I say, thinking that I don't either.

Abigail is not convinced. She is still standing on the sofa.

'Where do you think he went?' I ask her, edging a little further into the room and trying to be helpful.

She looks around. 'I don't know. Under the sofa?'

I get down on my hands and knees and look under the sofa. 'I can't see anything.' I wonder if Hammy has an underground network of tunnels beneath the floorboards so he can move from room to room. 'I'm sure he's gone now,' I say. 'He's a very intelligent hamster.'

Abigail finally climbs back into her sleeping bag.

'Someone turn that light out,' the girl in the onesie says.

'Go back to bed, Lou,' Sarah says.

'Sure,' I say. 'Night.'

No one responds. Abigail is patting her sleeping bag to make sure there is nothing inside.

'At least it wasn't a fish,' I say helpfully. 'Then you would have been really scared.'

The girl in the onesie opens her eyes. All three of them stare at me. I back slowly out of the room, closing the door behind me.

ON SATURDAY AFTERNOON I go to the station to watch the trains. I know that Dad is going to pick Mum up from the hospital and bring her home and I feel quite worried about this as I want Mum to be feeling better and not believing in things that aren't really happening - like she was before. I am hoping so much that she is well again that I don't want to be disappointed. I also know that, if she is better, nothing will still ever be the way it was because Dad will still be having an affair with Kaylee and Mum will still be angry, and they will probably still be getting a divorce. Despite all of this, I would still rather Mum be at home than in the hospital ward without any green colouring pencils, and with the giant insect sculptures outside on the roundabout.

I see Ray at the end of the platform with a pair of binoculars. Today he's wearing a grey cap and carrying a green rucksack.

I sit down on the bench, the one we sat on last time. It's the bench furthest away from the platform steps so very few people use it.

I watch the passengers getting off a train that pulls into the platform opposite. They are all rushing. They all have somewhere to go.

After a while Ray walks over and sits down next to me. He opens his rucksack and takes out his Thermos flask.

'Good couple of weeks?' he asks me.

'I guess,' I say. 'My nan moved in with us. My brother made a Boston Cream Pie. My dad got suspended from his job. I got beaten up at school. There's a new girl in my class and then there was a hamster in my sister's friend's sleeping bag.'

'You've got a lot going on,' Ray says thoughtfully.

'At least my mum's coming home.'

'That'll make a difference,' Ray says.

'How about you?' I ask.

'Spent yesterday at the allotment,' Ray says, unscrewing his flask. 'Harvested a pumpkin. Sowed a few sweet peas in the shed. Dug three new trenches.'

'That's good,' I say, thinking that things haven't been that great for me recently and that Ray must think my life is silly. I wonder if Ray has a job. 'Do you have a job?' I ask.

Ray smiles. 'I'm semi-retired. I've got a taxi. I don't advertise much anymore. I do a few jobs for old customers. I've got my regulars.' He reaches into his pocket and hands me a business card.

On the business card is a picture of a yellow car on a

black background. It's cartoon car with a smiley face. Next to the car it says *Ray's Taxis* in large red writing, along with a telephone number. I put the card in my pocket.

Ray takes something wrapped in kitchen foil from his rucksack. 'Here,' he says. 'Fancy a piece of flapjack? My wife made them.'

I know that I mustn't take sweets from strangers, or probably in fact, anything edible. We learnt this at school when we did Stranger Danger. At first I thought we were being told this because strangers might want to poison children but then we watched a video about a girl who was offered sweets from a man and when she reached out to take them he pulled her into his car and drove off with her. I always wondered what happened to that girl in the video. It was then I realised that strangers might use sweets as bait to pull children into cars. I never liked sweets as much as some children. I would be more susceptible to a cheese and pickle sandwich.

Although Ray has a taxi and it's his job to persuade people to travel in his car, right now we are sitting on a bench on a busy station platform. I can't see any cars. The flapjacks also look very nice and unlikely to be laced with poison. I gratefully accept.

After we have eaten our flapjacks, Ray reaches into his pocket again. 'Seen this?' he asks. He hands me a newspaper clipping. There is a picture of a train in a workshop and the headline, *Full Steam Ahead as Flying Scotsman Set to Return.*

'Do you know the Flying Scotsman?' Ray asks.

'The first train to reach a hundred miles an hour,' I say.

Ray looks impressed. 'That's her,' he says. 'The grand old lady of steam. Greatest locomotive in the world.' He screws the lid back on his flask. 'They're fixing her up,' he says.

'She must be very old now,' I say.

'She is indeed,' Ray says smiling. 'She took her first run back in 1923. She's on the tracks again after ninety years. Imagine that. Ninety years.' He turns to me. 'You keep an eye out for the old girl. She'll be out and about before too long.'

'I will,' I say.

Ray looks at the picture of The Flying Scotsman once more. We both look at it. 'You can't tell me,' Ray says. 'When you see her there, that that engine hasn't got a soul.' He sniffs and I think that he might be choking back a tear. He carefully folds the piece of newspaper and puts the article back in his pocket.

A train pulls up. Ray mutters a number and makes a note in his notepad. I see Sarah and the two girls from last night getting off the train with bags of shopping from Forever 21, and H&M and Roxy, and Victoria's Secret.

I don't enjoy shopping as I don't like crowds and I get hot in changing rooms. Mum takes me shopping after Christmas when the sales are on and it's even worse then. The only good thing about going shopping with Mum is that she has to stop regularly for cups of tea and she usually buys me a jam donut in the café at John Lewis.

Most of my clothes come from charity shops. I prefer to wear old clothes as new clothes make me itch. I have several old shirts and woolly jumpers which I bought from charity shops. When I wear these clothes Sarah pretends she isn't related to me.

I am not very good at deciding what to wear. Most of my other clothes come from GAP because the styles are simple and unconfusing. I have four pairs of GAP jeans, six T-shirts, three of them striped, and two GAP sweat-shirts. I like to wear certain colours on certain days of the week but that isn't always possible, either because Mum hasn't done the washing or because I don't own a T-shirt in the colour for that day. When I am older and have my own money, I will make sure I have enough coloured T-shirts to cover all the colours of the days of the week.

Today I am wearing my favourite baggy GAP jeans and a purple checked shirt that may have once belonged to Dad. I like to be comfortable.

'That's my sister,' I say to Ray. 'In the white jeans. With all the bags.'

Sarah looks at me and quickly looks away in disgust. The girl with the nose piercing is lighting a cigarette.

'I wouldn't have thought it,' Ray says.

'We're different,' I say.

'I'm not sure she's seen you,' Ray says.

'She has,' I say.

The train moves off and Sarah and her friends leave the platform with their bags. They move quickly past us. They are a blur of carrier bags and skinny jeans.

'My brother and I always looked very different,' Ray says. 'People used to say he was the milkman's son, or maybe that I was. I forget which.'

'Sometimes I imagine my real parents are living by a loch in Scotland,' I say. 'They home school me. I am an only child and I am very privileged. I am determined to make a success of my life in order to repay the love, attention, time and effort my parents have invested in me.'

'That's quite a thought,' Ray says. 'I've got an aunt in Scotland.'

'Does she live by a loch? I say.

'No,' Ray says. 'She's got a bungalow in Ayrshire.'

We sit quietly on our bench as the train pulls away, each lost in our own thoughts.

5

When I return home, Mum is in the kitchen peeling vegetables. It's as if she's never been away.

'Hi Mum,' I say.

'Hi Lou,' she says.

'You're back,' I say.

'Yes,' she says, putting down the vegetable peeler.

'Are you better?' I ask.

She doesn't answer, just wipes her hands on her jeans and we both move towards each other, and before I know it she is hugging me and saying, 'Oh, Lou.'

Usually I am not at all keen on people hugging me but I don't mind when it's my mum. My mum is one of the only people who I will let hug me. She knows it has to be quick and tight. Mikey knows that I don't like being hugged. Sometimes we touch fists which is our way of hugging. It suits me better.

Mum quickly releases me then studies me in that way parents do, looking at you as if they are trying to figure out if you have grown, or if there might be something different about you they didn't notice before.

Satisfied she hasn't missed anything, Mum returns to the vegetables. 'Would you like the fish or the potatoes?' she asks, dropping green beans into the steamer.

'The potatoes,' I say. 'And purple cabbage, because Saturday is a good day for purple vegetables.'

'Okay, Lou,' Mum says.

WE EAT DINNER together at the kitchen table, all five of us, which is weird after everything that has happened over the last few weeks. It's like we are pretending to be a real family.

Sarah is unhappy because she wanted to go out with her fireman boyfriend after she got back from shopping, but Dad said she had to stay home because we needed to have a family dinner and talk about 'the future'.

'Where's Nan?' Mikey asks.

'Bingo,' Dad says.

'Is she going to carry on living here?' I ask.

'No,' Mum says. 'She'll be leaving tomorrow.'

Dad frowns but doesn't say anything. He moves his mashed potato around on his plate.

'Your dad might move in with your nan for a little while,' Mum says, glancing sideways at Dad.

Dad looks up suddenly. 'I shouldn't think it will come to that,' he says. 'I expect to find somewhere fairly soon.'

'Will we have to move too?' I ask.

Mikey looks very worried about this. Mum tries to reassure us. 'We might have to move,' she says. 'But it won't be for a while yet.'

I feel very sad about having to move, although I try not to show it as I knew before I asked that it would be unlikely we could all stay in the house without Dad here. Houses are expensive. I feel sad for Mum, seeing as she waited ten years for the kitchen.

'Count me out,' Sarah says. 'I'm not sharing a room. Brett says I can stay with him. He rents a flat with his friend Liam. They pay someone to do the cleaning.'

'We'll talk about it,' Mum says.

Mikey looks upset. 'Will we have to move somewhere much smaller?' he asks Mum.

'No,' Mum says. 'I shouldn't think so. Not according to my lawyer anyway.'

I notice that Dad has turned very pale. This is new. No one has mentioned anything about a lawyer before.

Mikey looks relieved.

Everyone seems to be concentrating hard on eating their mashed potato and fish and green beans, peas and purple cabbage.

I'm glad Mum is back and that she is feeling better. Last time I saw her it was as though she had been abducted by aliens. There are different kinds of alien abductions. My friend Sam knows a lot about this as he is very interested in the subject. I don't mean the kind of abductions whereby the aliens perform experiments on humans while they are sleeping. No, I mean the body snatchery type, where aliens replace human beings with their own kind. In these cases, the human being still looks like a human being but isn't.

I know that Mum wasn't really abducted by aliens but I do want to know the truth about what happened. One day she was preparing our chicken Kievs like a normal Mum and the next she was performing cathartic fire rituals in our living room.

'Mum,' I say. 'Why did you steal from Debenhams and burn our photographs?'

Mum sighs. 'I wasn't well,' she says. Seeing how unsatisfied I look she adds, 'I had a slight brain dysfunction.'

'What kind of brain dysfunction?' I ask.

'Oh, just a touch of paranoid schizophrenia,' she says, in the way some people say *just a touch of flu*.

She puts down her knife and takes a sip of water. 'I've had a good rest.' She says this as if she's been away on a spa weekend in Hertfordshire, or on a walking holiday in

Wales, instead of in a hospital ward where she wasn't allowed a phone charger.

'Any more questions?' Mum asks.

Mikey solemnly shakes his head. Dad is still concentrating on his mashed potato. He has pushed it all together so that it forms a sort of tower on his plate. I wonder if he is building a replica of the mountain that the alien mother ship lands on like the man in that film by Stephen Spielberg, *Close Encounters of the Third Kind*. That film is one of Sam's favourites.

Sarah is looking down at her mobile phone on her lap. It seems our conversation about this family's future is already over.

'Good,' Mum says. 'It's important we communicate.'

I stab a pea with my fork and miss.

The pea rolls slowly off the table and onto the floor.

No one notices.

THE FOLLOWING WEEK we see Faith at lunch time. She scans the hall and I wonder if she's looking for us or just looking for a place to sit.

'Should I wave to her?' I ask Sam.

Sam shrugs. 'I guess so.'

I try to catch Faith's eye without drawing too much attention to myself as I am not always comfortable with lots of people looking at me. I do this by staring very intently at Faith, hoping she will look our way.

When she does look our way, I hold up my hand, kind of like an Indian chief. When she sees me, I give her a very small wave - like the Queen from her royal carriage.

Faith walks over and sits down at our table.

I notice she is carrying an apple and a book. This is

strange because mostly, at our school, books belong in the library. We keep textbooks in our lockers and we have to read a library book sometimes in our English class, but people do not usually carry books around with them like Faith is.

Sam and I like books a lot. I love to read because I can forget about myself and everything else, and you can always learn things from books. Like that time I read about how it's possible to tie someone up using just six inches of string.

One of my favourite books when I was younger that I still re-read sometimes is *The Wind in the Willows*. My favourite part of *The Wind in the Willows* is when Mole and Ratty get lost in the *Wild Wood* in the snow and Mole falls over and bangs his shin on Mr Badger's door-scraper. Then Mr Badger answers the door in his dressing gown and carpet slippers and says to Rat and Mole, 'This is not the sort of night for small animals to be out'.

Sam likes science fiction novels, especially those where scientists travel back into the past and meet famous people like Robin Hood or Shakespeare.

Sam and I don't usually carry our books around with us like Faith as this is considered geeky and uncool and we don't want to get teased. We try to remain invisible so as to avoid getting picked on. Until recently, when the whole Kaylee and Dad thing started, this has always worked pretty well for me. It's easy for me to be invisible.

Faith, I have noticed, is one of those people that everyone looks at when they enter a room, whereas I am one of those people who no one ever appears to see. Sometimes people even fall over me and then seem surprised to notice I'm there.

'What are you reading?' I ask Faith.

'*The Outsider*,' she says.

'What's it about?' Sam asks, because this is what you say when you haven't read a book.

'Death,' Faith says. 'Alienation. One man's indifference to an essentially absurd and godless universe.'

There is a moment's silence whilst Sam and I consider this.

'Sounds good,' Sam offers.

'Don't you believe in God?' I ask Faith.

'God is dead.'

'Are you having an existential crisis?' I ask Faith.

'Definitely,' Faith says.

Sam must have looked alarmed when Faith said 'God is dead' because Faith looks at him and says, 'It's okay. I didn't say it first.'

'Who did then?' Sam says.

'Nietzsche,' Faith says.

'Who's that?' Sam asks.

'German bloke with a large moustache,' Faith says, taking a bite of her apple. 'Graham told me about him.'

'I don't believe in God either,' Sam says. 'I believe in the Anunnaki, although I have to pretend I believe in God when I go and visit my gran because she goes to church and she gets very upset if I say I don't believe in God. I also have to pretend I like her date and pecan biscuits. She makes them because I'm not allergic to pecans.'

Faith looks thoughtful. 'What's the Anunnaki?'

I eat my sandwich whilst Sam explains to Faith that the Anunnaki are an extra-terrestrial race that came to earth around 5,000 BC when they genetically manipulated mankind by blending some of their own genes with the genes of our ancestors.

Faith listens and nods as if it could be possible.

'Who's Graham?' I ask Faith.

'One of my dads,' she says.

'You have two dads?' I ask.

'And two mums,' Faith says. 'Well, actually four now that Kate and Lizzie split up and Lizzie went to live with Fran, and now Kate lives with Susie and that's where I live most of the time.'

'That sounds complicated,' I say, thinking that two parents are difficult enough to cope with.

'Not really,' Faith says.

'No one can have more than two parents,' Sam says. 'It isn't possible.'

'Well, of course it isn't *biologically* possible,' Faith says. 'But, legally, I have three parents that entered into a platonic parenting agreement before I was born, only then Kate, that's my birthmum, met Lizzie when I was three and Lizzie was a big part of my life until I was ten when she moved out to be with Fran, which is why I go and stay with Lizzie and Fran sometimes. And then Susie moved in with us so that kind of makes four mums.'

Sam doesn't look convinced.

'What's platonic parenting?' I ask.

'When people decide to have a child together, but they are just friends. They don't have sex and they're not in love,' Faith clarifies whilst picking a pip out of her apple. 'So my parents met on a co-parenting website before I was born and got to know each other. My dads are both gay and wanted to have a child and my mum is also gay and wasn't in a relationship and was worried about her biological clock. I was made by artificial insemination at a posh clinic in London with real art on the walls. They had to try a few times.'

Faith looks from me to Sam. 'My parents have always been totally open about everything,' she says.

'I think that's great,' I say.

'Yeah,' Sam says after a moment of consideration. 'It's great.'

Faith shrugs. 'I was kind of a social experiment. It worked out pretty good. I have three bedrooms in different houses now, and I get to go on lots of holidays.'

'Do your mums and dads have any other children?' I ask Faith.

'No,' she says. 'One child between six is actually very good for the environment. The planet is already over-populated. Soon there won't be enough food for everyone, or enough countries with a temperate climate for people to live in.'

Suddenly my parents having three children seems excessive. I decide not to mention this. Annabel and Neil only had me because they also agree that the world is over-populated and are more familiar with ecological and environmental issues.

'Why did you leave your old school?' Sam asks.

Faith looks down at her apple core. 'I haven't been to school before,' she says. 'I was home educated.'

I can't believe what I'm hearing. I have never met anyone apart from myself in my alternative life with Annabel and Neil who has been home schooled, or 'home educated', as Faith calls it.

'Wow,' I say. 'That must have been great.'

'Yeah,' Faith says. 'Actually it was. I've only been here a couple of weeks and I can tell you, school is fucking depressing.'

'Were you home educated by your mums or your dads?' I ask Faith.

'Kind of both,' she says. 'On the days my mum had to work I would go to Graham and Will's. Graham lectures in philosophy at the university in town and Will writes articles for magazines so usually one of them would be at home, if my mum couldn't have me. We'd hang out and talk about stuff because my dads don't have a TV, and sometimes I'd get to go on these trips to museums or Stonehenge and places like that with a coach full of other Home Ed kids and their mums and dads.'

I think that I would like to tell Faith about Annabel and Neil and that they home educate me on the loch in the life I should have had, but I wonder if it might sound weird so I decide not to.

Sam goes to buy a bottle of water because any drink with sugar in it gives him a headache and Faith and I walk to our lockers. She waits for me whilst I get my stuff and then I wait for her whilst she gets her stuff. This is nice because we do this without talking about it first.

'Do you like R.E.M.?' Faith says, rummaging around in her locker.

'I'm not sure,' I say, thinking of rapid eye movement and sleep patterns but being aware that this might not be what Faith means. 'What is it?'

Faith hands me a CD. 'They're a band,' she says. 'They're really cool. I think you might like them. You can have this CD. The original is Will's but this one's a copy.'

'Thanks,' I say. The album cover is of a group called 'Til Tuesday'. In the foreground is a girl with very puffed up white-blonde hair wearing a tank-top.

'Don't worry about the cover,' Faith says. 'Stuff gets mixed up in our house. Inside it's R.E.M.'

I slide the CD inside my science textbook. No one has ever given me a CD of a cool band that belongs to their dad before, or even any CD of any band before.

Faith and I walk into registration together. I think that I will listen to the CD when I get home. Faith is busy applying more purple lip gloss. She seems to have forgotten about giving me the CD already.

After school I collect my bag and my coat from my locker and leave the building. I am walking very fast, partly because it looks like it might rain and partly because I don't like school and am always keen to get home as quickly as possible.

I have my head down as I cross the playing field on my way to the gate. I am whispering very fast a poem I like about being on a train which goes like this:

Faster than fairies, faster than witches,
Bridges and houses, hedges and ditches;
And charging along like troops in a battle,
All through the meadows the horses and cattle...

I pass a group of boys from my year and it is my own fault for having my head down and whispering the poem to myself and not paying attention to what is happening around me because as I am rushing past, one of the boys puts his foot out and trips me up.

'Your dad's a paedo!' he shouts.

I fall over, face down. In fact, I don't just fall, I seem to fly momentarily through the air, my coat flapping out at the side like wings before I land, my arms and my legs sticking out like a starfish.

Luckily the grass is soft and muddy, I have lots of layers of clothing on and am not too hurt.

The boys are laughing.

'Careful,' the one who tripped me up says loudly as they move away from me.

'Watch where you're going,' another one shouts.

'Don't stack it!'

They walk away still laughing whilst I pick myself up. My white school shirt is muddy from the wet ground and my glasses have landed in a nearby puddle that is probably a hole used for goalposts.

I stand up and wipe my glasses. I try not to show the boys that I'm upset but it doesn't matter as they aren't looking at me anymore. My coat is muddy as well but I tell myself I can easily wipe it down when I get home.

I watch the boys walk through the open gate that leads from the school playing field to the farmer's fields. I can only hope they didn't film me falling over or take a picture of me on their phones. My school is very strict about things like that and they would get into big trouble if they had filmed me falling over but it did happen once to a girl called Isabel. There was a video going round of her being tripped up in the corridor and when she fell you could see her pink knickers. It would be just my luck that it would happen to me, although I don't wear pink knickers and I always wear tights.

I didn't see any of them holding a phone but it all happened so quickly and then I had my face in the mud.

I notice that above me the sky is darkening. The clouds are moving together to form one big cloud. I doubt I will make it home before it rains.

I look around. The school playing field is now deserted. For a moment it seems as though I am the only person in the world, just one girl standing in the middle of a school playing field under a very dark sky with mud on her shirt and her coat, and muddy water on her glasses.

Although I want to be at home, somewhere warm and safe, just for a second it feels nice, in a happy/sad kind of way, to be the only person alone on a school playing field with mud on her coat and muddy water on her glasses, and even though I am cold, and possibly bruised after being tripped up, it's nice to stand alone under the sky with no one around to bother me.

There is a loud clap of thunder and then it begins to rain. Big, fat droplets are falling on my head and soaking my already muddy shirt. My hair is getting wet. My face is wet. My tights are wet. I button up my coat, tightly grip the straps of my rucksack, put my head down and run.

I do not want to get struck by lightning on the school playing field.

I read something once about a girl being struck by lightning who was saved by the under-wiring in her bra.

I do not have under-wiring in my bra.

When I get home Mikey is the only one in, although I notice Dad has finally got around to painting to living room walls. It seems that our house used to be full of people and now it is mostly me and Mikey. We are like the only survivors of a shipwreck, sitting on a tiny desert island keeping a fire going in case of passing ships. Only in our case the island is the kitchen table and instead of making fire Mikey makes cake.

Mum has gone back to work now and she seems to be going out a lot in the evenings in order to avoid Dad, but

Dad is never in anyway as he goes out in the evenings to avoid Mum. Sarah is never in because she is always out with her friends or her new boyfriend. She has started staying at his flat now when he has his days off or when he doesn't have to work nights.

Mum is going to classes at the gym which she has never done before. She has bought lots of new tops and leggings and a swimming costume, and they are always on the drying rack in the kitchen. She has stuck the gym class timetable on the fridge and circled in blue biro things like *Tai Chi,* and and *Body Balance* and *Aqua Aerobics* and *Nova.* I am especially unsure about what this *Nova* is so I decide to google it. The first definition I get says: *A star showing a sudden large increase in brightness and then slowly returning to its original state over a few months,* which makes sense. The second definition says: *A combination of freestyle fitness yoga and Pilates in a language you can understand,* which sounds silly to me although I guess it must be that one.

Mikey walks into the kitchen.

'What have you got in the oven?' I ask.

'Banana loaf. You can have some when it's done. Have you seen this?' he says, looking a little upset and passing me the local paper that comes through the letter box every Thursday.

I look at the paper. There is a small article that says, *Teacher Suspended over Relationship with Student.* The article doesn't say much, it just mentions our school and that a male teacher has been suspended after conducting an inappropriate relationship with a sixth form student.

'Nan will know now,' I say. 'He can't keep it from her.'

'Everyone will know,' Mikey says, looking depressed.

I suddenly think of something I haven't thought of

before that makes me very worried. 'Will Dad go to prison?' I ask.

'No,' Mikey says firmly.

'Is it because Kaylee is over sixteen and they love each other?'

'I guess so,' Mikey says, and then, 'What's happened to your shirt?'

'I fell over.'

'Bad luck,' Mikey says whilst bending down to check his loaf in the oven.

I leave the kitchen and go into the garage. There's a small, ancient CD player with a radio that Dad uses sometimes if he's cycling on his exercise bike or doing 'jobs' that involve him being in the garage.

I unplug the CD player. I have my laptop which has a CD slot but it's Dad's old laptop and the speakers aren't very good. I know my CD from Faith will sound much better if I put it in a proper CD player.

Mikey watches me as I bring the CD player into the kitchen. He doesn't say anything. A lot of stuff has been moved around in our house recently. I think this is because Dad will be leaving soon and he is trying to figure out what to take with him without it looking like he is taking anything.

I go upstairs. Once I shut my bedroom door I suddenly feel very tired and I have to sit on the floor for a while. This happens to me sometimes, especially after school. I have a special place on the floor next to my bed and my book shelf and I sit there, sometimes for quite a long time. I like to sit there and just be very still and very quiet. Sometimes I cry and that makes me feel better, but I don't always cry. Lots of times I am happy just to be there on the floor by myself. I think I have to sit here in order to gather myself back together again. Maybe it's because of being tripped up after school or because of seeing the article about Dad in the paper but I know I have to sit here today.

I sit on the floor for a while until I hear Mum come in from work and start to make dinner. I get up, plug the CD player in and take the CD from inside my science text book.

Faith has written on it in very large writing. 'In Time: The Best of R.E.M. 1988-2003' I know it's Faith's handwriting because I recognise it from her homework diary. She has very messy handwriting.

I don't have many CDs because by the time I was born the internet was fully evolved and it's easy to listen to music for free if you don't mind adverts. Mum and Dad have a CD collection downstairs. It's clearly divided into Mum's section and Dad's section. Mum and Dad never listen to music through the internet as they say the quality is bad.

One Christmas Mum bought me some Motown CDs of artists like The Four Tops and Diana Ross and The Supremes. Most of these CDs are now in Mikey's bedroom. Mikey especially likes The Supremes. He often plays 'You Can't Hurry Love' to cheer himself up.

Mum and Dad have always had very different tastes in music. Dad likes bands like Madness which Mum hates. Mum likes bands like New Order and The Cure because they remind her of the late 1980s, when she was still young and free. She used to play a song called 'True Faith,' very loud whenever she hovered which used to drive Dad crazy as he hates New Order.

The only band my parents both liked when we were younger was The Beautiful South. We used to go and visit my Granny Eve and my granddad Jim, my mum's parents who live in Cornwall, every summer and, as The Beautiful South was the only band my parents both liked and Sarah, Mikey and I also liked, we used to always listen to The Beautiful South. Dad especially liked the song where the singer recites all the names of his ex-girlfriends and says 'I love you from the bottom of my pencil case'.

One summer, when we got in the car, Sarah said she didn't like The Beautiful South anymore and that if she had to listen to one more Beautiful South song, she would throw herself out of the window and onto the motorway and they'd have to collect her limbs, put them in the plastic bags we kept for Mikey's travel sickness, and try to re-assemble her before the funeral.

Dad said that wasn't funny. He was so cross and disappointed in Sarah for no longer liking The Beautiful South and spoiling our 'driving and listening to family music' ritual that we had to drive all the way there in silence. The entire six hours.

I never used to enjoy these car journeys because I was the smallest which meant I had to sit in the middle. Mikey always got travel sick and once threw up on me twice on the same journey. One year Sarah developed a game where she would kick my bare shin very hard and then when I yelled out pretend that she hadn't done anything and that I was just being weird by spontaneously yelling 'ouch!' every five minutes.

No one believed me until we arrived in Cornwall and they saw my left leg was purple. Sarah was grounded for the first day of our holiday and had to stay in whilst we went to the beach.

I sit on the floor and listen to my R.E.M. CD until Mum

calls me down for dinner. Listening to the CD makes me feel happy, partly because the music makes me feel happy and partly because Faith thought to give it to me.

I think that I will tell Faith I especially like three songs. The one where the man is 'losing his religion', the one where he is 'pushing an elephant up the stairs', and looking for answers 'from the great beyond', and the one where he talks about the man on the moon and sings 'yeah yeah yeah' a lot.

THE NEXT DAY is Friday and Faith isn't in school. I wonder if she is sick.

I always think I would be much better off at home, learning what I want to learn in a way that I can remember. Sometimes I *really* don't want to go into school and I have, occasionally, had days off sick when I haven't really been sick. I don't do this very often as I don't like lying. When I was younger it was very hard for me to take days off sick as both Mum and Dad work and it would have meant that one of them would have had to stay home with me. I used to feel very guilty about this as I knew Mum and Dad needed to go to work. Usually, if I had a cold, I would have to go to school. Mum would give me fizzy vitamin C tablets in the morning and send me in with a wad of tissues soaked in Olbas oil that I would keep up my sleeve.

Once when I was younger, I took a day off school sick and Mrs De Souza from next door came round to look after me. I told Mum never to ask her again as she sat next to me on the sofa all day watching programs about people who found old objects in their lofts and thought they might be valuable, and then she gave me tinned soup.

Mrs De Souza made me feel very uncomfortable by being so close to me all the time and putting damp flannels on my forehead.

I hope Faith isn't too sick.

We have P.E. in the afternoon. It's our last lesson of the day. P.E. is one of my least favourite subjects. I always feel cold, whether we are in the school hall or the gym, or outside, and I hate the getting changed part. The getting changed part is the worst.

The worst thing of all is if you forget your P.E. kit because if you forget your P.E. kit you have to wear 'spare kit'.

'Spare kit' is a big plastic carrier bag filled with a random collection of old P.E. clothes that no one has claimed. The clothes always smell funny and are too big or too small and everyone knows there are period stains in the shorts. Also, written on the clothes in large white writing, is 'spare kit' so if you are forced to wear 'spare kit' everyone will know just by looking at the back of your shorts or tracksuit bottoms. There are a pair of old plimsolls in 'spare kit' and if they are too big you are forced to wear extra socks and if they are too small you have to wear your ordinary school shoes which always looks ridiculous.

Luckily I have remembered my P.E. kit.

We have to line up outside the sports hall whilst Mrs Jones, with her whistle and her clipboard, who, like my dad, always wears shorts whatever the weather, takes the register.

Then we are let into the changing rooms.

I hate the changing rooms as they are always noisy with girls talking and Mrs Jones is always coming in and telling us to hurry up.

I get a spot in the corner and begin to get changed, careful to avoid looking at anyone else because if you look too long at anyone else in the changing rooms, you are called a lesbian. As I take my clothes off and put my P.E. kit on, I place my clothes in a line on the bench so I don't lose them.

I don't like losing things. Sometimes even just losing the smallest thing that I don't really need at that moment can make me feel panicky.

I begin to roll my tights up, starting at the toes, thinking that I will put them in the pocket of my blazer so I don't lose them.

'Look at Louise. She's so *weird*.'

I turn around, half dressed in my tracksuit trousers and camisole. Cherry Wiles is staring at me. Bryony Silver turns round and looks at me too.

'Yeah, she's a freak,' Bryony says.

More and more of the girls are turning to look at me. There is a group of girls in my class generally thought of as the 'popular girls' and now they are all looking at me.

'She's not even wearing a proper bra,' one of the other girls says.

This is not true. I am wearing a proper bra from Debenhams that came from the underwear department. It's just that it doesn't have under-wiring as I find under-wiring very uncomfortable.

'She doesn't need to,' Cherry says, and they all laugh at me.

'What's she done with her tights?' Bryony says, looking at my tightly rolled tight ball which I was about to put in my blazer pocket.

'Look at her clothes on the bench,' Lianne Parks says. 'It's so *weird*.'

I try to speak in order to defend myself but I can't. This happens to me sometimes in stressful situations. I can't seem to form the words I want to say. I want to tell them to go away, to leave me alone, that I don't care what they think of me, although I do.

I open my mouth but no words come out.

'Say it, don't spray it,' Lianne says, causing them all to laugh.

I try to speak again but I can't seem to say anything. Instead I flap my hands, something I can't help doing but had not intended to do.

They are all shouting things about me now.

'Nutter!'

'Freak!'

'Weirdo!'

'Look - she's flapping like a chicken. She's not even human.'

Bryony walks over and stands very close to me. For a moment I think she is going to hit me but then she leans over and sweeps my clothes off the bench and onto the floor.

All the girls begin to laugh again.

The sight of my clothes on the floor makes me feel very distressed. I make a sound in my throat, a sort of small wail. I had not intended to do this either, but I can't help it.

The room begins to spin. All the girls are laughing at me and pointing and all my clothes are out of order and on the floor and I will probably lose something. I feel very confused and I wish they would stop laughing because it's hurting my ears.

I put my hands over my ears and sit on the floor. I don't realise I am doing it at first but I am rocking from side to side. I just want it all to go away.

'Whatever is going on in here?'

I open my eyes at the sound of Mrs Jones' voice very loud and very close to me. I take my hands away from my ears.

All the girls grow quiet and pretend to be getting on with the business of changing into their P.E. kit.

I am still on the floor, now hugging my knees, still rocking a little and surrounded by my clothes.

'Get up Louise.'

I look at Mrs Jones but I can't speak. I want to tell her that I can't get up just yet, that I will need to stay here for a few minutes longer and that I would like to talk to her but I can't do that just yet either.

'I said get up!'

I just sit and look at her. I can't get up.

She looks at me in disgust then turns to the rest of the class. 'Does anyone know what happened here?'

I wince because Mrs Jones' voice sounds like a dog barking.

All the girls are shaking their heads. 'She just freaked out, Miss. She threw her clothes on the floor.'

Mrs Jones walks over and stands in front of me.

'I said, GET UP, Louise.'

I try to get up but I have to do this very slowly and it makes me feel sick.

'Get your stuff together and go and see Mr Dodd. Tell him you were being disruptive. I don't want you in this class.'

I start to pick my clothes up off the floor and get changed back into my uniform. I can feel all the girls looking at me whilst trying to pretend they're not.

Finally, Mrs Jones and the other girls leave for their P.E. lesson. They all stare at me as they walk past.

I decide this is one of the worst P.E. lessons ever.

When I get to Mr Dodd's office he does not look pleased to see me.

I try to explain that Mrs Jones has sent me for 'being disruptive'. I explain it all very quickly because I have been rehearsing it in my head on the way to his office to make sure I get it right. Sometimes after I get panicky and can't speak, when my speech does come back, the words all comes out at once.

Mr Dodd doesn't appear to have been listening to me. He looks stressed. When I arrived he was gathering papers from his office and rubbing the bald spot on his head.

He says that I must remain in 'isolation' for the rest of the afternoon.

'Isolation' is where they put you if you get sent out of a classroom or if you do something very bad. It just means that you have to sit in an office under the supervision of a teacher for the remainder of the lesson, or sometimes the entire day.

'Isolation' is supposed to be a punishment and, although I don't like the thought of a teacher thinking I have done something wrong, I don't like most of my classes or other people very much so, for me, 'Isolation' is not much of a punishment.

'Where did you say you'd come from?' Mr Dodd says.

'Outside,' I say, because I am thinking that I just had to walk all the way around the building to get to Mr Dodd's office.

Mr Dodd glares at me. 'Don't be smart,' he says.

This makes me feel confused because I wasn't trying to be smart, I was only trying to answer the question.

'Your name. Your form tutor,' Mr Dodd says impatiently.

I take a deep breath before I answer because I am still finding it difficult to speak. 'My name is Louise Coulson. My form tutor is Mr Wexhall.'

Mr Dodd gives me a funny look. 'Well, I can't take you on,' he says. 'I've got a meeting.'

I'm not sure what he means by this as 'taking on' implies the taking up of a project of some sort. I am not a project. I am just supposed to sit somewhere in silence and read my textbooks, or contemplate my badness and how I will reform myself.

'Go and see Mr Lawrence,' Mr Dodd says, ushering me out of his office and locking the door behind him. 'He'll take you. Did Mrs Jones give you anything to do?'

I shake my head.

Mr Dodd sighs. 'Go to your locker and get a book, or some homework or something.'

I nod.

Mr Dodd gives me one last glance then turns and walks quickly away, leaving me standing outside his office, still holding my P.E. bag.

I go to my locker and put away my P.E. bag. The corridor and locker area are quiet. I wish they could always be like this. I take out my pencil case and English exercise book, along with a play we are reading called *Death of a Salesman*. I am enjoying the play. Our English teacher says it is about a man who has been 'left empty' after the end of his 'American dream'.

I am feeling a little better now. Mostly because I don't have to do P.E. and the others do, and because I am going to see Mr Lawrence and I like Mr Lawrence.

Mr Lawrence is our art teacher. I have had him for two years now. He's quite strict and sometimes makes us do our art in silence. I don't mind this as I get very absorbed in what I am doing and find other people's noise a distraction.

If he comes round to see you at your desk, you are very lucky as he will always spend a lot of time with you, helping you with your technique.

Mr Lawrence wears brightly coloured jackets and scarves and sometimes he tells us stories, like the one about how his grandfather arrived in London in 1952 from an island called Saint John in the Caribbean with only a linen suit, a small suitcase and half a bottle of rum. I like Mr Lawrence's stories. I always remember them.

When I enter the art room it's full of Year Elevens. No one takes any notice of me.

'Louise.' Mr Lawrence notices me lingering by the door. Today he's wearing a red velvet jacket rolled up at the sleeves and a blue paisley scarf. 'And what can I do for you?' he says, getting up from his desk.

'I'm in Isolation,' I say. 'I'm supposed to sit in your office. Mr Dodd has a meeting.'

Mr Lawrence raises an eyebrow. 'Isolation? How did that happen then?'

I begin to follow Mr Lawrence into his office. The door is open. I've been in before because some of the art supplies are kept in here, like the smallest brushes, and tracing paper.

I don't feel much like talking so I just say, 'I'm not sure,' which is true anyway.

Mr Lawrence smiles and I feel I should try and say something else so I say. 'My things were on the floor in the changing room and I flapped my hands and sat on the floor and Mrs Jones told me she couldn't have me in her class anymore.'

Mr Lawrence looks at me for a moment. He seems to

be considering something. He smiles at me again. It seems like a kind smile. I can't always tell when smiles are real or fake. Mr Lawrence has kind eyes and, today, a kind smile too, which makes me feel better. 'Well,' he says finally. 'Make yourself at home.' He gestures towards his desk and chair, meaning for me to sit down. 'I'll be in and out,' he says. 'Give me a shout if you need anything. Do you have something to do?'

I nod because I have *Death of a Salesman* to read.

Mr Lawrence looks at *Death of a Salesman* and smiles. He picks up a book on his desk. 'If not, I was going to suggest this one,' he says. 'I'm reading it at lunch times.'

I look at the book Mr Lawrence is holding. He is using a bent train ticket as a bookmark. The book is called *Jude the Obscure*.

'Have you read it?' Mr Lawrence asks me.

I shake my head. 'What's it about?' I say, because that is what you usually say when you haven't read something.

Mr Lawrence looks thoughtful. 'It's about a man,' he says. 'He's young at first, but then he gets older. He tries very hard, but he doesn't seem to succeed.'

I nod because I don't know what else to say about this man who gets older and doesn't seem to succeed. Even though Mr Lawrence is one of my favourite teachers, I am still surprised that he hasn't told me off and that he doesn't seem disappointed that I have been sent to him in 'isolation'. I am also surprised that now he is telling me about the book he is reading called *Jude the Obscure* with the picture of the bearded man on the cover.

'It's the people who are different who make the difference, Lou. You remember that,' Mr Lawrence adjusts his scarf.

I nod again.

'Right,' he says. 'I'd better get back to the class.'

I sit at the desk in the art office surrounded by all the books and art supplies and the aprons hanging on the peg rail, and *Jude The Obscure.*

I don't do anything for a while because I feel quite exhausted and need to gather myself together. I look at the grain of the wood on Mr Lawrence's desk. I trace my finger along the grooves and over the embedded splashes of paint and ink.

I feel a little calmer.

The Year Elevens in the classroom are very quiet and must be absorbed in their art work. I can hear the murmur of voices and catch the odd word as they talk to each other and as Mr Lawrence talks to them. I can hear the swishing of brushes in jam jars. I like all these sounds and I like it that I can hear the sounds without anyone looking at me because I am hidden behind the door at the desk.

I read *Death of a Salesman* for a while. Then I decide to look at Mr Lawrence's book. I open it very carefully and begin to read.

The school master was leaving the village, and everybody seemed sorry.

I think that I would be very sorry if Mr Lawrence left our school. I don't get any further than the first line because the bell rings and it's time to go home.

When I get home Dad is in the living room putting his football annuals from the bottom shelf of the bookcase into a large cardboard box.

'Hi, Dad,' I say.

'Hi Lou,' he says, trying to cover up what he is doing by standing in front of the box.

'I think you should go and see your nan,' he says.

'Does she know about you and Kaylee now?' I ask.

'Yes,' Dad says. 'She knows. It's all fine, Lou. You don't need to worry, but I would like you to go and see her. She says she doesn't see enough of you. I'll drop you round there if you like. You know she'll feed you. I'll pick you up later.'

I must be looking less than impressed with this idea, because Dad says, 'Come on, Lou.'

'What about Sarah and Mikey?' I ask.

Dad sighs. 'Sarah's being Sarah, and Mikey has to study. He has a mock exam on Monday so he's off the hook.'

Whenever people say things like this to me I can't help visualising what they say. I think of a giant hook and of Mikey attached by the collar of his shirt being pulled down and let off.

I am not going to be let off the hook. I am firmly on the hook.

'Okay,' I say reluctantly. 'I'll go.'

'Good,' Dad says. 'She'll be pleased.'

It's true, I think to myself, as I go upstairs to get changed out of my school uniform. Nan does always feed us when we go round to her flat. She still makes me boiled eggs and soldiers as I used to like boiled eggs and soldiers a lot when I was little. She also keeps chocolate Viennetta ice cream cake in her freezer for when we come round to see her.

I don't like going to other people's houses very much but I know Nan's flat already which makes me less anxious, and I know I won't have to stay long as Nan gets tired and sometimes falls asleep in front of the TV which means I can change the channel to a nature program. I also like to see Clive. Sometimes Clive will come and sit next to me on the sofa. I like to stroke him for a very long time as stroking Clive makes me feel happy and calm. Clive seems to like it too. He purrs and lifts his chin so I can stroke underneath it.

WHEN WE ARRIVE at Nan's, Dad drops me outside.

'Aren't you coming in?' I ask.

'Not this time,' Dad says. 'Text me when you want picking up.'

'Okay,' I say, getting out of the car.

I walk up the path to Nan's flat. I notice she has a new garden gnome with a red pointy hat and a spade.

When I was younger I used to be very frightened of Nan's garden gnomes. I used to imagine they would come alive and run after me and try to bite my ankles.

I have gotten a bit more used to them since then.

I ring Nan's door bell.

'Lou?' Nan opens the door. She looks surprised. She steps back to let me in.

'Hi, Nan,' I say.

'What are you doing here?' she asks me.

'I've come to see you,' I say.

'It's a bit inconvenient,' Nan says. 'I'm going out.'

I look back towards the driveway. Dad has already driven away.

'Well, never mind,' she says. 'I suppose you could come with me. Come in and sit down for a minute. I'll do you some eggs and soldiers.'

I sit down on the edge of Nan's sofa. Nan turns the TV

off as she knows I don't like to talk when the TV is on, especially when Nan has it on because she has it very loud.

'Where are you going?' I ask.

'The Spiritualist Church,' Nan says. 'I always go on a Friday.'

'Dad must have forgotten,' I say.

Nan smiles. 'He's in love, that's why. His brain has turned to mush.'

I try very hard not to think of Dad's brain turning to mush as it is not a nice image.

'You know then?' I ask tentatively, as Nan goes over to the kitchen area and puts a saucepan on for my eggs.

'Know what?' Nan says.

'About Dad having an affair with a sixth form student called Kaylee Deal, and it being in the paper, and Mum and Dad having a trial separation with a view to its becoming permanent, and Dad sleeping on the sofa under the frog duvet, and Mum going to gym classes.'

Nan turns round holding an egg in each hand. She peers closely at me. 'Yes, I think I knew most of that. Two eggs?'

I nod.

After Nan has put the eggs in the water and the timer is ticking away,she comes and sits next to me.

Clive jumps up onto my lap and I stroke him behind the ears and under his chin.

'It might be a good thing for your mum too,' Nan says. 'A change is as good as a rest.'

I want to say that it hasn't felt very restful in our house recently but I don't say anything. I continue to stroke Clive.

'And she seems a nice young girl,' Nan says. 'Very perky.'

'Who?' I say.

'Kaylee of course,' Nan says. 'They came round for tea last Saturday.'

'I didn't know that,' I say.

'We can't all know everything,' Nan says, getting up to put my toast on. 'And it would be nice to have another grandchild or two, before I pop off.'

'Pop off where?' I say.

Nan smiles at me. The timer makes a noise and she quickly turns the eggs off.

I can't imagine that having children is high on Kaylee's list of priorities but I decide not to tell Nan that.

Clive starts to purr. I like it when he purrs. I feel like I have a special relationship with Clive that only we understand. Animals are so much easier to get along with than people. Annabel and Neil understand my need to be around animals which is why we have Renzo. Whenever I ask Mum and Dad for a cat or a dog they say that one escaped hamster is enough for our house. Then they make excuses. They say a cat would hunt out Hammy and eat him, or that I wouldn't have time to walk a dog and the dog would be sad when we went on holiday, which means they don't want to pay for kennels.

I always have time to walk Renzo.

When I am older and have my own house I will definitely have animals. I think I will have a cottage in the county somewhere. I will have a cat and a dog, and maybe some sheep and chickens too. My eggs will always be fresh and I'll make the bread for my soldiers.

I have always wanted chickens. When I was much younger and I discovered that chicks came from eggs because I saw them being hatched under artificial conditions in a chicken factory on TV, I decided I would hatch my own chicks. I borrowed some eggs from the fridge and put them under my bed. I turned on my torch and kept the light on them for several days before the torch battery ran out and Mum said *what's that smell?* when she came in in the morning to wake me for school. I showed Mum the eggs under the bed. One of them had cracked and had made a sticky mess on the carpet.

'I just hope she doesn't wait as long as your mother did, or I shall never see them,' Nan says, bringing my eggs and soldiers over and putting them on the table.

I realise Nan is still talking about more grandchildren. Mum had Sarah at twenty-seven which Mum thinks was ridiculously early and Nan thinks was ridiculously late.

Clive jumps off my lap. He knows I have to sit at the table to eat and, if he's lucky, I might give him something when Nan isn't looking.

I sit down and tap my eggs with my spoon which I always do before sliding the tops off.

'Hurry up,' Nan says. 'We need to leave in twenty minutes.'

I remember that Nan is going to her Spiritualist Church. I'm not sure I want to go as I know Nan goes there to try and contact my granddad and that there will be other people there also trying to contact relatives and friends who have died. My nan says my granddad has never 'come through' but still she continues to go, just in case he does.

My dad says the Spiritualist Church is a con and wherever Granddad is, he isn't coming back. Mum said once under her breath that he wouldn't come back anyway as he didn't like being nagged when he was alive, and certainly wouldn't come back for more now he's dead.

'I'm not sure I want to speak to any dead people,' I say,

carefully scooping out the yolk and spreading it onto a solider.

'Oh, don't worry,' Nan says. 'It's the medium's night off. We've got an angel evening.'

'What's that?' I say.

'I don't know,' Nan says. 'We'll find out won't we. I just hope Gloria has stocked up the biscuit tin. Last week Julie's husband ate all the custard creams.'

6

WHEN we arrive, it's more like a village hall than a real church. There aren't any crosses or other religious stuff.

There's a circle of chairs in the middle of the hall and a lot of people are busy standing and talking to each other or draping their coats over pairs of chairs. In order to secure a good spot, I think. There are a lot of chairs with coats over them but no one sitting there. 'Like the Germans and their sun-loungers,' Dad would say.

I don't like lots of people talking all at once so I hide behind Nan and try to remain invisible.

'This is my granddaughter, Louise,' Nan says, to a tall woman with long dangly moon earrings and to another woman, much younger, who has black curly hair and a turquoise headscarf, and who is wearing a tight purple jumper.

I don't like purple very much, and I don't think it goes with turquoise. At least not *that* purple and *that* turquoise.

And the way Nan says 'this is my granddaughter,' it's difficult to tell if she's proud or apologising for me.

'Ah, a rainbow child,' the lady with the curly hair says, attempting to touch me.

'I don't think so,' I say, backing away very quickly.

'Pat, this is Tula,' the tall lady with the moon earrings says to Nan. My nan's name is Pat. 'She'll be hosting tonight. We're very lucky to get her.'

'It's wonderful to meet you both,' Tula says. 'Please, take a seat.'

Once we are sitting down I take out my phone and google 'rainbow child'.

Apparently rainbow children are children born in the new millennium who have never been incarnated before which means they have no karma or past lives. They like colours and are often psychic. They are full of energy and have an enthusiasm for life and tend to avoid being born into dysfunctional families.

That definitely isn't me.

Everyone sits down and Tula introduces herself as a lightworker who works specifically with angels who are God's missionaries. She says it like some people say they work with children or alcoholics.

Then we sing a couple of hymns, *All Things Bright and Beautiful* and *Cross Over the Road My Friend*. Luckily we used to sing these hymns at primary school so I know most of the words.

After we have sung the two hymns, we sing an ABBA song called *I Have a Dream*. Everyone sings very loudly, and a little out of tune, at the 'I believe in angels' part. Luckily I know the words to this too as Mikey likes ABBA.

After all the singing, Tula begins to tell us about angels. She tells us there are archangels and guardian angels. We each have a guardian angel and the archangels kind of oversee things, a bit like Mr Dodd. She tells us we can call on our guardian angel, or even an archangel, anytime we are in need; if we are feeling sad or desperate, or are suffering a bereavement or even, she says, for smaller things too, like if we lose our car keys, or can't decide which shoes to wear to a wedding, or forget what we wanted to buy from the supermarket when we get there.

She shows us pictures of the archangels and other angels in a giant scrapbook. I think that it must have taken her a very long time to put the scrap book together. Probably she has been collecting angel images since she was very little. Then she tells us what each angel specialises in: matters of the heart, healing past traumas, or helping you get a new job. So we don't waste time by calling on the wrong angel I guess.

Then she asks us to share our angel stories. I don't have any angel stories. Sarah once told me, when we were younger, that there was a goblin living down at the bottom of our garden and I believed her for quite a while, but I've never thought much about angels.

We all listen very politely to a woman who said she once met her guardian angel at an Esso garage in Stevenage and he sold her a packet of cigarettes. She said she knew he was her angel immediately and she left the garage feeling calm and peaceful and with an enormous sense of gratitude.

I wonder if her angel should have refused to sell her the cigarettes. Surely that would be looking out for her? I'm not sure angels should be promoting lung cancer.

Perhaps Tula thinks this too as she frowns at the story about the angel at the Esso garage and says it's rare for angels to manifest themselves in human form.

Then Tula tells us we will do an angel visualisation. She instructs us to uncross our legs and place our feet flat on the floor, rest our hands on our laps, and sit with a straight back.

We have to close our eyes and listen to nothing but the sound of her voice.

Firstly, she tells us to relax. We have to relax each part of our body, bit by bit starting with the top of our heads and then the space between our eyebrows that Tula calls our 'third eye centre of consciousness'. Then she tells us to focus on our breathing and make sure it's calm and even and that we are breathing from our tummies not our chests, and that our tummies are sticking out and expanding when we breathe in and falling back when we breathe out. As I can't see my tummy, I'm not sure it's working right.

Tula tells us we are in a forest.

I try to imagine I'm in a forest but the forest is dark and scary so I open my eyes a tiny bit and I see everyone else sitting in the circle with their eyes closed. Even Tula has her eyes shut. I close my eyes again and try to go back to my forest. I am not at all sure about being in this forest on my own. All I can think of is when Mole gets lost in the *Wild Wood* in *The Wind in the Willows* and hears the pattering of small feet all around him and sees evil faces in holes in the ground and has to hide inside a tree until Ratty comes to rescue him.

Tula tells us the forest is quiet and very beautiful. The sunlight is shining through the thick canopy of leaves above us. The birds are singing.

This makes me feel a little better. Now my forest is in daylight and not so scary. Still, I am worried about stinging nettles. I once got stung by a stinging nettle and it hurt a lot and was very itchy. I decide that I am carrying antihistamine cream in my pocket. Tula hasn't said anything about us carrying antihistamine cream but it makes sense to me. In fact, she hasn't said anything about us carrying anything at all. We don't seem at all prepared to be wandering around in this forest.

I decide that I am carrying a rucksack with cheese and pickle sandwiches and a re-usable BPA free bottle of water inside it. I have a compass, and maybe firelighters in case I need to make a fire.

Tula tells us to look around and take note of what we can see in the forest but I am busy thinking about what's inside my rucksack. I have added an Ordnance Survey map and a Kendall Mint bar.

She tells us to listen to the birds and the other sounds of the forest. She asks us to concentrate on what we can feel, the sunlight on our faces, or maybe the soft ground or fallen leaves beneath our feet. I am thinking perhaps I should add a tent as we seem to have been in this forest a very long time and maybe it will grow dark and I will definitely need to put a tent up before it grows dark. I can't guarantee finding a tree with a large enough hollow inside it to hide in like Mole did.

She tells us that we have come to a clearing in the forest and in the clearing is a temple. I'm not sure what a temple looks like. All I can think of are those Japanese houses you see on blue china plates that seem to have many roofs with points that curl upwards towards the sky. My temple looks like one of those.

Tula tells us to go through the doors of the temple. I decide to leave my rucksack on the steps. It's probably safe. I haven't seen anyone else the entire time I have been in this forest.

Tula tells us that inside the temple is an altar. She says standing at the altar is our guardian angel, surrounded by white or yellow light, waiting to love and embrace us.

I am standing in my temple looking at the alter but there is no angel.

I check my phone which appears to be conveniently in

my pocket with the antihistamine cream. Maybe she, or he, is late.

Tula is still talking about our angels, how much they want to love us and offer us guidance.

I can hear Tula's voice telling us that we should now be saying goodbye to our angel and leaving our temple. I feel something sharp digging into me and wonder if it's my angel. Perhaps she's invisible and has been at the altar all the time.

I open my eyes. Nan is elbowing me in the ribs. 'Lou,' she whispers. 'It's finished.'

I look around me. Everyone else has their eyes open. Some people are talking to each other. The visualisation must be over. I am tempted to close my eyes again to see if my angel has arrived. Can angels be late, like humans, caught up in angel traffic?

I blink a few times, adjusting to the light in the room which now seems very bright.

'Did you meet your angel, Lou?' Nan asks me.

'No.' I say. 'Did you meet yours?'

'Yes,' Nan says. 'Don't worry about not seeing your angel. It's very unlikely, the first time you try.'

'What did your angel look like?' I ask. 'Was she beautiful, with golden wings?'

Nan smiles dreamily. 'My angel was a he,' she says. 'He looked like a young Cliff Richard. I didn't notice his wings.'

I WAKE UP on Saturday morning to a very loud noise. I don't like loud noises. I find them very disturbing.

It also feels colder than normal. I am as sensitive to heat fluctuations and changes in temperature, as I am to loud noises.

I kneel up on my bed and look out of my bedroom window.

Mr De Souza is using a machine to blow leaves around his back garden. He's herding the leaves together to make a big pile that might, if I was younger of course, have been fun to jump in.

The leaves are mostly just blowing around in the air. Mr De Souza is wearing a mask which looks to me like the kind of mask that should come with a snorkel. Perhaps that was the only mask he had to hand.

It's the end of October and fallen leaves are a naturally occurring phenomenon. What I am witnessing here is one man's solitary attempt, in his own small way, to conquer nature.

Like Mr. De Souza's ancient lawn mower, his leaf blowing machine must use petrol.

Petroleum comes from crude oil which is one of the world's limited and non-renewable resources. I know this because I sometimes listen in our science lessons when something interesting is being taught to us and, very occasionally, I remember facts.

The gases released from crude oil can be very harmful which is why you should never stand too close to the exhaust of a bus or lorry when it stops at traffic lights.

The fact that Mr De Souza is using this highly toxic resource that comes from deep within the foundations of the earth just to blow leaves around his back garden seems to me a little crazy.

But then lots of things don't make sense to me.

I decide to get out of bed and investigate the source of the coldness.

When I reach the top of the stairs I see that the front

door is open. There is one of Dad's old boots wedged between the door and the frame.

I go downstairs and open the door fully.

Mum is outside in her old jeans and jumper. The sleeves of her jumper are rolled up to her elbows and she's wearing rubber gloves.

She has a bucket of soapy water at her feet. She seems to be scrubbing at something underneath our front window.

I step outside onto the driveway. I only am wearing my pyjamas and socks.

There are letters written in white paint on the brick-work underneath our window: EDO. There was another letter that Mum has already scrubbed off. I can see by the shape of the water mark on the wall that it was a P.

PEDO.

I think this must be a reference to Dad. Clearly there wasn't room to write paedophile on the wall after they had written the first letters so large. Or perhaps they just didn't know how to spell it. They have already missed out an A.

I bet a group of boys from my school did this.

'Hi Lou,' Mum says, noticing me standing there.

'Hi Mum,' I say.

'Did you have a nice evening,' she says, scrubbing at the E. 'I didn't see you last night.'

'Yes,' I say. 'I went to the spiritualist church with Nan for an angel evening. We did an angel visualisation only my angel wasn't there.'

'Well, never mind,' Mum says, dunking the scrubbing brush into the water. 'We can't always expect people to be there for us when we need them.'

'But Tula told us angels are always there when we need them.'

'Who's Tula?' Mum says, scrubbing at the top of the E.

'A lightworker,' I say.

Mum looks confused.

'Do you know who did this?' I ask, attempting to change the subject.

'No,' Mum says, stopping her scrubbing and staring at the large white letters.

Mikey appears from inside the house with another scrubbing brush and the small red bucket from Lakeland. He is fully dressed which makes me feel even more self-conscious that I am once again standing in the drive-way in my pyjamas. Why does this keep happening?

Mikey sets to work on the O. I guess they will meet in the middle at the D.

'Dad should be doing this,' Mikey says crossly.

Mum sighs. 'Let's just get it done.'

'Do you want me to help?' I ask.

'It's okay Lou. We've got it covered,' Mum says, re-suming her scrubbing in a very determined kind of way.

'Where *is* Dad?' I ask.

'He didn't come back last night,' Mum says. 'I think he's gone away for the weekend.'

'With—?'

'Yes, with Kaylee,' Mum says.

'He never said anything,' I say.

Mum turns and looks at me. 'I think it was probably a last-minute decision,' she says.

'Maybe she has a swim tournament?' Mikey says help-fully.

We all stare at the wall for a moment. Mum begins to scrub again. 'Who knows?' she says. 'Who knows…' She looks weary.

I don't need to ask where Sarah is because if she's in

the house she will definitely be in bed. She hasn't got up before 1.00pm at the weekends since she was eleven.

Next door's front door opens and Mrs De Souza steps outside in her dressing gown in order to collect a catalogue from her door mat.

When she sees us all outside the front of our house, Mum and Mikey in their rubber gloves with their scrubbing brushes and me in my pyjamas, she stares at us.

She frowns and disappears very quickly inside.

'I think we scared her off,' Mum says. 'Or maybe she's upset because we never returned her shredder.'

'I'll drop it back later,' Mikey says.

A couple walking their dog pass by the house and I begin to feel very exposed. 'I think I better go and get dressed,' I say.

'Shall I make scones?' Mikey says, finishing off the O.

'Yes!' Mum and I say at the same time.

We all laugh.

At least we can laugh, I think, even if the front of our house has been vandalized and the neighbours aren't speaking to us.

On Monday morning Faith is back at school. I sit next to her in registration. She's doodling stars in her homework diary.

'Were you sick?' I ask her.

'Kind of,' she says. 'I have bad days, you know. The darkness descends.' She adds a half moon to her doodles, in amongst the stars.

I wonder about Faith's bad days, whether she has to sit on the floor like I do and whether she suffers from anxiety attacks like I sometimes get where I can't breathe and can't speak and am sometimes sick.

'Do you have anxiety attacks?' I ask Faith.

Faith stops doodling stars and looks closely at me. 'I prefer to call them moments of lucidity.'

'Why? I ask, unsure of what she means but very interested.

'Because they are a result of the realisation of my own nothingness.' Faith says, adding a shooting star to her doodles, or maybe a meteorite.

'I see,' I say, not totally sure that I do see, but wanting to know more about Faith's 'moments of lucidity'. I don't often meet people who have strange moods and do weird things like I do without meaning to. It's hard for me to figure out why I get my panic attacks. Sometimes the reason is obvious, like if I've had a bad day at school or if Mum mixes up my socks and knickers in my underwear drawer which she often does, but other times they seem to happen for no reason at all.

'Sometimes I have anxiety attacks and I can't breathe and then I have to sit on the floor and I can't speak for a long time,' I say.

'You're very lucky,' Faith says. 'In our anxiety we recognise our freedom and can become authentically ourselves.'

I must be looking confused because Faith puts down her pen and says very profoundly, as if clarifying her point. 'Angst is the shadowy queen of all moods.' She sounds as though she's quoting.

'Did the German guy say that?' I ask. 'The shadowy queen thing?'

'No,' Faith says. 'A different German guy said it. Graham met him once at a convention.'

I don't feel much like myself when I have to sit on the floor,' I say. 'I feel like I've lost myself.'

Faith shrugs. 'We must first be destroyed before we can be free,' she says. 'Being yourself is scary. But this fear should not be confused with the fear of external objects.'

Now she really has lost me. The fear of external objects?

Mikey and I once had a babysitter who told us she was frightened of coat hangers. Only empty ones. She said they looked sinister. Maybe this is what Faith means. Maybe animals can also be included in this fear of external objects.

'Like spiders?' I ask, thinking that Mum is frightened of spiders.

'Exactly,' Faith says. 'Like spiders.'

Mr Wexhall interrupts us by taking the register. Faith no longer says 'over here' when her name is called. She has gotten used to registers now. She just says 'here' like everybody else.

After he has taken the register, Mr Wexhall gives us sheets of lined paper and tells us that we are not too young to start thinking about what job we might want when we are older and have completed our education.

He says he will give us five minutes to write down what job or jobs we think we might want to do and what qualifications we might need in order to 'pursue our chosen careers'. He says it doesn't matter if we aren't sure yet, it is just an exercise to get us to 'start thinking about our options'.

I sit and stare at the blank piece of paper in front of me.

It seems very white, and very empty.

I look at Sam who is busy writing down a list of GCSEs and A Levels and Higher Education degrees he will need in order to study the universe and discover extra-terrestrial life.

'Do you have a black colouring pencil?' Faith asks me.

'Sure,' I say, opening my pencil case.

I give Faith the black colouring pencil and return to my blank piece of paper.

I am thirteen and a half years old. How can I be expected to know what I want to do with the rest of my life? I can't even roller-blade in a straight line, which may, or may not, be something to do with the undiagnosed dyspraxia.

All I can think of is that I would rather work with animals than people. Not tiny pottery animals like the Year Ten girl in our assembly. Real animals, like sheep and chickens and horses and hedgehogs. Hedgehogs are in decline because people's gardens are too tidy and there aren't enough hedgerows and hedges anymore which is where hedgehogs like to live. I read this in an online article I found about hedgehogs. I also found out that there is a hedgehog hospital in Hertfordshire. They take in sick and injured hedgehogs that people bring to the hospital, although a hedgehog once arrived by itself in a taxi from Watford.

I take my red pen, because it's Monday and red is a good colour for Monday. I write on the top of my piece of paper. ANIMALS and underneath HEDGEHOGS.

'Right,' Mr Wexhall says. 'Let's go round shall we?'

He starts with the boys by the window. One of them wants to be a professional footballer and says he doesn't need any qualifications. Another says he wants to be a plumber because that's what his dad does and there is good money to be earned, as well as the possibility of seeing women in their dressing gowns.

Then Mr Wexhall asks the group of girls who sit on the back row, the girls who all hate me and who always laugh at me, what they have written.

Sitting there today are Lianne Parks who punched me in the eye and Bryony Silver who threw my P.E. kit on the floor and called me a freak. They especially don't like me.

Lianne says she's going to be a mobile hairdresser and Bryony says she's going be a nail technician.

'What is that exactly?' Mr Wexhall says, looking confused.

Bryony and Lianne roll their eyes. 'Someone who does nails, Sir.' Bryony says as if Mr Wexhall is the stupidest person in the world.

Bryony and Lianne's friend, Bonnie Jackson, says she's going to be a receptionist in a car showroom because that's what her sister does and she gets asked out on lots of dates by the men she works with who sell cars.

Bryony and Lianne nod approvingly.

Mr Wexhall takes off his glasses and rubs them very slowly with the piece of cloth he keeps in the top pocket of his tweed jacket. He glances at the clock on the wall. There's still seven minutes before the bell is due to ring for first lesson.

He looks wearily around the room. Three girls are texting on their mobiles. Two of the boys appear to be having an arm wrestling competition. One girl is plaiting another girl's hair. A boy called Matthew Markson has his hand on Bonnie Jackson's thigh. Even though it is October, Bonnie is wearing long socks instead of tights so her thighs are bare.

I can see Mr Wexhall watching the hand on the thigh. It begins to creep up Bonnie's skirt. Mr Wexhall looks away.

'If I could just have your attention for five more minutes, please.'

A few people look up.

Mr Wexhall glances over in our direction. I pretend to be studying my homework diary.

'We haven't heard from this table yet,' he says. He looks hopefully at Sam. 'Sam?'

Sam blushes. He isn't very good at talking in front of lots of people.

'Spit it out, rosy red cheeks,' one of the boys by the window says.

Sam blushes even more. 'It's Rosacea.' he mutters.

'I can see you've written *something*,' Mr Wexhall says, still looking at Sam.

'Astrobiology,' Sam whispers.

'What?' Mr Wexhall says.

'Astrobiology,' Sam says, a little louder this time so Mr Wexhall can hear. He begins to gain confidence. 'When I've completed my GCSEs and my A levels in the required STEM subjects which will probably be Maths, Geography, Physics, Chemistry and Biology, and my first degree in Physics and Astronomy, and my MA in Astrophysics and then my PhD in Astrobiology...' Sam stops talking and looks down at the desk. 'Then I will go and work for NASA and join the search for extra-terrestrial life. My mum and I worked it all out when I was seven,' he adds quietly.

The room is suddenly very silent.

'Geek,' someone mutters.

'Nerd.'

'Well, at least *someone* has a plan,' Mr Wexhall says. 'Even if it is - ambitious.'

'I have a plan,' Bryony says huffily. 'There is always a demand for nail art.'

I glance at Faith, who is looking very bored.

Mr Wexhall returns his gaze to our table. 'What about you Amanda?'

Amanda is sitting at the table with me and Faith and Sam. Zero isn't in today, and everyone knows of his ambition anyway.

'A Nuw-sery school teacher,' she says softly. Amanda has difficulty pronouncing her r's.

'Very good,' Mr Wexhall says.

'I can do a deg-wee in it,' Amanda says.

'What the fuck is a *deg-wee*,' Bryony says, under her breath.

'Personally,' Lianne says. 'I wouldn't want to be covered in other people's children's sick and piss every day.'

All the boys laugh. Not because what Lianne has said is funny, just because she has the potential to make your life hell if you don't agree with her.

Mr Wexhall frowns. He has clearly heard this remark but decides to ignore it.

'What about you Louise?'

I look down at my piece of paper. I pray for the bell to ring.

'I can see you've written something too,' Mr Wexhall says, leaning forward.

'I - I'm not sure...' I say, stalling for time.

Amanda gives me a sympathetic look.

Mr Wexhall isn't giving up. 'Come on Louise. What does it say?'

I don't know why but I hold up my piece of paper. 'Animals,' I say.

The class erupts into laughter.

'Shhh!' Mr Wexhall says, glancing angrily around the classroom. He returns to me. 'What do you mean, Louise? You want to work with them?'

'Yes,' I say weakly.

Bryony giggles. 'She wants to work in a zoo.'

One of the boys is making monkey noises.

'She *is* a zoo,' Lianne says.

'What sort of animals?' Mr Wexhall asks.

Why can't he leave me alone, I think. Why does the bell not ring?

'Sheep,' I say because it's the first thing I can think of that isn't a hedgehog.

Everyone laughs.

'Baa,' Lianne says.

'That *entire* table's a farmyard,' Bryony whispers, which is clearly a reference to Faith's surname.

I think of that expression about the ground opening up and swallowing someone. I imagine a Lou size hole under my chair that I might be able to slip into. It isn't there.

'Oh, shut the fuck up.'

Everyone looks at Faith. She has spoken extremely loudly. Loudly enough that no one can pretend they didn't hear her, even Mr Wexhall. Faith is staring at Lianne and Bryony who both fall silent.

Mr Wexhall looks visibly angry. He's going to send her out, I think. She'll be in isolation, get detention for a week, they'll suspend her, expel her. It seems as though the whole class is holding its breath.

'Do you have something to contribute, Faith?' Mr Wexhall says. Faith turns away from the girls. Mr Wexhall clears his throat. Faith looks at him. Mr Wexhall looks very slightly intimidated. 'What have you written?' he asks.

I can hear Lianne sucking in air from the back row. She's livid, I think. Livid that Faith got away with talking to her like that and that Mr Wexhall isn't going to send her out for swearing even though *she* swears all the time.

Faith holds up her piece of paper. She has coloured in

the whole of one side in my black colouring pencil. She had to sharpen it twice.

She points towards the white side. 'This,' she says, 'represents my being-towards,' then she turns the paper over. 'Death,' she says, pointing to the black side.

Mr Wexhall stares at Faith. He doesn't seem to know what to say.

'Would you like to explain, perhaps, what you mean, and how this...' he gestures towards Faith's piece of paper, 'relates to your future career choice?'

'Sure,' Faith says, slowly putting her piece of paper back down on the desk. 'All of my potential and limitations as a human being are measured against my inevitable death. I will live my life in relation to death and my own finitude, as a being-towards-death.'

Mr Wexhall continues to stare at Faith like she is an alien from outer space.

'Bunch of freaks,' Lianne mutters.

'Is that from the German guy too?' I whisper.

'A different one,' Faith says.

'Another different one again?' I say, wondering how many German men there can be.

'Yes,' Faith says. 'Heidegger.'

'But,' Mr Wexhall says, looking totally confused, 'how are you going to earn a *living*?'

'Oh that,' Faith says, as if it's a stupid question. 'I'm going to be a dentist. Good health starts in the mouth.'

The bell finally rings and everyone quickly begins to gather their stuff together.

Mr Wexhall takes his glasses off. He rubs his head in same way I saw Mr Dodd rubbing his head in his office. My dad does this too sometimes. Perhaps they have head rubbing competitions.

Mr Wexhall stands up as everyone rushes past him on their way out the door. He looks very weary, as if not quite sure how he got here. All he wanted to do was play the trombone.

I feel worried for Faith. 'Lianne will be after you now,' I say to Faith as we walk to our Maths lesson. 'Bryony too.'

'I'm not worried about them,' Faith says.

'They won't let you get away with it,' I say. 'They already hate me.'

Faith smiles. 'The Philistines are upon us, Mr Lloyd.'

'Yes,' I say, nodding very seriously but wondering who Mr Lloyd is and making a mental note to look the word 'Philistines' up later.

'Hey,' Faith says. 'That reminds me, how did you get on with R.E.M?'

'I really like them,' I say truthfully. 'I like the song about the man on the moon, and the one where he's losing his religion.'

'Yes,' Faith says. 'It happens to us all.'

'Especially Nietzsche,' I say, smiling.

Faith turns and looks at me. She laughs. 'Exactly,' she says.

It's the first time I've heard Faith laugh. It's nice because she is laughing with me, at something I've said, rather than at me, which is what most people seem to do.

'Here,' she says. 'I've got another one for you.'

She reaches inside her textbook and hands me a shiny silver CD, this time without a case. I look at the CD and it takes me a moment to figure out what she has written as all the letters are in different colours and in a circle around the edge. FLEETWOOD MAC.

'Thanks,' I say.

'No problem,' Faith says as we enter our maths class.

'And by the way,' she adds. 'I like hedgehogs too. Hedgehogs are cool.'

I REALISE ON Wednesday that I haven't seen Dad for several days.

It's early evening, Mikey is in the kitchen making pear muffins and Mum is on her way out to her gym class.

'I've left you a pasta bake,' she says, adjusting her hair in the mirror that hangs in the hallway. 'Just heat up the oven and put it in for thirty-five minutes. There's salad in the fridge if you want salad with it.'

'Where's Dad?' I ask.

'Oh, he moved out,' Mum says, opening the front door.

'Moved out where?' I ask, completely astounded that no one thought to tell me this important piece of news.

'Oh, I don't know,' Mum says. 'He's living somewhere in town I think.'

'When did he move out?' I ask.

Mum sighs. 'I really don't know, Lou. Last weekend? I'm sorry, love, but I'll be late for Chi Ball and Steve doesn't like us to be late. He says it disrupts the energy of the class.'

Mum grabs her car keys. 'Don't forget the pasta bake,' she says, before closing the door, leaving me alone in the hallway.

After I hear her car turn in the driveway I go slowly through to the kitchen. Mikey is lining a muffin tray with paper cases. He's wearing Mum's Cath Kidston apron again. The one with the tiny blue flowers. The kitchen smells of flour and eggs, and kind of fruity.

'Did you know Dad's moved out?' I ask him.

Mikey turns and looks at me. 'It's unofficial,' he says. 'We're not supposed to know yet.'

'But Mum just told me,' I say, feeling confused because 'unofficial' means not officially confirmed and Mum seemed quite sure that he *had* moved out even if she wasn't sure *when* he moved out.

'She let the cat out of the bag then,' Mikey says, putting the remaining paper cases back in the cupboard.

Of course I can't help thinking of a cat being let out of a bag. In this instance it's a black cat and a brown paper bag. It looks grateful.

Mikey must have seen me looking confused. 'He wants to tell us himself,' he says. 'But I know he's already found somewhere to live.'

'How do you know?'

'The estate agent rang yesterday. She thought I was Dad. She said, *the keys are ready now*.'

'What did you say?' I ask.

Mikey is checking the oven temperature. He's very particular about oven temperatures.

'I told her to call him on his mobile.'

I pause to consider this as Mikey returns to his mixing bowl.

'Will we have to pretend that we don't know he's moved out when he tells us he's moved out?' I say, thinking that I am not very good at lying.

Once when I was five and Sarah was ten, she told me I had to give her all my Easter eggs or the goblin in the garden would creep into my room in the middle of the night and dance on the end of my bed. She knew this would scare me. She told me I had to tell Mum and Dad that I didn't want my Easter eggs because I didn't like chocolate anymore which would have been a lie because I like chocolate a lot. I fully intended to tell the lie, firstly because I wanted to please Sarah and secondly because I was afraid of the goblin, but I just couldn't do it. When Mum asked me why I wasn't eating my Easter eggs I told her I had to give them to Sarah otherwise the goblin would come. Mum got cross with Sarah and took away her Easter eggs and Sarah was cross with me, and all because I couldn't lie, although I did enjoy my Easter eggs.

Mikey looks thoughtful. He knows I'm not good at lying. 'We could *try* and pretend we don't know,' he suggests. He begins to spoon the mixture into the paper cases and I can tell by the way he is doing it he is concentrating very hard on getting it right and not spilling any.

'Okay,' I say, thinking that pretending I don't know something might not be the same as lying and that I might be able to do it.

I decide to go upstairs and leave Mikey to his muffins.

I run my hand over the smooth wood of the bannister. Dad sanded it down three years ago and painted the part underneath in a white paint called Dover Cliffs. I remember because he covered the stairs in old bed-sheets and I had to keep bringing him cups of tea whilst he painted. I wonder if he thought he'd be moving out so soon.

When I reach the top of the stairs, I pause outside Mum and Dad's bedroom.

I don't know why but I turn the handle and go in.

The bedroom looks the same but different. I try to work out what it is.

I realise there are no books (usually sports biographies) or odd socks by Dad's side of the bed.

His bedside table, always covered in loose change and

old pens and the glasses he has to use for reading things up close but never admits he needs, is completely empty. All that's left is the lamp that matches Mum's on the other side. Even his old red alarm clock has gone.

I wonder why he decided to take the alarm clock but not the lamp. Did he hold them both and try and make a decision? Alarm clock, lamp… Alarm clock, lamp… Did he leave the lamp because it matches the one on the other side? Why bother, if no one is going to use it? Won't he need a lamp in his new house?

All these things confuse and distress me.

I open the wardrobe. Mum's clothes are still there, on the left hand side, but the right hand side has been cleared out. There are just a bunch of empty coat hangers.

Our baby sitter was right. They do look sinister.

I shut the wardrobe and decide I don't want to look around anymore.

I leave Mum and Dad's bedroom, or now just 'Mum's room', and go into my own room.

I decide I need to sit on the floor for a while.

I know I mustn't forget the pasta bake, and maybe Mikey will let me have a pear muffin. I think that I will take the muffin upstairs, climb under my duvet with it, and watch the penguins in *Frozen Planet* build their nests of stones in Antarctica.

I will try to forget that Dad doesn't live with us anymore, and about the empty coat hangers.

I think that the first thing I will do is put on my new CD from Faith.

I slowly reach for my school bag and retrieve the CD from my maths exercise book.

I put the disk in the CD player, sit back down on the floor and wait for it to begin.

At first I'm not sure about the music but then I quite like it. I like a song about thunder only happening when it rains and another about someone who must 'go their own way'. I like it because I think of Dad, and that he must 'go his own way' even if it makes me feel sad.

I listen until I begin to smell the pear muffins and I know that Mikey will soon be finishing in the kitchen.

7

I WAKE in the night feeling strange. There is an ache in my tummy very low down and I feel a bit sick.

When I go the bathroom, I notice there's blood in the toilet bowl and on my favourite rabbit pyjamas.

There is blood on my legs and then, as I try desperately to wipe it away, on my hands too. It looks like a scene from a 1990s horror movie, the kind that Sarah and her friends like to watch on the free film channels. The girl has been stabbed in the stomach by a man in a mask (or maybe it's a female, there's the twist). She looks down at her bloody hands and then into the black and soulless eyes of her unknown killer, then she falls to the floor and dies.

This does not happen to me.

I am not alarmed.

I am good in a crisis and I realise immediately that this must be my period.

I know this because in my final year of primary school I had to attend a 'mothers' and daughters' evening' with my mum. We sat at our school desks with the afternoon's mental maths questions still on the white board whilst our teacher, Mrs Kingston, talked to us all about periods and our reproductive systems, and all the girls in my class looked very embarrassed and all the mothers sat around smiling knowingly, or checking their watches to make sure they made it home in time for the next episode of *Happy Valley*.

I wrap myself in my dressing gown. I have to take my pyjama bottoms off and soak them in the sink to get the blood out. I wash my hands and clean myself up, giving myself time to think.

When I attended the mothers' and daughters' evening, we were given a small bag, like a party bag, containing some leaflets and a sample pad, but I'm pretty sure Dad threw the bag away by mistake when we got home, thinking it was meant for the recycling. I have no idea what happened to that sample pad.

I try to think quickly. Mum will be asleep and I don't want to bother her for such a minor emergency but I know I can't rely on toilet tissue to soak up all the blood for the rest of the night and the Co-op shuts at eight and the clock in the bathroom says quarter past twelve.

This means I only have one other option.

Sarah's room.

I open the bathroom door and tiptoe out onto the landing holding a wad of toilet tissue. I go back into my bedroom and quickly change into some fresh pyjamas and old underwear I should probably have discarded years ago.

I tiptoe back out onto the landing, this time in clean pyjamas and with a wad of toilet tissue between my legs. It is quite hard to tiptoe under these conditions and, as I don't want to turn the landing light on, I have to feel my way. I look like a giant insect, my knees and toes bent, my legs and arms all stuck out at unnatural angles.

I approach Sarah's bedroom door and relax my outstretched limbs. The toilet tissue seems to be doing its job for now. Luckily Sarah is away tonight, staying with her fireman boyfriend. She has been spending a lot of time with him recently. I wonder if she has moved out too and someone has forgotten to tell me.

I cautiously turn the door handle. The pain in my tummy is increasing.

I step inside and switch on the light.

There are clothes everywhere; on the bed, on the floor. There are clothes spilling out of the open wardrobes. Dresses, tops and skinny jeans in various colours have been draped over the open doors and are falling off coat hangers (no sinister coat hangers here).

I look down. I have stepped on something sticky which, on closer inspection, appears to be some sort of hair serum that is oozing out of its container and onto the floor.

There are lots of shoes scattered across the floor; trainers, flip-flops, spiky high-heels, high boots with thick heels and even a fluffy white ski-boot. All the shoes appear to be odd.

The mirror by the door is smeared with black streaks of mascara and lipsticks in various shades. There are hairbrushes and hair pins and hair straighteners and hair curlers and large clips with jagged jaws, and other dangerous looking electrical appliances all laying on the floor in front of me.

The walls are covered with peeling posters of men, most of them semi-dressed, whose faces I vaguely recognise but who I couldn't name. There are also photographs of Sarah.

Everywhere I look there are photographs of Sarah. There are photographs of Sarah and her boyfriend, of Sarah and her friends, of Sarah in night clubs, of Sarah eating ice-cream on Brighton Pier, of Sarah by the London Eye, of Sarah on holiday in Spain with her friends last summer, of Sarah at her prom, of Sarah when she was younger singing into a microphone, and even of Sarah falling out of what appears to be a pink limousine. There is a collection of photographs that Sarah has arranged on her wall so that they spell out her name: SARAH.

I begin to feel dizzy. The photographs seem to be screaming at me, I exist! I AM SARAH!

I take a deep breath.

I must not forget my mission.

I move towards Sarah's bedside table. The top drawer is filled with jewellery and more hair brushes and sheets of loose paperwork that look like they could be important, and should really be filed away.

I have a special green folder for important documents that says on the front 'Important Documents,' even though I don't have that many important documents yet. This is where I keep my passport and my library card.

I really don't like going through Sarah's things. I have to keep telling myself that this an emergency and that I have no other option.

I wonder if Sarah will know I've been in her room. I used to read a lot of Nancy Drew books and I know that there are ways you can tell if someone has been in your room and opened a private drawer. I wonder if Sarah has left a single hair trapped in the top drawer of her bedside cabinet and when she gets back she will see that the single hair has fallen into the drawer and will know that someone has been in her room.

I think that this is unlikely. Sarah doesn't read much. She has fashion magazines but I suspect she mostly looks at the pictures. The only thing I know she reads for sure are the labels on clothes when she's out shopping. She will have to check the size and price and whether they need dry cleaning because Mum said if Sarah buys any more clothes that need dry cleaning, she can pay for the dry cleaning herself.

I hear a loud scuffling rustling sound behind me that makes me jump.

I immediately freeze. I have been discovered.

I turn around very slowly.

There's no one there.

I hear the noise again. It seems to be coming from under Sarah's desk.

I approach the desk cautiously. I bend down and there is Hammy. He's rustling around inside an old packet of salted peanuts that has fallen out of Sarah's wastepaper basket. The wastepaper basket has been knocked over. There's a pile of old tissues and crisp packets, and chocolate wrappers along with the salted peanuts.

'Hi, Hammy,' I whisper.

He seems to be enjoying the salted peanuts. I can see he has his cheeks full. He has probably stored some away for later.

No wonder he has been ignoring the humane trap Dad bought before he left with the food/bait inside it. The humane trap is a clear plastic box. Mum leaves it on the kitchen floor in the evenings. Hammy is supposed to go inside when he sees or smells the food which then activates the door of the trap to close behind him.

I wonder if Hammy tipped the wastepaper basket over himself. It would not surprise me. He is a very resourceful hamster.

I decide to leave Hammy where he is. I hope the peanuts don't make him unwell. I would try and catch him but it could take a while and I have more pressing issues to attend to.

I try the bottom drawer of Sarah's bedside cabinet and there they are, pads! I quickly grab a handful along with a few tampons.

I close the drawer triumphantly. My mission has been successful.

On second thoughts I open the drawer again and take out the instructions from inside the tampon box.

I navigate my way back across the bedroom floor, carefully avoiding the spilt hair serum. I turn out the light. I pull the door over but don't shut it fully so Hammy can leave if he wants to (although I still suspect an under floor tunnel system), and return to the bathroom with my new collection of period catching equipment.

I feel like a warrior who has been forced into enemy territory and who has not only survived, but returned with treasure. Even if my treasure is only sanitary towels and tampons.

I CATCH UP with Faith at break time. It's always difficult for me to find somewhere to go at break and lunch times where I can remain invisible and hide out until the bell rings. The canteen is usually a safe bet as there are more teachers around, but even then someone like Bryony Silver might come up to you and tell you to come outside now so Lianne Parks can hit you, and I don't like the canteen that much anyway because it's very loud.

I find Faith outside by the technology block. We have started to hang around together. I thought I had better warn her that hanging around me might not be a good thing because I often get picked on and am considered to be a weirdo, and also because of what's happening with my dad and Kaylee, but when I tried to tell Faith this she just looked at me and said 'Lou, what the hell are you talking about. I don't give a shit,' which kind of put an end to the conversation.

Faith is very smart and I'm sure would have already figured out what people think of me.

Now whenever Lianne and Bryony and Cherry and Bonnie see us their eyes narrow and they turn away.

Faith doesn't seem to notice this. Neither does she seem to notice that the boys laugh whenever they see us together.

As we walk across the playground they call out to us.

'Watch out - here comes Little and Large!'

'Laurel and Hardy!'

'Sharky and George!'

We ignore them, or Faith does anyway, and I copy Faith. I have to walk extra fast to catch up with her.

I'm not sure yet if I can consider Faith my friend. I have made this mistake before, thinking that someone is a friend but then they turn out not to be a friend. Like the girl in my primary school who told me she had discovered a secret world, like Narnia, that you could only get to from inside the cleaning cupboard and when I walked inside the cleaning cupboard she shut me in and I could hear lots of girls outside the cupboard laughing and I realised it was a trick and that she wasn't really my friend.

I'm not sure I can truly consider Sam my friend, either, as I don't see him outside school much. Sam and I are more like two of the same species who are sometimes drawn to one another out of a necessity for survival.

'What's up with you, Lou?' Faith says, looking at me. 'You look pale.'

'I got my period,' I say.

'Your first one?' Faith says, looking at me in disbelief.

I nod.

'I got mine when I was ten and a half,' Faith says.

'I'm a late developer,' I say, because that's what my mum always says to me.

'Are you in pain?' Faith asks.

I nod again. I am still feeling slightly sick. My tummy aches. I have to keep stopping to sit down, and I feel kind of heavy. I seem to only be able to move around very slowly and, even though it seems to be doing the job, I have an irrational fear that my tampon will fall out.

'Come on,' Faith says, 'I know something that will help.'

She begins to march away from me, through the gates and onto the school field.

I quickly follow her, wondering why a cure for my period pain involves us crossing the school field.

We walk past clusters of girls in their winter coats, some of them eating their break snacks, others looking at their mobile phones.

We walk past a haphazard game of football involving several Year Seven boys. Four school blazers are being used as goalposts.

The ball flies towards us.

'Watch it!' Faith shouts as we both jump out of the way of the ball.

'Offside!' someone yells from beyond the makeshift goalposts.

'Sorry,' one of the boys mutters, collecting the ball from our feet.

Faith shakes her head and we carry on walking. No one usually goes this far down the school field at break time. I can't see how this is going to help my period pain. In fact, it's making it worse. I could do with sitting down but there is nowhere to sit now except the ground which will be cold and which I noticed for the first time this morning was frosted.

We are walking towards the fence and the back gate that leads to the fields I use as a cut through.

There are very few people around now apart from the huddle of grebo kids by the gate. This is where they usually hang out, as far away from anyone else as they can possibly get.

I don't know why they're called grebos, they just are and always have been.

They usually wear black hoodies, sometimes with the names of heavy metal bands on. Quite often they carry skate boards and have many piercings and wear bicycle chain jewellery.

They keep themselves to themselves and don't mix with the other kids.

We seem to be heading straight for them.

'We can't talk to them,' I whisper, as Faith strides ahead of me.

Faith turns and looks at me. 'Of course we can,' she says. 'Who says we can't?'

I can't think of how to explain to Faith that there are some people you just don't talk to in school.

As we get closer we can hear music coming from a phone. They always like to play their music whenever they can. Most of them are sitting, or sort of lounging on the grass. They don't seem bothered that it might be cold, or wet. One guy is standing up with his skateboard. He has a black hat pulled down low over his super greasy hair.

'AC/DC,' Faith mutters. 'That's like, totally retro.'

'What?' I say. But it's too late.

'Hey!' Faith shouts to them.

They all look us. None of them move.

I notice the guy with the skateboard has a bicycle chain hanging from his baggy trouser pocket. He takes it out and swings it like he's practicing for a bicycle chain swinging competition, or perhaps figuring out how much damage it might be able to do to a human skull.

Faith has really gone and done it now I think. We're toast.

We are standing very close to the grebos. All six of them. All boys.

They smell like sweat and car oil and something else. Something - herby.

The guys all stare at us. They look more at Faith. They seem to be trying to figure her out.

Eventually one of the guys on the ground speaks. He seems to be oldest and the biggest of the group.

'Yo,' he says slowly. 'What's up?'

After he says this the others seem to relax.

The guy with the bicycle chain is still practicing his swinging but in more of a care-free kind of way.

The older, bigger guy on the ground is propped up on one elbow smoking. He takes a long drag on his roll-up, closing his eyes then opening them again. 'Anything we can help you girls with?' he says slowly.

'My friend here,' Faith says, indicating me. 'Isn't feeling too great. She's in pain,' she adds.

I stare at the ground. I can feel all the pairs of eyes looking at me.

'She needs something to take away her pain,' Faith says. 'We thought you could help us out.'

'You want a joint?' the guy on the ground says.

'You got it,' Faith says.

'Sure,' the guy says. 'No problem. We can provide.'

I lift my eyes. The guy with the skateboard is grinning at Faith who is politely ignoring him. The guy on the ground is reaching into his jacket pocket and pulling out what looks to me like a tiny ball of tin foil.

Then I realise Faith has just asked them for drugs, and not the pharmaceutical kind. She's asked for cannabis. This is not good. This is terrible. Drugs are bad. Last year we had a group of actors visit our school to tell us how bad drugs are. They performed a play in which one of them nearly died from taking too many drugs. All her friends tried to help her but she was too in love with drugs to be helped like a normal person. Then at the end we were all given leaflets about how bad drugs are and badges with the slogan 2 SMART 4 DRUGS written on them.

The leaflets told us that cannabis can be particularly damaging to the developing teenage brain. It can shut down cells and reduce IQs. Basically it can make you stupid.

Faith is now reaching into her blazer pocket. She takes out a crumpled note.

The guy on the ground waves it away. 'This one's on me,' he says. 'Consider it a free trial.'

He slowly sits up and places a cigarette paper on his knee. 'You want it neat?' he says.

Faith rolls her eyes. 'What do we look like - pot heads? And don't give us any rubbish. We want the real deal or we're not interested.'

The guy smiles and turns to one of his friends. 'They want the pricy stuff.' He shrugs. 'Pass us the baccy, Ginger.'

A tall skinny guy with red hair, wearing a Nirvana jumper throws a packet of tobacco to the guy who is making the joint.

When he's finished making it he hands it to Faith. 'This is the good stuff. You need a light?'

'No thanks. Come on Lou.' Faith begins to turn away.

'You're not going to enjoy it here with us?' the guy calls after her.

'No,' Faith says.

'See you around then,' the guy with the skateboard says.

'Yeah,' Faith says, calling back over her shoulder. 'See you around.'

We walk until we are quite far away from the group of grebos. I am so surprised that Faith just went up to them and asked them for drugs and they gave them to her and that we survived that I don't know what to say about it.

We stop by a tree along the back fence.

'Faith,' I say. 'It was very kind of you but—'

'It's all right,' Faith says, reaching into her pocket and producing a tiny box of matches. 'You don't have to. It was just an idea. It will help though - with your period pain.'

I watch Faith light the small white stick. She takes a drag and closes her eyes.

I look around to make sure no one can see us. 'Drugs are very bad for you,' I say.

'Yes,' Faith says. 'They are. But I consider this to be more of a medicinal herb.'

'Really?'

Faith looks at me. Her face has relaxed. 'Sure,' she says. 'Cannabis has been used in medicine for hundreds of years. You've just got to make sure you've got the good stuff.'

I watch Faith smoking and think that for once in my life I might just take a risk.

'What if I get addicted?' I say.

'Well, don't,' Faith says.

'What if it makes me stupid?'

Faith looks sceptical. 'From half a joint?'

This seems like a reasonable kind of answer. And anyway I am not a person that gets addicted to things in that way. I sometimes like to have the same things over and over again, like I once ate a bowl of bran flakes for breakfast and one slice of toast with honey for approximately two years before Mum persuaded me to try and 'mix up my breakfasts' a little. I don't think this is the same thing as an addiction and, anyway, I would never be brave enough to ask the grebos for it myself, and where else would I get it?

'I'll try it,' I say.

'You sure?' Faith says.

I nod.

'It may not do much good anyway,' Faith says. 'They were pretty stingy. I'm not sure a fly could get stoned on this, although it is making me feel mellow...'

'Mellow?'

'Chilled out,' Faith says, handing me the white stick. 'Breathe it in as far as you can,' she says.

The first time I do this I cough, but the second time I try I seem to get it right. Now I know what the herby smell was that seemed to surround the grebos.

We pass the joint backwards and forwards between us. I definitely seem to have got the hang of inhaling it down into my lungs then slowly blowing it out again.

'How are you feeling?' Faith asks me.

'A little better,' I say, having no idea whether this is

due to the marijuana herb/drug taking effect, or the rush of adrenaline I have received simply by taking it, or the fact that my period pain seems to come in waves, like labour pain. I have never been in labour but I have seen it on TV.

'Good,' Faith says lazily as I pass her the joint again.

The huddle of grebos begins to disperse. We can see other people walking off the field and towards the Technology Block.

'The bell must have gone,' I say.

'We better get going,' Faith says. 'Here, you can have the last drag.'

I take the joint from Faith then hand it back to her. She drops it to the ground and stamps on it very hard.

As we make our way across the field I realise I feel calm and, in fact, a little spaced out. I feel as if nothing can bother me and as if I have nothing to worry about.

I feel like Dylan the rabbit in *The Magic Roundabout,* the one who always looked spaced out and sleepy. Mum used to make us watch the original Magic Roundabout episodes with her when we were younger as she liked them and thought that we would too. Then she bought us a film called *Dougal and the Blue Cat.* I was terrified of that film.

I didn't like *The Magic Roundabout* much anyway. I thought it was pretty scary, what with the strange coloured trees and the people with large heads, but I was especially frightened of the evil blue cat who wanted to turn the entire world blue.

I think, as we cross the field, that my idea of hell would be being stuck inside an endless episode of *The Magic Roundabout.*

'What are you thinking about?' Faith says. 'You've screwed your eyes up.'

'I was thinking that hell would be being stuck inside *The Magic Roundabout*,' I say.

Faith pauses to consider this. 'Hell is other people,' she says.

We enter the building and head towards our lockers. I think that although I enjoyed the joint from the grebos I don't intend on having another one. My period pain has gone but I have a slight headache, and I don't ever want to think of *The Magic Roundabout* again.

When I get in from school Dad is home but Mum isn't which is strange as Dad doesn't live here anymore. I know Dad is home because his car is in the drive.

I wonder if someone has found out that I smoked marijuana at break time. I imagine entering the house to find Dad standing in the hallway with a grave face. There will be two police officers sitting at the kitchen table. They will have parked their car around the corner in order to conceal their visit and make sure I don't run away before they have a chance to arrest me. I will have been expelled from school, like Dad. No other school will have me and I will be sent to a Juvenile Detention Centre where I will have to wear an orange jumpsuit and learn engineering skills. The police officers in the kitchen will be shaking their heads and thinking *Well, what could you expect from a family of criminals*? First Mum steals clothes from Debenhams, then Dad gets suspended from school for an inappropriate relationship with a student. Even Mikey has been using Dad's PayPal account to buy baking supplies. Perhaps Sarah is really and truly the saint of this family, only she disguises it well.

I put my key in the door and open it slowly. There is no one in the hallway at least.

'Hi, Lou,' Dad calls out from the kitchen, as if everything is normal.

I drop my school bag in the hallway and walk through to the kitchen.

'How was your day?' Dad asks, smiling. He looks edgy and nervous, not at ease in his own kitchen. He's holding a small pile of post which he must have been sorting through before I arrived. He hastily puts the post down on the kitchen table.

I look around for police officers. There are none, which doesn't explain Dad's odd behaviour.

'Okay,' I say, wondering if Mum told him I got my period.

'Mikey's in the living room,' Dad says. 'I thought we could have a chat. You know - a family get together.'

I nod. Dad's sudden enthusiasm is a little scary.

'What about Mum and Sarah?' I ask.

'Sarah's upstairs. I thought you could give her a shout for me. Your mother's out. I think it might be better if it's just the four of us this time. Run up and get Sarah for me.'

'Are you sure she's in?' I say.

'Yes,' Dad says. 'Didn't you see the hallway?'

I didn't notice, but when I go back and look I can see what Dad means. Sarah's shoes are lying abandoned in the place where she kicked them off, one on the door mat, one on the bottom step of the stairs. Her coat has been slung over the bannisters. On the hallway table is an assortment of items Sarah must have discarded from her pockets; a pair of sunglasses, a bunch of keys with a fake Juicy Couture key ring, a lime-green leopard print purse and a pink lip gloss that has so much gunk around the opening it seems to have welded itself to the table.

I go upstairs. I can hear music coming from Sarah's room, something with a beat that makes me feel overwhelmed.

I take a deep breath and knock on the door.

The door opens a crack and Sarah's face appears. 'What?'

'Dad wants to have family meeting,' I say. 'In the living room. Now,' I add just to make sure she's got it.

The door opens more fully. Sarah folds her arms across her chest. She's wearing a T-shirt with a palm tree on the front that says *Hawaii Beach,* and her favourite black velvet tracksuit bottoms with the pink trim that she changes into after school. I am not surprised she changes as soon as she gets in. Skinny jeans have never looked very comfortable to me.

'I don't want to speak to him.'

'I don't think it's optional,' I say, as politely as I can.

Sarah studies me for a moment. She looks at me in the same way she used to look at the ants on our patio, right before she squashed them.

'Fine,' she says.

She pushes past me onto the landing. I follow her down the stairs.

'Have you moved out too?' I ask her back.

Sarah turns around and frowns at me. 'Don't be stupid. I get free rent and food here.'

We enter the living room. Mikey and Dad are sitting on the sofa. Mikey is watching *Junior Bake Off*. Mary Berry is talking about the taste of what looks to me like treacle tart. Dad looks perplexed. Mikey turns off the TV when we sit down.

I sit on the other side of Dad. Sarah sits on the other sofa, as far away from us as she can. I notice a small grease stain on the thigh of her velvet tracksuit bottoms. She hasn't got any socks on. The pink nail varnish on her toes is chipped.

I wonder if her feet are cold. I always wear socks unless I am wearing tights for school. I love socks, especially bright coloured socks, or very soft and fluffy ones.

'Hello, love,' Dad says to Sarah.

Sarah looks suddenly confused, as if he's caught her out and she isn't sure how to respond.

'Yeah,' she mutters, which isn't really a response.

Dad rearranges a magazine on the coffee table. 'The thing is,' he says. 'I wanted to tell you that I'm moving out.'

'We know,' I say.

Sarah rolls her eyes, probably at my inability to keep a secret.

Mikey nods in agreement with me.

'Well,' Dad says, faltering slightly. 'That's great. I mean - you've had some time to get used to it then.'

'You've been sleeping under the frog duvet since the fifth of September, that's seven weeks and three days.' I say helpfully.

'We've had time,' Mikey says.

'I see,' Dad says.

'It's really no big deal. All my friends' parents are divorced.' Sarah examines her nails. She seems to have changed her tune. I know she's still upset about Dad. She's trying not to show it. 'Except Hannah's parents,' she says. 'But they invite young bisexual women they meet on the internet into their bedroom whenever her dad gets his bonus.'

Dad coughs. He looks uncomfortable. 'Right.'

'Approximately forty-two percent of UK marriages end in divorce,' I say. 'I googled it.'

Mikey is looking at something on his mobile. 'It's less than one percent for same-sex couples within twenty-nine months,' he says, proudly. 'And lesbians are twice as likely to get divorced than gay men.'

Dad looks confused.

'What's that got to do with anything?' Sarah says.

Mikey blushes and puts his phone down.

Dad takes a deep breath. 'Anyway, I'd like to have you all round of course. Show you the flat.'

'You're in a flat?' Mikey says. 'Where?"

'Will *she* be there?' Sarah says.

'Yes, we're in a flat. It's - cosy. Yes, Kaylee might be there.'

Sarah looks disgusted. Mikey looks worried.

'Is it in town?' I ask Dad.

Dad smiles at me. 'It's by the station, Lou.'

Dad knows that I will like this piece of information and he's right. I'm being bribed by Dad's proximity to trains and I know it.

'Can you watch the trains from your flat?' I ask. I can't help feeling excited.

'Well, sort of,' Dad says. 'If you lean out of the bathroom window at a certain angle. You can hear them anyway,' he adds hopefully, trying not to lose me.

'Oh,' I say, feeling let down.

'How many bedrooms does it have?' Sarah says, in a bored tone to show she's not really interested even though she is.

'Two,' Dad says. 'Although one's kind of more of a storage room...'

'You mean a cupboard,' Mikey says.

'Two!' Sarah looks horrified.

'We've got a futon,' Dad says. 'In the living room. You're all welcome to stay,' he says looking at each of us. 'But perhaps just - one at a time.'

We all stare at him.

Dad clears his throat. 'It's a great location,' he says, sounding like an estate agent. 'Very close to - amenities. In fact, it's above a shop.'

Sarah's eyes light up.

'A chip shop,' Dad says. 'They do very good—'

'I can't believe you're living above a chip shop!' Sarah wails. 'That's totally gross.'

Dad looks confused. 'But it's very good,' he says. 'It's been featured in—'

'I don't *care,*' Sarah says, interrupting him again. 'A chip shop is a chip shop. I bet it smells.'

'But you eat chips,' Dad says.

To this, Sarah can say nothing.

'The cod is exceptional,' Dad says. 'They use beer in the batter. And last night Kaylee and I went for the plaice.'

I suddenly think of Dad and Kaylee sitting on their futon eating fish and chips with beer batter straight from the wrapping paper. It's a weird thought.

'Are we done?' Sarah says, standing and folding her arms over her chest, obscuring *Hawaii Beach.*

'Yes,' Dad says. 'We're done. Thank you.'

Sarah rolls her eyes and leaves the room.

'It may take Sarah a while,' Dad says thoughtfully. 'To get used to the changes. But I'd really like the two of you to come round on Saturday.' He looks hopefully at me and Mikey.

Mikey and I exchange glances.

'Okay...' Mikey says slowly.

'Great!' Dad says. 'And you, Lou?'

'I guess so.'

Dad grins. He thumps Mikey on the shoulder in a manly kind of way. Mikey winces. 'Excellent,' Dad says. 'I knew I could rely on you two.'

8

ON Friday evening I'm alone in my room sitting on my bed watching a documentary about dormice. The hazel dormouse is the only dormouse native to the United Kingdom. Like hedgehogs, their numbers are in decline and they are vulnerable to extinction.

There is a knock at my bedroom door. Mum enters wearing a pair of new leggings and a sports top. She's holding a small bottle of water.

I pause the dormice.

'I'm off to Tai Chi,' Mum says.

I nod, waiting for her to tell me something, although I can't think what it might be as we have already had dinner; fishcakes with sweetcorn and spinach.

Mum lingers in the doorway.

'I was wondering if you might like to come with me,' she says hopefully.

I look away from the frozen dormouse on my screen and up at Mum, who is smiling at me.

'No thanks,' I say, thinking of Nan's angel evening and wondering why my family are keen to involve me in their recreational activities.

'It might be fun,' Mum says. 'Steve would like to meet you.'

'Who's Steve?' I ask.

'He teaches the class,' Mum says. 'It'll be quiet. It's Friday night.'

Mum is saying this because she knows I don't like loud

environments. I especially don't like gyms, which is where Mum's Tai Chi class will be. I don't like the loud music and the noise of the machines and all the sweaty people moving very fast but going nowhere.

'I don't think so,' I say.

Mum sighs. 'It won't kill you, Lou. You should get out more.'

I look at Mum but say nothing, hoping this discussion will soon end. It's clear she isn't giving up. 'It's very calming, Tai Chi.' She backtracks a little, fearing she has come on too strong and has offended me, ruining her chances altogether. 'There are lots of beginners,' she says. 'It's only an hour. I thought it might be something we could do together.'

Mum studies the label on her water bottle. She is doing her best to look like a mother who doesn't get to spend the quality time with her children she wishes she could.

I close my laptop. 'Fine,' I say.

Mum brightens. 'We leave in five minutes,' she says. 'Wear comfortable clothing.'

She shuts my bedroom door and leaves me to get ready. When do I ever not wear comfortable clothing? I think to myself as I swap my favourite boyfriend style jeans (that's what the label called them) for a pair of faded blue leggings and an oversize grey T-shirt. I put on a GAP sweatshirt with a hood in case I'm cold. Gyms are often air conditioned and I hate air conditioning.

I go downstairs. Mum is already by the front door. I put my trainers on whilst she checks her hair in the mirror.

We get into the car. 'I'm so glad you decided to come, Lou,' Mum says, as we pull out of the drive. She waves to

Mr De Souza who is putting out his rubbish. He seems to have a lot of rubbish. I expect he isn't recycling.

I stare out of the window at the houses and the other cars and a woman walking a tiny dog in a pink jacket. I think that at Annabel and Neil's, right now, we are all sitting on our designer sofas in the living area after dinner reading our books. Neil has put the log burning stove on. The logs are crackling and hissing as they burn. Outside, the sun is setting over the loch. It's very beautiful. There is a bowl of roasted chestnuts on the coffee table. Annabel has just taken them out of the AGA. Renzo is dozing on the rug in front of the fire. Annabel and Neil are both sipping mulled wine from tall elegant glasses and I am drinking hot chocolate with full fat unpasteurised milk from my favourite blue spotty mug.

I notice we are nearly in town. I feel quite nervous at the thought of going to this gym. I often get very anxious when I have to go somewhere I haven't been before because I don't know what it will be like.

'Here we are,' Mum says, as we turn into a smaller road and then into a large car park.

We quickly find a space. Mum checks her hair in the mirror one last time before we get out of the car. She seems to be doing this a lot recently.

We walk up to the large glass doors of the gym entrance.

'Will I get in?' I ask Mum, suddenly feeling worried. 'Don't you have to be a member?'

'I already thought of that,' Mum says. 'I worked out a system so we don't have to pay any extra.'

I frown. This sounds like one of Dad's avoiding-paying-for-parking type ideas.

'As soon as the girl at reception turns her back, we'll go through,' Mum whispers. 'You'll take my membership card and go through first. You have to swipe the card on the reader and then you can push through the metal turnstile. I'll be right behind you. Once you've swiped, leave the card on top of the barrier next to the bit where you swipe. I'll quickly put my hand over the card and grab it. Then I can re-swipe. I'll be a matter of seconds.'

Already this is sounding complicated, and I don't like breaking rules. Rules are not meant to be broken.

Mum is peering through the glass doors. 'Now,' she hisses. 'She's walked away from her screen.'

Mum thrusts her membership card into my hand and pushes me in front of her.

A man with wet hair, a towel, and his swimming goggles still around his neck, holds the door open for us. I notice he's wearing jeans with flip-flops. There is nothing weirder, I think, than jeans and flip-flops. Especially in November.

I cross the reception area as confidently as I can, not liking this at all. I try not to look at the receptionist who is busy talking to man in a suit. I swipe the card and hear the click that releases the barrier. Mum is right behind me. I let go of the card and it immediately falls to the floor.

'Whoops,' I say.

Now I am one side of the barrier and Mum is trapped on the other. She is looking very panicky.

I reach down for the card. I pick it up and pass it to Mum. This now looks incredibly suspicious. 'You dropped your card, Mum,' I say, hating having to lie but knowing Mum will be mortified if she gets caught attempting to smuggle me into the gym.

'Thanks,' Mum says.

The receptionist has reappeared and is staring at us.

Mum makes it through. She rushes past me and we quickly walk up the stairs to the upper floor which I guess is where the Tai Chi class must be.

'Well done, Lou,' Mum says. 'That's saved me a tenner.'

I don't feel I can comment on this.

We have to walk across the main area of the gym. There are bikes and running machines all facing giant TVs tuned into different channels. The thumping dance music that's playing in the gym doesn't seem to relate to anything on the TV screens. There are lots of sweaty people. There is an area of torturous looking contraptions that people are sitting in or pulling parts of and grimacing. A large sign on the wall says RESISTANCE TRAINING AREA. I wonder why there is a separate area for people who are resistant to training.

We reach a door that says STUDIO 2. There are some guys with arm muscles bigger than my thighs lifting weights by the studio door.

'This is it,' Mum says, as she opens the door.

Inside the studio it's much darker. I like that it's dark. The lights in the gym were far too bright for me. I can hear a tinkling sound. I realise it's music playing faintly. It sounds like wind-chimes.

One side of the room is covered with mirrors. There are a few women doing stretching exercises. Several others are having a conversation along by the back wall. There are piles of jumpers and trainers and handbags positioned along this wall.

Most of the women seem old. In fact I would say, apart from me, that Mum must be the youngest in the room.

One of the women is wearing a Christmas jumper with a robin on the front. It looks hand-knitted. Another woman is wearing pink tracksuit trousers and a blue headband and a large white T-shirt that says *I completed the 10K run for Alzheimer's 1999*.

Mum walks over to them. 'Hi, Gwen,' they say.

'This is my daughter, Lou,' Mum says. The two women smile at me. Sometimes I find it difficult to look at people and make eye contact with them. This is one of those moments. 'Hi,' I say, trying to focus on the robin. It's a very fat robin with a round white belly and a bobbly eye.

'Have you been to Tai Chi before?' the woman in the Alzheimer's T-shirt asks me.

I manage to shake my head.

'Oh, you'll love it,' the robin lady says. 'Steve's very good.'

The Alzheimer's lady nods in agreement. 'The best,' she says.

Mum is taking her jacket and her trainers off so I do the same. We make a neat pile of our stuff whilst the two women wander off to talk to someone else.

'Come on,' Mum says. 'Let's go and say hi.'

It's then I notice a man in the corner of the room by a small hi-fi system. He is the only man in the room. He is putting a CD back into a CD case.

I walk over to him with Mum. 'Hi, Steve.' Mum is smiling at the man. 'This is Lou,' she says.

Steve is tall. He has shoulder length brown hair and a beard with lots of white bits in it. He is very crinkly around his eyes. He's wearing striped trousers that look like a giant tea towel. I imagine he bought them on a beach somewhere, along with a coconut and a straw.

'Hello,' Steve says. 'We're glad you could join us this evening.'

'Thanks,' I say awkwardly, not sure Steve should be speaking on behalf of everyone in the room.

Mum keeps smiling at Steve. 'I've been reading that book you lent me. I'm sorry I forgot to bring it.' Mum smooths down her hair, even though it is already super smooth.

What book? I wonder. Mum usually only reads romance novels, or occasionally crime novels, although I know she sometimes skips the gory parts.

Steve nods. 'It's a great read.'

'What book?' I say.

'The Tibetan Book of the Dead,' Steve says.

Mum is still looking at Steve in a dreamy kind of way, as if he holds all the secrets she wants to know.

'What's it about?' I say, because this is what you say when you haven't read a book.

'Transitional states of consciousness,' Steve says, smiling at me.

I'm not sure what this means but I think that one day I might read this book.

A man comes into the studio and lays down on the floor with his jumper over his head. I can't help but stare at him.

'Don't mind Brian,' Steve says. 'He's in preparation.'

In preparation for what? I wonder.

'Come on Lou,' Mum says, 'Let's get a good spot.'

We carefully walk around the man lying in the middle of the floor with his jumper over his head and stand facing the large wall of mirrors.

'We have to stand a little apart,' Mum says. 'Find your own space.'

I notice the other women in the room are each finding their own space behind us. I imagine an invisible circle around myself. I hope no one invades my space. I don't like people invading my space.

Once in my primary school, we did a P.E. class where we were each told to stay on our own mats. A girl called Shelly Block stood on my mat so I hit her because she stood on my mat and broke the rules. I got sent out of the class and had to write out twenty times, *I will not hit other children.* When I tried to explain that it was Shelly who broke the rules, my teacher got very cross and said I must *take responsibility*.

Steve stands in front of the class. His hair is now tied back into a ponytail.

'Let's begin,' he says.

The jumper man lying on the floor slowly gets up. I notice he has a pink crystal hanging on a bit of black string around his neck.

'We'll do some warm up exercises,' Steve says, probably for my benefit as clearly I am the only new person in the class.

Steve tells us to stand with our feet shoulder width apart. We have to bend our knees and let our arms hang loose, and then swing them.

This is very difficult for me. I try to copy Steve but his body has gone all floppy and I can't make mine do the same.

I can see myself in the mirrors in front of me that cover the entire wall. I don't like mirrors and I usually try not to look in them. Mum and I are at the front of the class. I often sit at the front of my classes in school because it means I can't see all the other people in the room so I feel less nervous, but here, because of the mirrors, I can see everyone and they can see me.

'Let your body be like jelly,' Steve says encouragingly, looking over in my direction.

I look at myself in the mirror. My knees are bent awkwardly like I am half way to sitting on the floor. My arms are rigid, like tree branches moving quickly up and down in a strong gale.

'Like jelly, Lou,' Mum whispers to me.

I give her a look which I hope explains that I am trying my best to be like jelly and I can't help it if I look more like an awkward tree flailing in the wind.

There is a loud thud followed by a yell that comes from somewhere just outside the room. The loud thud makes the studio floor shake. I imagine that one of the beefy guys outside has dropped his weights.

All the women in the class begin to tut. They sound like hens. Some of them are looking at Steve and shaking their heads.

Steve looks towards the studio doors. He also shakes his head. 'It's so difficult,' he says. 'Trying to teach a mind-body-spirit class under these conditions.'

All the women nod in agreement, including Mum. I think that until a few weeks ago Mum probably didn't know what a 'mind-body-spirit class' was. I wonder if the Welsh doctor we met at the hospital encouraged her to do these classes along with the colouring.

Steve tells us our warm up exercises are over. I am very grateful.

'Now,' Steve says. 'We'll do the sequence.'

All the women nod. They prepare themselves by shaking their arms and legs. Steve looks at me. 'Don't worry, Lou. Just follow along as best you can.'

Everyone turns and looks at me. I look down at my feet. I can feel I have gone very red. I don't like people looking at me.

'Let's take a moment to centre ourselves,' Steve says.

I slowly lift my eyes when I am sure people are no longer looking at me. Steve and lots of the women are standing with their eyes closed. The man with the pink crystal smiles at me in the mirror. I don't smile back in case he thinks I'm a rainbow child.

Then Steve opens his eyes. 'Let's begin, he says. Everyone opens their eyes except for me and the crystal man as we never closed them.

Steve keeps his knees bent. He places one foot out in front of the other and begins to slowly move his hands. All the women, Mum, and the crystal man copy him. I also try to copy him. At first I think this will be easy but then I realise it isn't.

Steve is standing in front of us and I try as best I can to mimic his movements. This is difficult. When Steve lifts his left arm, I lift my right arm as he is standing facing us and I use him like a mirror, only I realise this is wrong as everyone else is lifting the opposite arm to me.

'Left arm, Lou,' Mum whispers to me. 'No, *right* leg.'

This is proving to be impossible.

Steve is calling out things as he moves. 'Drive the monkey away,' he says, stepping back and sweeping his hands down in a graceful movement.

I catch a glimpse of myself in the mirror. I have stepped back on the wrong leg and look like I am swatting flies with my arms.

'Grasp the bird's tail,' Steve calls out, withdrawing his arms then pushing them forward, one hand on top of the other.

I try to copy him, not unaware I have missed out several moves in the middle and that I am still standing with the wrong leg forward.

I quickly change my feet over. When I look back at Steve, he has changed position again. It's impossible to keep up with him. I can't understand why I am the only person finding this so difficult. I can only think about moving one of my limbs at a time. I can't seem to be able to move two or three of them at once and in different directions like Steve is doing.

'Single whip,' Steve calls out, changing position again. Everyone copies him. Even Mum seems to be managing to keep up. I wonder if she has been practicing at home with YouTube videos.

After a while Steve glances behind him at the class. He draws his feet together. His hands sweep down to his sides. All the women and the crystal man copy him so I do the same, grateful that we seem to be stopping. I expect Steve to take a bow and everyone to clap but this doesn't happen.

Steve closes his eyes. 'Feel the flow of energy in the room,' he says. He opens his eyes. 'Remember not to force the movements. Use your mind. Be like water.'

A few of the women are nodding.

'We'll take a five minute break,' Steve says. 'Then we'll run through again. The whole thing this time.'

My heart 'sinks'. This is exactly how it feels anyway. I can't believe we have to do it again. The whole thing? How much more is there?

The women go to the back wall to take sips of their water or check their phones. The crystal man lies on the floor again with his jumper back over his head.

Mum offers me her water and I take a sip even though I'm not really thirsty. 'Well done, Lou. You're doing great. Isn't it relaxing?'

I look at Mum and I don't know what to say. This is one of the most un-relaxing things I have ever done.

Mum notices my expression. 'It gets easier,' she says. 'Once you know the moves.'

Steve returns to the front of the class and the women hastily screw the caps back on their water bottles or put their phones back in the pockets of their coats. The jumper/crystal man gets up.

'Mum,' I say quickly. 'I think it may be more beneficial for me to just watch this part.'

Mum smiles at me. 'Okay,' she says. 'You can watch.'

I feel very relieved. I find a space in the darkest corner of the room and sit on the floor amongst the bags and coats and jumpers. I hug my knees to my chest and rock backwards and forwards a little because I find it comforting and sometimes I need to do things that are comforting. I especially need to do this after standing in front of so many mirrors with all those people watching me trying to do Tai Chi.

I watch Steve and the man with the pink crystal and all the women doing the sequence and I begin to feel more relaxed. Perhaps for me, Tai Chi is something that is more relaxing when you are not the person having to do it.

Dad picks me and Mikey up on Saturday morning. We're going to see his flat. Mikey knocks on my bedroom door to tell me that Dad is here.

'Where?' I ask, looking out of my bedroom window. I can't see any sign of Dad and I have been listening for his car. 'How do you know?' I ask Mikey.

'He texted me,' Mikey says.

Mikey and I leave the house together. We walk to the end of the driveway.

'There,' Mikey says, pointing along the road.

I see Dad's car parked several houses down. 'What's he doing there?'

Mikey shrugs and we walk down the road to where Dad has parked.

When we climb in we notice Dad is wearing sunglasses and a baseball cap. I sit in the back and Mikey sits in the front. Dad's on his own. There's no sign of Kaylee.

'Thought I'd keep a low profile,' Dad says.

'But you're our Dad,' I say.

'And I always will be,' Dad says, starting the engine.

Mr Griffin who lives at number six is walking along the road with Rocky, his Yorkshire Terrier. Mr Griffin organises the neighbourhood watch meetings that Mum and Dad never attend. I know this because he posts leaflets through our doors about these meetings, along with notifications about burglaries in our area or cars with foreign number plates that have been seen parked on our road. These notifications always go straight into the recycling.

Mr Griffin frowns at Dad's car. Dad pulls the baseball cap down over his eyes.

Mr Griffin knows a lot of things about a lot of people. He always talks to the women who work in the Co-op. Mum says we should never tell the ladies in the Co-op anything we don't want lots of other people to know.

A griffin is actually a mythical animal, part lion, part eagle. Mr Griffin does not look part lion or part eagle. He wears a brown rain mac and green cord trousers and, when it rains, brown wellies. These are his dog-walking clothes. In the summer he wears a large hat with a wide brim. *There goes Dundee and snappy* Dad used to say as Mr Griffin walked past our house with Rocky. Mum told me that Dad called Mr Griffin 'Dundee' because his hat reminded Dad of the hat the man wore in the film *Crocodile Dundee.*

'So how are you both?' Dad asks us, once we have left our road.

'Fine,' Mikey says, staring out of the window.

'Okay,' I say.

'Good,' Dad says, removing his sunglasses and putting them on the dashboard. This, for Dad, counts as a successful conversation, but then I wonder what else could really be expected from two teenagers.

As we drive towards town, I wonder whether we should have bought Dad and Kaylee something, like a *Welcome to your New Home* card, or a balloon, or a plant (preferably a plant as I don't like balloons). Mum often buys people plants when they move house or have a baby or leave their jobs. She says they are always better than flowers because flowers die. Mum is usually the one who waters the plants in our house. I wonder if Kaylee waters plants. Maybe she is too young to think about watering plants. Perhaps, if I do get a plant, it should be a cactus, something that requires very little water, just in case Kaylee is not a plant watering person.

We are already in the car though and heading into town. Probably it is too late for the plant. Instead I look at a drop of rain on the window outside that is slowly sliding down the glass.

Dad eventually pulls into a small road which appears to have no end to it. It has what you would call 'a dead end'. I know where we are. We are in a road close to the back of the station. There is a long stay car park near here that Mum and Dad sometimes use if they need to get a train somewhere or are going to London for the day.

'This is it,' Dad says.

At the end of the road is a pub called *The Green Man*. The pub is closed because it's Saturday morning. Then there is a row of terraced houses, all tightly squashed together. There's a convenience shop, and then a fish and chip shop. It's the only fish and chip shop on the street so I guess it must be the one Dad lives above. It's called *This Must Be the Plaice* which is written in large black writing on a sign over the door. Under the writing are swirls of blue meant to be the sea. There is a palm tree at one end of the sign and a large yellow sun with lots of rays at the other end.

Dad pulls into a parking space across the road.

'It can be difficult to park sometimes,' he says. 'You have to have a permit.'

Mikey and I nod as if we are interested and Dad turns the engine off.

We cross the road and enter through a door that's at the side of the fish and chip shop. Dad has a key for this door. Inside, there's a long passage and, at the end of the passage, a door with *kitchen* written on it. The passage smells kind of greasy, like old cooking oil.

'This way,' Dad says. We follow him up a flight of stairs. I notice the carpet is very worn. It's a funny brown colour although it may not have been that colour originally.

Dad takes another key from his pocket and opens the door to his new flat.

We follow him through. There is a small hallway and off the hallway on the left are three doors, two of them closed. There is another door at the end of the hallway which I guess must be the bathroom as it's open a crack and I can see black and white tiles on the floor. The walls in the hallway are all patchy. They need re-painting. The floor is reddish coloured wood. It has a few stains on it. Some of them look like drops of paint. Someone, sometime, obviously tried to paint the hallway. It wasn't recently.

Dad turns off to the right and we follow him into the living room. There is a small TV, a futon, a deckchair I recognise from our garage, a drying rack, a table with a sheet over it, and a few cardboard boxes stacked in the corner. There's a single shelf full of small objects, photo frames and ornaments, and a medal which I guess must be Kaylee's swimming medal which she showed us in assembly.

I look at a poster on the wall that has lots of different types of fish on it. The poster says *Fish, Shellfish and Molluscs*.

'Marley was throwing that out,' Dad says, noticing me looking at the poster. 'He had it on the wall in the shop downstairs. I thought it would do until we get some pictures of our own.'

I nod whilst trying to read the names of all the fish. I think that I would like this poster for my bedroom wall. It could go next to the three-toed sloth.

Sarah's friend with the fish phobia would not like this poster at all.

I notice the paint on the windowsill is peeling, flaking off onto the floor beneath. Still, I like Dad's windows because they are old. I guess that before this was a fish and chip shop with a flat above it, it was a house. I think that I wouldn't mind sitting by Dad's windows and looking at the peeling paint on the windowsill. Sometimes I can sit for a very long time not doing very much, just looking at peeling paint on a windowsill, or blades of grass in the garden. Other people don't seem to be able to do things like that. They get bored.

'We're still getting straight,' Dad says apologetically.

'What's with the deckchair?' Mikey asks.

'Oh,' Dad says guiltily. 'I borrowed it. We're a bit short of stuff at the moment. The futon isn't really big enough for three.'

I sit down on the futon. Mikey sits next to me. Neither of us are quite sure what to do.

'I'll get you a drink,' Dad says. 'Apple juice? The tap water here is a little brown.'

'Okay,' Mikey says.

'Thanks,' I say.

Dad smiles and quickly disappears through the door which must be the kitchen.

I stare at the deckchair. It has a swirly nineteen seventies print, orange and brown flowers. I think it might have come from our granny Eve's house before they moved to Cornwall. It's very strange to see it here.

The futon smells funny. It smells kind of - herby. Then I recognise the smell. It is the smell that was hanging around the grebos. The smell of marijuana.

Are Dad and Kaylee smoking pot?

Dad returns with two glasses of apple juice. It's the apple juice I like. The cloudy type. This makes me feel pleased, that Dad remembered which apple juice I prefer.

Mikey takes a sip of his, then puts his glass down on the floor as there is no coffee table.

'Where did you get this futon?' I ask Dad, pretending to admire it.

'Gumtree,' Dad says, looking pleased with himself. 'A couple up the road sold it to us last week for twenty quid. Kaylee and I carried it back.'

I nod, thinking of Dad and Kaylee struggling up the road with the futon. I wonder if they argued about which way to go and who should take which end, like Mum and Dad used to whenever they moved furniture.

'Where is Kaylee?" Mikey says, looking nervously around, as if Kaylee might appear from somewhere.

'She's got swim practice,' Dad says, sitting in the deck-chair. 'And I thought it might be nice, you know, just the three if us. So you can both get used to the place.'

Dad leans back in the deckchair. He looks like he should be on a beach somewhere, wearing his sunglasses and with a hat over his eyes. He sits up, clearly not at ease in the deckchair. He perches precariously on the edge, as if worried the deckchair will swallow him up.

'Do you have a garden?' Mikey asks.

'No,' Dad says. 'But the park's not far.'

'What's under the sheet?' I ask, looking towards the table with the sheet over it.

Dad grins. 'It's the pool table.'

Mikey and I exchange glances.

A couple of years ago Dad decided we were watching too much TV and that we should be doing more activities together as a family. Knowing that none of us are sporty, he decided not to push the issue and instead he bought the pool table. *Something we can do together, even in the winter,* he said. I think he had this idea that we could make teams. Him and Sarah against me and Mikey for example.

The first problem was that nobody was really interest-ed in playing pool. The second problem was that Mum said the table was too big to have in the house, and that her newly created 'snug,' previously the playroom, was not to be turned into a pool room, especially as nobody wanted to play pool anyway.

The pool table was banished to the garage. Dad main-tained his enthusiasm that we could all still play together in the garage. Nobody shared this enthusiasm. The pool table was covered with a sheet and left in the back of the garage amongst the odd chairs and parts of bicycles and Dad's home brew kit which was also never really a success. Once Dad made a batch of wine that tasted like vinegar. He told us it would taste much better if we left it for a while. We tried the wine again at Christmas but it still tasted like vinegar. Mum spat it out all over her roast potatoes. Another time Dad tried to make beer but the air-lock blew and the garage floor was covered in a brown, sticky, stinky mess which stuck to our bike tyres.

The home brew kit was left in a corner of the garage along with the pool table. Over time stuff in boxes from Mum's 'clear outs' began to appear on top of the pool table, and everyone forgot about it.

'I rescued it,' Dad says, looking fondly at the table.

I wonder what Kaylee thinks about this addition to the living room.

I notice that hanging on the drying rack is a red top and a pair of faded jeans. The clothes are much too small to be Dad's. They must be Kaylee's. The zip on the jeans is open and the top button is undone. I wonder if Kaylee hung the jeans on the drying rack or whether Dad did it for her.

I hear the rumble of a train passing but I can't see it.

'Can I go and look at the trains?' I ask Dad.

'Sure,' Dad says. 'But like I said…'

'I know,' I say, sliding off the futon. 'I have to watch them in the bathroom.'

'Help yourself,' Dad says. 'Don't look at the shower curtain. We need to replace it.'

I go into the hallway and find the door to the bathroom. The bathroom floor is covered in chipped back and white tiles laid out like a chessboard. The loo seat has a tropical fish print.

There is something green and furry growing on the

shower curtain that hangs over the bath. I decide not to get too close to it.

Above the sink, next to the bath and shower controls, is a deep window ledge and, above that, the window.

I have to climb up on the edge of the bath and clear a space on the ledge so I can sit there. I move some stuff out of the way: razors, cotton wool balls, and half empty bottles of shampoo and conditioner that must belong to Kaylee. I guess she has to wash her hair a lot because of the chlorine, or maybe she wears one of those little rubber hats when she swims.

Out of the window I can see the train line. It's a large window and it isn't frosted which is useful for looking at trains.

I wait a little while, looking at the track. I count the numbers of sleepers I can see. I wonder how many sleepers there might be for every mile of track. I have to wait quite a long time for a train but I don't mind.

At last I hear a train approaching. I lean to the left so I can see it better. There it is! The train passes and I can see right into the carriages. I catch sight of a man reading a newspaper, a woman in a yellow coat looking out of the window. They are all gone in a matter of seconds.

I wonder if anyone saw me at the window. I expect they didn't. I wonder what Dad and Kaylee do when they shower. Do they mind that a train might come past and that someone on the train might see them naked?

There's a knock on the bathroom door. I hadn't realised I had shut it.

'Lou?' Dad says through the door. 'Are you okay?'

'Yes,' I say. 'I was watching the train and counting the sleepers.' I hop down from the window ledge and open the door.

'Okay,' Dad says. 'But would you like to come and have fish and chips?' He holds up a carrier bag. 'I've just been down to get it.'

'Thanks,' I say, following Dad through to the living room.

At first Mikey and I sit on the futon again and Dad takes the deckchair. Dad then decides the deckchair isn't safe to eat fish and chips on so he sits on the floor. Mikey and I join Dad on the floor. Perhaps Dad deserves to eat his fish and chips alone on the floor, but it seems neither Mikey or I are comfortable with this.

Dad spreads out a newspaper and puts the wrapped parcels on top. He grabs extra salt, vinegar and a bottle of ketchup from the kitchen. Clearly he and Kaylee are well stocked on fish and chip condiments. We all sit together on the floor, having an inside fish and chip picnic which, for some reason, reminds me of the floating tea party in *Mary Poppins*, only no one is laughing.

Dad dishes out the fish and chips. 'The shop has been owned by Marley's family for over forty years,' he tells us as we begin to eat.

Mikey and I pretend to be suitably impressed. It seems important that we take an interest in these new, and rather strange aspects of Dad's life.

'I got you fortune cookies,' Dad says, after we've finished. He hands me and Mikey a fortune cookie each. They're wrapped in red shiny wrapper.

'I thought fortune cookies were Chinese?' Mikey says.

Dad shrugs. 'Marley says the Chinese take-away got his vinegar sachets. Tit for tat, he said. He's got a whole box of them downstairs.'

Mikey and I open our fortune cookies. Mine says, *To be more healthy, eat more Chinese food*. Mikey's says, *Better to press shirt than press luck.* We are both disappointed.

'But weren't the fish and chips good!' Dad says, trying not to let the fortune cookies get us down.

'Sure,' Mikey says.

'The best,' I say.

Dad looks pleased.

After we've finished our fish and chips and fortune cookies and Dad has cleared everything away, he asks us what we'd like to do next.

'I have to get back,' Mikey says. 'I have revision.'

Dad looks disappointed. 'On a Saturday?'

'Yes.'

'How about you, Lou?'

'I think I'll go back too,' I say.

'All right,' Dad says, looking defeated. 'At least you've seen the place.'

Dad takes us home in his car. I try to remember the route in case I ever have to walk to Dad's flat, although I can't think of a situation when this would be necessary.

Dad stops just before our house again. It's clear he isn't going to drive any closer.

'When will we see you again?' I say because I feel that one of us should ask Dad this question.

Dad turns and looks at me. 'Whenever you want,' he says cheerfully. 'There are no rules here.'

'You mean we don't have set days or anything?' Mikey asks.

'No,' Dad says, thinking carefully. 'Not set days exactly. But I was hoping we could make this a regular thing.' He looks hopefully from me to Mikey.

'You want a schedule?' Mikey asks.

'I want to see you,' Dad says.

Mikey thinks about this. 'How about just as and when,' he says firmly. 'No plans.'

Dad's face falls.

I nod to show I agree with Mikey. 'As and when,' I say.

'Well, all right,' Dad says, opening the car door. 'Don't leave it too long though. I'll forget what you look like.' He's trying to be cheerful, although I can tell he feels hurt.

After we have said goodbye to Dad and we are walking up the drive, I ask Mikey if he thinks we are being hard on him.

'No,' Mikey says. 'He brought it on himself.'

I think that Mikey is probably right, but I know that people are not perfect, even parents. In fact, especially parents. I also know that sometimes people have to do the things that are right for them, even if this makes other people upset or angry. I can't help feeling sorry for Dad. He still loves us and wants us to eat the best fish and chips and remembers which apple juice I like, even though he can't be with Mum anymore and wants to be with Kaylee now.

Despite all this, I wish Dad hadn't left and we could still be a family. It seems everyone is angry with Dad. Our family has been divided. As I think about this division, I imagine my family standing together. A large crack appears in the ground, splitting the earth and separating Dad from Mum, Sarah and Mikey. Dad is out there on his own. Then I imagine myself. I am straddling the widening crack. I have one foot in Dad's territory and one in Mum's. It is not a comfortable place to be.

9

IN registration on Monday morning Mr Wexhall says he is going to give us another task. He begins handing out sheets of paper.

'How was your weekend?' Faith says to me.

'I went to my dad's new flat,' I whisper back. 'I looked at trains from the bathroom window and we ate fish and chips on the floor.'

'Cool,' Faith says.

'What did you do?'

'I went to a modern art gallery with Graham and Will and we saw a floating head made out of blood.'

'Cool,' I say.

Mr Wexhall tells us that we will each write a personal statement. He says we live in a world where self promotion and the ability to talk about ourselves and our strengths is very important. He says this exercise will prepare us for the CV writing we will practice in Year Eleven. He says not to worry about the exercise too much, just to write a short statement that explains who we are. He says we should try to write two statements if we can, one in the third person and one in first person. He writes an example of third person on the board.

Mr Wexhall is a secondary school teacher who works at Westlands Comprehensive.

Then he writes an example of first person on the board.

I am a secondary school teacher who works at Westlands Comprehensive.

These are just the examples. Now we are all supposed to be quiet and get on with the task. This is so that Mr Wexhall has time to check his emails and his lesson plans before his first class.

I think that I will write the third person one first. I write:

> *Louise Coulson is a person aged thirteen and a half. She likes to be left to her own devices. She has a dog called Renzo but it should be noted that Renzo lives in an alternate universe along with her real/imaginary parents. Louise Coulson cannot juggle or walk a tightrope or perform any additional circus tricks. She likes cheese and pickle sandwiches and endorses the fact that the world is round and that she cannot, therefore, fall off.*

I am quite pleased with my statement. Now I try to write the first person one.

> *My name is Louise Coulson. I am socially shy and awkward but I am happy to be your friend if you'll be mine as long as there are clear boundaries. I like quiet places, nature programs and small mammals native to the British Isles. I also like trains and train timetables and old-fashioned stations with bridges. I used to eat a lot of bran flakes but now I don't. I sometimes find it hard to be around people and even harder to talk to them. People often look at me as if I am from another planet. As far as I am aware at this moment in time, this is not the case.*

I am slightly less pleased with this one but I think that it will do.

The bell rings and Mr Wexhall hastily collects our pieces of paper. I hand mine in and hope for the best.

I'M SITTING EATING my lunch with Faith and Sam. Faith has finished her rocket and mozzarella sandwiches and is re-applying a dark lipstick to her lips.

'Don't they tell you off for wearing that?' I ask Faith, watching her apply her lipstick.

Faith shrugs. 'Probably. I believe I have the right to express myself in whatever way I choose. I'm exercising my freedom.'

Sam is still eating his rice and carrot sticks with egg free mayonnaise.

'But we're not free,' he says. 'We have to go to school.'

Faith frowns. 'That's true,' she says. 'Maybe we should skip it this afternoon.'

Sam and I look at Faith as though she's crazy.

'Skip school?' I ask. 'You mean, just leave?'

'Why not?' Faith says.

'Because it's against the rules,' I say.

'I don't agree with the rules,' Faith says.

I think about this for a moment. I don't like breaking rules, but I like school even less. 'When would we do this?' I ask Faith.

Sam looks at me as if he can't believe I am contemplating this unthinkable idea. Skipping school could definitely result in us being suspended and our parents being thrown into prison.

'Now,' Faith says.

I must be looking thoughtful because Faith quickly adds, 'It's your decision, Lou. I can't say what the consequences of your decision will be, but you are free to choose and no one can take that freedom away from you.'

'I'm in,' I say, thinking that it feels good to make a decision, and that I don't want to let Faith down.

Sam is looking very worried. He closes the lid on his lunchbox, leaving several carrot sticks untouched. 'You'll have to count me out, I'm afraid. I'm going to see the new Star Wars on Saturday and I'll definitely be grounded if I'm caught skipping school.'

'We understand,' Faith says. 'We all have priorities.'

Sam looks relieved. He opens his lunch box and resumes eating his carrot sticks.

'Where will we go?' I ask Faith.

Faith tucks her lipstick inside her blazer pocket. 'We'll go to the park and stare at tree roots and contemplate the nauseating grotesqueness of being.'

'Okay,' I say.

Faith and I clear our lunch things away and get ready to leave the canteen.

'Good luck,' Sam says to me. He quickly gathers his lunch things. 'I'm going to the library to wait for the bell.'

'Thank you,' I say, feeling like the character in a movie who has been nominated to stay behind on the alien planet with only the light spacecraft (the equivalent of a dingy) in order to administer the detonator that will destroy the planet and save the world. I am a hero but the future is uncertain.

Sam quickly hurries away. As Faith and I leave the canteen, I wonder if I will really be able to do this, to break the rules.

'Do you have any clothes with you that aren't school clothes?' Faith asks me as we walk along the corridor.

I mentally scan the contents of my locker. 'I've got a

GAP sweatshirt,' I say. 'And navy jogging bottoms in my P.E. kit.' We are allowed to wear plain jogging bottoms in the winter for P.E. if we have to go outside, even though they are not strictly school uniform.

'That's good,' Faith says. 'I've got a pair of jeans.'

We reach our lockers and collect our bags. I find my GAP sweatshirt, the jogging bottoms and my P.E. trainers. I put them all in my bag, taking out as many books as I can to make it less heavy.

We put our coats on. We are allowed to wear our coats outside in the playground in the winter so this will not arouse suspicion.

Faith and I cross the school playground together. We have to walk along the side of the Science Block which leads into the school car park where all the teachers park their cars. At the end of the car park is the gate. Once we go through the gate we are free. Unfortunately, the school office window and reception area looks out onto the car park. It is more than likely that we will be seen.

I wonder how we are going to do this. I imagine Faith and I are ninjas, darting behind cars, or perhaps even hiding underneath them as we try to navigate our way unseen across the harsh and dangerous terrain that is the car park. We will have to move quickly. Perhaps Faith will want us to make balaclavas out of our tights in order to hide our identity. I imagine myself doing a forward roll in between two parked cars. I will appear as nothing but a blur on the security camera.

'Did you see something just then?' the receptionist in the office will ask her colleague.

'No,' he'll say. 'It must have been your imagination.'

As we approach the entrance to the car park, I grow nervous, even though I am prepared to do whatever it takes to secure our freedom. I can feel the adrenaline flowing through my veins or blood vessels, or wherever it is adrenaline flows.

'How are we going to do this?' I whisper to Faith, hoping she has formulated a plan.

Faith stops and looks at me. 'We'll just walk across the car park and go out the gate,' she says.

I don't know what to say to this. I'm extremely confused by this plan. 'Just like that?' I ask.

'Just like that,' she says.

I'm still confused. Faith must have seen my expression because she says. 'It'll be fine, Lou. All we have to do is look like two people who have a legitimate and honest reason for leaving school this afternoon. Try to look like you know exactly what you're doing and where you're going.'

I think that I rarely know either of these things.

'Ready?' Faith asks me.

I nod, thinking that I will just have to trust Faith's plan even though it isn't much of a plan.

We walk, rather boldly I think, right across the middle of the car park in a steady and determined kind of way, keeping our eyes focused on the gate. I glance across at Faith. She looks relaxed, not at all like a person who is breaking rules. I concentrate on the gate. I remember Faith's plan and try very hard to look like a person with an honest and legitimate reason for leaving school in the middle of the day. I lift my chin in a way that I think indicates this. I begin, in my head, to hum the theme tune to *The Great Escape*, a famous old film that Sarah, Mikey and I watched last Christmas Day whilst Dad was asleep and Mum was on the phone to our Uncle Simon.

I hear a noise to the left of us. I look over and see our

religious studies teacher, Miss Briggs, lifting the boot of her car. I notice she's wearing her Timberland boots again and her hair is messy. Clearly she is still having relationship trouble.

She's taking a heavy bag of text books out of her boot whilst frowning at something on the screen of her mobile phone. As she closes the boot I notice she has two paw-print stickers stuck to the rear window and, underneath, another sticker that says *Be a fruit loop in a world full of Cheerios!* I wonder if the sticker was a gift.

There's no chance of Miss Briggs not noticing us. Oh well, I think, we gave it our best shot.

I'm ready to turn around and go back, but Faith keeps on walking. Miss Briggs looks up.

'Hi, Miss,' Faith says.

Now we have no chance of remaining inconspicuous.

'Oh, hello girls,' Miss Briggs smiles at us briefly before looking at her phone again. It's clear she doesn't want to engage in conversation with us on her lunch break. Faith keeps walking, so I do too. Miss Briggs locks the boot of her car and rushes away.

We finally make it to the gate. We walk easily through and out onto the pavement. I expect some sort of high pitched alarm to go off and for teachers to come running after us with tasers but nothing happens. I still can't believe Miss Briggs didn't ask us what we were doing in the car park. I can't believe they didn't see us through the office windows or catch us on the security camera.

'Keep walking,' Faith whispers.

So WE KEEP walking. We are on the housing estate at the back of the school. If we take a right, we will reach the parade of shops. There is an Indian take-away that Dad used to drive to sometimes. I used to like to go with him as they gave you chilli peanuts in little bowls to snack on whilst you waited for your curry.

'How much money do you have?' Faith asks me.

'I've got eleven pounds,' I say. 'For emergencies.'

'I've got fifteen,' Faith says. 'Will always makes me keep fifteen pounds on me in case I have to take a taxi somewhere. We'll take the bus into town. It's too quiet here. We'll stand out less in town. We can go to the bigger park and hang out there.'

'We can get the bus from outside the shops,' I say.

'Great,' Faith says. 'But first we have to get changed.' Faith points to two graffiti covered concrete blocks at the edge of the park. 'Over there.'

'Oh, no,' I say. 'Those are the public toilets.'

I don't like public toilets. When we were little Mum used to avoid public toilets at all costs. If one of us really had to go she would first supply us with a packet of travel tissues then stand outside the door and shout, *Remember to hover! Don't touch the seat!*

'We have no choice,' Faith says solemnly.

We both look towards the concrete blocks.

'I'll go in first,' Faith says. 'You keep watch.'

I stand outside the door, not quite sure if I am meant to be looking out for teachers, or the police, or just other people who might want to use to toilet.

I think that I look suspicious. I take my phone out of my pocket and check the weather for something to do. Apparently it's going to rain. I wonder what people used to do before the invention of mobile phones when they were waiting for someone and trying not to look suspicious. Perhaps they looked at their watches or smoked a cigarette. Perhaps that's why smoking used to be so popular. It's a sort of non-activity that passes for an activity. What about non smokers? Maybe they just stared at the sky and pretended they were interested in nephology, which is the study of clouds.

I recently watched a program on climate change which told me that the study of cloud formations is called nephology. It also said that by the time I am a pensioner the UK will be very hot in the summer and that there will be lots of floods. For this reason, when I am older and have my own money I intend to buy a boat like Annabel and Neil's, just in case.

Faith comes out of the toilet wearing her jeans and her P.E. trainers. She has stuffed her skirt and blazer into her bag.

'I know it isn't visible beneath my coat,' she says. 'But we can't be too careful.'

I go into the toilet and hang my bag on a hook on the back of the door. The floor is disgusting and I decide to try and keep as much of my stuff as possible away from it.

The inside of the toilet is covered in graffiti. Above the sink someone has written in black marker pen *Shaz is havin Daryl Flynns baby!* Underneath it someone else has written in red pen, *No she isn't* and underneath that someone else has written. *Shes having Ryan Bakers!* I wonder who these people are. The person who wrote *No she isn't* has tiny spidery handwriting and the other two people have a poor grasp of grammar.

I take off one shoe, then realise that I don't want to put my foot on the floor. I hop to my bag and take out my jogging bottoms. I remove the left leg of my tights and, still balancing on one leg, put the left leg of my jogging bottoms on. Now the spare leg of my jogging bottoms is flapping around and I don't want the bottom to touch the floor so I hold it between my teeth as I reach into my bag for my left trainer.

I put the trainer on the floor, then ease my foot in, using my free hand to undo the laces. I have to do this in a strange crouching position as I still have the end of the right leg of my jogging bottoms between my teeth.

Once the trainer is on, I take off my right shoe and the right leg of my tights and ease the right leg of my jogging bottoms on. At one point, I almost lose my balance and end up grabbing the sink. Luckily I have anti bacterial hand gel in my bag.

I hop to my bag, find the gel, and apply it to the hand that touched the sink, still standing on one leg. Then I take out my right trainer and put it on the floor in order to put it on. Once the trainer is on, I feel strangely proud of myself.

I wrap my shoes in the plastic carrier bag my trainers were in and put them in the bottom of my school bag. I take my coat off and drape it over my bag. Then I take my blazer off and put that in my bag along with my school shoes, skirt and tights, making room for it by taking out my GAP sweatshirt.

I quickly put my GAP sweatshirt on and then my coat. I am ready!

When I go outside, Faith is leaning against the wall looking at the sky.

'Cool,' she says. 'Let's go.'

THERE IS NO one else waiting at the bus stop. It's funny to think of the bell ringing and of everyone at school going to their lockers and collecting their stuff whilst Faith and I are waiting for a bus.

When the bus arrives, we buy two child tickets and find a seat together near the back. The bus driver doesn't seem at all suspicious of us.

'This feels great,' Faith says as the bus pulls away. 'Better than weed. Freedom is nothing but a chance to be better. Camus said that.'

'What will happen when they realise we're missing?' I say.

'Try to make peace with your anxiety,' Faith says, leaning back in her seat. 'It's inevitable. Better to feel something than to feel nothing.'

The bus pulls up at the next stop. An elderly lady with a shopping trolley is slowly getting off. A man in scruffy clothes, holding a can of what looks like lager, runs along the pavement towards the bus. The driver quickly closes the doors and begins to pull out of the bus stop.

'Son of a bitch!' the man yells as we drive away.

'School's hard for me,' Faith says. 'Will always says I'm not one to follow the herd.'

I imagine cows in a field. I imagine one cow breaking free of the herd and trotting off in a different direction to all the others. This is Faith.

'You're not either,' Faith says, looking at me.

'Not what?' I say.

'You don't follow the herd,' Faith says.

'Don't I?' I ask, imagining another cow breaking free.

'No,' Faith says. 'You never will. You're not the sort. If we get into trouble you can say it was my fault, that it was my idea, that I made you skip school.'

'Thanks,' I say. 'But I would never do that. I shall take full responsibility for my decision.'

Faith nods. 'You're a good friend, Lou.'

This makes me feel happy. I'm not sure I've been anyone's good friend before. Mum used to invite girls over to the house when I was younger but they always wanted to play stupid games involving mummies and babies whereas I wanted to play a game I had invented about a spacecraft that was on its way to another planet, in another galaxy, with a similar atmosphere to earth called Zefron. On board the spacecraft lived a small community of people and two of every animal, a kind of Noah's Ark in space. When we arrived on Zefron, it was our job to settle the animals into their new environments and build a settlement and report back any difficulties to planet Earth. Sometimes these difficulties might be something small, like a bad harvest, other times it might be something slightly more major like giant crab-like aliens with candy striped legs wanting to claim planet Zefron as their own.

I did find two girls in my junior school who were happy to play this game for a while at break and lunch times. The three of us played the game every day under my careful supervision until one day they both said they were bored and that they were fed up with me always making up the rules. I said I had to make up the rules as I was the only one who knew about Zefron. After that I had to play it by myself.

The bus pulls up outside Debenhams.

'This is where my mum had a short psychotic episode and tried to steal clothes,' I say. 'She didn't mean to steal them. She didn't really know what she was doing.'

'At least she took action,' Faith says.

We begin to walk towards the park.

'She's better now,' I say. 'She's joined a gym.'

It begins to rain and we walk more quickly. I have forgotten what we are supposed to be doing in the park. I think it had something to do with tree roots.

When we are in the park Faith and I find a willow tree to protect ourselves from the rain. Under the tree we are dry. The rain drips easily off the long thin leaves. It looks like the tree is crying.

Even though it's raining, I don't feel cold. I think the fact that I am excited to be skipping school and standing under a willow tree with Faith is making me feel warmer than I would usually feel.

'Maybe we should do the contemplating the tree thing another time?' I suggest to Faith.

'No,' Faith says. 'Now is a good time.' She stares very hard at the tree. She peers closely at the bark.

I also look at the tree, although I am not quite sure what I am supposed to be looking for.

'Why does the tree exist?' Faith says. 'Its randomness overwhelms me.'

I look at the tree again. It's a nice tree. It does not overwhelm me.

'We should hug it,' Faith says. 'Before we go.'

This surprises me. Faith, hug a tree? This is the person the other girls in our year move out of the way of when she passes them in the corridor.

'It's therapeutic,' Faith says. 'We've used the tree for shelter. We should give some love back.'

This makes sense to me. 'Okay,' I say. 'Let's hug the tree.'

Faith moves around to the other side of the trunk. We both lean in and hug the tree. My arms are below Faith's, our hands almost touch each other's shoulders.

'It's as alive as we are,' Faith says.

'I hope it likes its hug,' I say.

'Can you feel its vibration?' Faith asks me. 'All living things vibrate.'

I rest my cheek against the rough bark of the tree. There's a tingling sensation in my arms. 'I can feel it,' I say.

'It has an energy,' Faith says. 'Just like us. We're here now, living, just like the tree is.' Faith pauses. 'All energy is borrowed and one day we have to give it back.'

'It that Nietzsche?' I say.

'No,' Faith says from the other side of the tree. 'It's from *Avatar*.'

'I love that film,' I say.

'Yeah,' Faith says. 'That was one hell of a tree.'

Faith and I release the willow tree. 'That felt good,' I say.

'What did I tell you,' Faith says. 'In Japan they hang out with trees. They call it forest bathing.'

The rain has finally stopped. We pick up our school bags and dart underneath the wet, drooping leaves.

On the other side of the park there's a street with a row of small shops. We pass the shop my dad always calls the hippy shop. It sells incense sticks, and statues of fairies, and crystals. I wonder if this is the shop where the crystal man at the Tai Chi class bought his pink crystal.

We stop at an Italian ice-cream café and stand under the blue and white striped awning. We carefully avoid the big fat drops of rain still sliding down the awning and onto the pavement.

'Let's go for ice cream,' Faith says, peering into the shop.

'In November?' I say.

'Sure,' Faith says.

We enter the café. There are no customers, just a young guy leaning against the back counter looking at his phone. He wears a red striped apron over a thick woolly jumper. He has a paper hat balanced on his head. He doesn't look happy to be here.

He puts his phone away as Faith and I walk up to the counter.

'What can I get you?' the guy says. 'Hot chocolate? Babyccino?'

Faith looks steadily at the guy. She narrows her eyes. 'No,' she says. 'We'll have two filter coffees.'

The guy behind the counter raises his eyebrows.

'And ice-cream,' Faith adds.

The guy glances towards the windows as if to confirm that it's still cold and wet outside. He shrugs. 'The two scoop sundaes are £4.50 each. You can choose your toppings. Sprinkles are free but nuts are an extra 50p.'

'Fine,' Faith says, reaching into her pocket. 'I'll get these,' she says to me, pulling out a tiny brown leather purse with a red sombrero hat stitched onto the front of it.

'Don't ask,' Faith says. 'Susie bought it back for me from Mexico. She'd notice if I never used it. We won't have the nuts,' Faith says, handing the guy her fifteen pounds. She puts the purse back in her pocket.

'Shouldn't you kids be in school?' the guy says, opening the till and searching for change.

'We're home schooled,' Faith says calmly.

'Oh, yeah,' the guy raises his eyebrow again. He looks sceptical. 'Both of you?' he says, handing Faith her change. 'You don't look much like sisters.'

'We're not sisters,' Faith says. 'We're friends.'

'Right,' the guy says. He picks up the ice cream scooper. 'So what are you having?'

Faith has mint choc chip over salted caramel and I have raspberry ripple over double chocolate. Faith has dark chocolate sauce and I have strawberry sauce because Monday is a good day for red foods. We both have sprinkles.

We take our ice creams over to a table covered in a red and white checked table cloth. The guy brings us our coffees.

We eat our ice cream with long spoons, sipping our coffees in order to stay warm.

I'm not sure if I really like coffee. Sometimes it tastes very bitter. Mum always has her coffee black. Dad has his very milky and with two cubes of brown sugar. Mum calls him a wimp. Nan doesn't drink much coffee. Mostly she drinks weak tea as she says coffee gives her heart palpitations and makes her stressed and that's why the French are so skinny and smoke a lot; they have to calm themselves down from all the black coffee they drink. This coffee is white. It tastes nice, especially after I take a bite of my ice cream, which is very cold and very sweet.

Faith glances over at the ice cream guy. 'Don't you think he's cute?' she asks me.

I must have looked surprised because Faith smiles and says, 'I know. Six gay parents and I turn out straight. It's a drag, but what can you do.'

I look over at the guy again. I think that he looks grumpy, not cute. He looks like the kind of guy who would take you to the cinema to see a film he wanted to see, eat all the popcorn, then make you take the bus home. I decide not to say this to Faith. Instead I say, 'I guess you can't help being what you are.'

Faith studies me for a moment. 'I know,' she says

finally. 'But I feel I've disappointed my mums. Fran's always trying to promote the risk-free elements of lesbian sex.'

'Perhaps you're rebelling?' I say helpfully. 'Going through a heterosexual phase?'

'Perhaps,' Faith says. 'It's a shame. At this stage in my emotional, sexual and intellectual development, I'd prefer to think of my sexuality as fluid.'

'My brother's gay,' I say, thinking about Mikey. 'I'm not sure if he knows yet, but I'm sure he is.'

'How old is he?' Faith asks me.

'He's fifteen and three quarters.'

'He'll know,' Faith says.

WE DECIDE TO take the bus back to Faith's house.

'We'll go to my mum's,' she says. 'They won't be home from work yet and you shouldn't arrive home from school too early. It will look suspicious.'

'Okay,' I say, feeling curious about Faith's house.

Faith lives on the other side of town in a small suburb, kind of like where I live.

'The suburbs suck,' Faith says, as we get off the bus. 'As soon as I finish school, I'm outta here.'

'Where will you go?' I ask as we walk along the pavement. I notice the sign that says Laburnum Drive.

Faith shrugs. She adjusts her school bag on her shoulder. 'Anywhere that isn't here. A big city. Somewhere where no one knows their neighbours and the levels of air pollutants are particularly lethal, and where I'm never more than six feet away from a rat.'

'It's an aspiration,' I say. 'Not so many trees to hug though.'

'No,' Faith says. 'I'll have to take regular forest bathing holidays.'

I think that I would like to live in a big city because there would be lots of stations and libraries and art galleries and zoos and maybe an aquarium where I could go and look at all the brightly coloured fish, but I would also worry about living in a big city. I don't like crowds and lots of noise and I find other people extremely overwhelming. I also have a terrible sense of direction and can't find my way very easily, unless I can picture the route I need to take in my mind and there aren't too many corners.

This is why I think I might be better off in the country with sheep and chickens and, hopefully, hedgehogs.

We turn up Faith's driveway. She lives at number twenty-six. I'm disappointed that the house looks so normal. I suppose most people's houses do look normal. There are a lot of plants in pots outside the front door.

'These are Susie's,' Faith says, gesturing to the plants. 'She works in a garden centre. She brings home all the nearly-dead plants that the centre wants to throw away. She tries to bring them back to life.'

'Like a plant doctor,' I say.

'Yeah,' Faith says. 'A plant doctor. She'll like that.'

Faith lets us in with her key. We hang up our coats and kick off our shoes. I notice there is a small framed fish skeleton hanging on the wall in the hallway.

As we go past, I look into the living room. There's a TV and two sofas and a large glass coffee table with magazines on it, and another plant. On the wall there's a large photograph of a block of flats which I think is an unusual choice of photograph for a living room wall, although some people might think this about my three-toed sloth poster and ABC train time-table. I like the photograph of the block of flats, all the tiny symmetrical squares, some of them coloured.

'That's my mum's,' Faith says. 'She likes photographs of buildings, and sometimes bridges. She works in an architect's office.'

'I like it.'

'Let's go up to my room,' Faith says.

Faith's bedroom is quite messy. Not anywhere near as messy as Sarah's but much messier than mine. She has a huge poster of a small man in a hat that says *Tom Waits,* and a framed old-fashioned picture of a man and a woman smoking cigarettes in a café.

I notice Faith has only made a half-hearted attempt to make the bed. She has a black duvet cover and yellow pillows. There is a yellow bean bag on the floor. She has a large glass tank on a small table over by her desk and bookshelf. The tank has its own lights. I wander over to it. Inside there are some branches and plants, a large rock and a sort of tube.

I bend down and look inside the tube. I can see a pair of eyes looking back at me.

'That's Jonathan,' Faith says, watching me.

'Who's Jonathan?'

'He's a bearded dragon,' Faith says. 'He'll probably come out soon. He can be shy.'

I back away from the tank. Jonathan begins to slowly emerge from the tube. He's very scaly with funny spread-out toes and a small spiky beard. Faith and I watch him climb to the top of his rock.

'He likes it up there,' she says. 'He sunbathes. I once asked my parents for a baby brother so they bought me Jonathan instead. I consider him a fair substitute.'

'He looks like he's thinking about something important.'

'Yeah,' Faith says. 'He always looks like that. Or like he has just had to make a difficult decision and must now face the consequences.'

We both watch Jonathan on his rock. He suspiciously eyes us up. Then he lifts a front leg as if he's saying hello.

'He waved at us!'

'He does that sometimes,' Faith says. 'He comes out and sits on his rock whenever there's someone new in the house. He also comes close to the glass and watches me whenever I do my maths homework. I think he must like maths. He likes Bob Dylan too. His favourite album is *Desire*. He bobs his head to it. Although he's also pretty partial to *Blood on the Tracks*.'

'That's cool,' I say.

Faith turns to me. 'I'm glad you came over Lou,' she says. 'There's no one else at school as interesting as you.'

I don't know what to say. No one has ever said this to me before. Sometimes when I talk about the things I like, trains, or small mammals native to the British Isles, or my favourite Sir David Attenborough documentaries, other people, usually my family, will nod and say 'that's interesting', in a way that means they aren't really that interested.

'You're different to other people,' Faith says. 'You see the big things and the little things. Most people, they just see the stuff in the middle.'

'Thanks,' I say, not sure what to make of this.

Faith shrugs, 'It's just the way you are.' She looks at me very seriously. 'I have to say one thing though.'

'What?' I ask, pulling at the sleeve of my jumper.

'You shouldn't try to be invisible all the time. Sometimes it's like you're trying to be part of the furniture or something, you know?'

'It's a survival mechanism,' I say.

'You gotta just be you,' Faith says. 'Don't worry about anyone else. If they don't want to hang out with you, it's their loss.'

'Maybe,' I say, unconvinced.

Faith ignores me. 'You have to own who you are,' she says. 'Just walk in and say, yep this is me. If they don't like it, they can fuck off.'

'Thanks,' I say. 'But being me makes everything more difficult,'

'But who else can you be?' Faith says. 'You said so yourself.'

'I admit you've got a point,' I say thoughtfully.

We both look at Jonathan who appears to have been eavesdropping.

'Let's listen to music,' Faith says. 'Something upbeat.'

I sit on the edge of Faith's bed and watch as she goes to her CD player. She picks up a couple of CDs and studies them before choosing one and sliding it in.

'Jonathan likes Bruce Springsteen,' Faith says. 'Especially the *Born in the USA* album, which is weird as he was born here, in a pet shop, and his ancestors came from Australia.'

The song starts to play. It's a song I know about a man who says we're just dancing in the dark.

Faith is standing by her CD player. She starts to move her shoulders in a funny kind of way like she has a twitch. Then she begins to do the same thing with her hip. She shuts her eyes. She's making strange jerky movements with her elbows. For a moment I'm worried she's having a fit, then I realise she's dancing.

I stand up. Bruce Springsteen is still singing about not being able to light a fire without a spark. I shut my eyes too. I sway a little to the music. I move my shoulders and make a swinging movement with my arms. It feels good.

I open my eyes. Faith is hopping about now, bobbing her head up and down and spinning round on the spot. I begin to jump around like Faith, moving my head from side to side and letting my hips follow. I stick my elbows out and punch the air. Faith opens her eyes and smiles at me. She looks like she's having fun. We're both having fun and not caring what anyone else might think about us. Even Jonathan looks amused.

Here we are, I think, just two weird kids in a bedroom somewhere in the east of England doing a funny, geeky dance because it makes us feel happy.

10

WHEN I arrive home from skipping off school, there is a man hanging upside down in our living room doorway.

There's a large metal bar attached to the top of the door frame. Strapped to the bar are two huge upside down boots. The man has his feet strapped into these boots. He has his arms folded across his chest and his eyes shut. His ponytail is touching the floor.

It takes me a moment to realise it's Steve from Tai Chi, only upside down.

I put down my school bag and the upside down Steve opens his eyes.

'Hi,' he says.

'Hi,' I say.

'Gravity boots,' he says, as if this explains everything. Seeing my confused expression he adds, 'Hope you don't mind me hanging out here. My doors are a little short.'

'No,' I say, feeling bewildered.

'Better check the rice,' Steve says, swinging himself upwards. He holds on to the bar with one hand and fiddles with the straps on the boots with the other. He releases his socked feet and swings to the ground.

I follow him through to the kitchen. Mum is there tidying the kitchen table. Usually there is a random selection of stuff like unopened letters and take-away leaflets and books or magazines that get pushed into the middle of the table at meal times but today it seems Mum has decided to clear the table completely.

'Lou,' Mum says, 'You remember our friend Steve?'

'Yes,' I say, wondering when Steve the Tai Chi man became 'our friend Steve'.

Steve stretches then wanders over to the hob and lifts the lid on something simmering on our hob top. I notice a giant pile of chopped vegetables on the chopping board.

Sarah appears in the kitchen wearing a tiny pair of denim shorts and a cropped fluffy jumper.

'Steve's making dinner tonight,' Mum says, as if it's the most normal thing in the world.

Sarah glances at Steve. She doesn't seem at all fazed to see a strange, pony-tailed man in our kitchen. She takes two slices of bread from the bread bin. 'Count me out,' she says, dropping the two slices of bread into the toaster. 'I'm going to the pub.'

'That's a shame,' Mums says.

'It's nice to meet you,' Steve says.

'Sure,' Sarah says, concentrating on her toast. 'Whatever you say.'

Mikey enters, looking confused. Perhaps because there is a strange man in our kitchen wearing green socks and boiling rice on our hob.

'You remember Steve,' Mum says. 'From the supermarket.'

Mikey looks at Steve as if trying to place him.

'Last Thursday,' Mum says helpfully. 'We couldn't find the mustard and we bumped into Steve who helped us find it.'

Mikey nods. He still looks confused.

'Mustard is always with the other condiments,' I say. 'Next to the pickle.'

'And so it was,' Steve says, winking at Mum.

I decide we have been set up. There is no way Mikey and Mum 'accidentally' bumped into Steve in the supermarket, and there was clearly an agenda in her taking me along to her Tai Chi class. Mum wanted us to meet Steve. Perhaps she felt it would lessen the shock somehow if we first met him outside the house. I can imagine the section in the parenting manual that advised Mum to do this. *Introduce your children to your new boyfriend on neutral territory so that when he comes into your home he is not seen as an intruder but as an established friend.*

The best Mum could manage was a Tai Chi class and a trip to Sainsbury's? And what about Sarah? Perhaps it doesn't matter. Sarah isn't as sensitive as me and Mikey.

Sarah's toast pops out of the toaster. She grabs a plate, a butter knife and the entire jar of peanut butter.

'Enjoy,' she says, glancing at the boiling rice. She leaves the kitchen carrying her plate of toast and with the peanut butter jar tucked under her arm.

'What are we having for dinner?' Mikey asks.

'Brown rice and vegetables,' Steve says.

Mikey looks disappointed.

'I'm macrobiotic,' Steve says.

'Oh,' Mikey says. 'Do you inject?'

'No,' Steve says, dropping the vegetables into the steamer. 'It isn't a medical condition. More a lifestyle choice.'

'Steve eats a lot of rice,' Mum says, as if it's the most fascinating thing in the world.

'Whole grain is very grounding,' Steve says, carrying the saucepan over to the sink in order to drain off the remaining water.

'Actually, my friend Sam breaks out in a rash every

time he eats whole grain.' I say. 'He can tolerate small amounts of refined white grain much more easily.'

Steve frowns.

'I guess there are exceptions,' Mum says quickly.

'How long have you been - macrobiotic,' Mikey says, pronouncing the word very slowly.

'Since nineteen eighty-six,' Steve says proudly, dishing out the rice onto four plates. 'I've given us a good mix of ying and yang veggies.'

Neither Mikey or I are interested enough to ask what 'ying and yang veggies' are.

We sit down to eat.

Steve picks up his fork. 'Of course you must eat however you like to enjoy your dinner,' he says. 'But I try to chew each mouthful at least twenty times and really concentrate on my food. It's much better for your digestion.'

Mikey and I exchange glances. Clearly this meal could take a while. At least no one noticed I arrived home half an hour late because I skipped school this afternoon.

AFTER DINNER I go up to my bedroom and sit on the floor for a while. I feel the need to be quiet, to spend some time by myself. I decide that, although fun, this day has been quite overwhelming, what with skipping school with Faith, hugging trees, eating ice cream, meeting Jonathan the bearded dragon, dancing to Bruce Springsteen, and then arriving home to find Macro Steve hanging upside down in our living room doorway.

I think that I will now watch a nature documentary. I select *The Life of Mammals* and am just about to press play when my mobile phone rings.

This is very unusual. I do not use my phone as much as other people. I don't spend a lot of time chatting to friends like some people do. This is partly because I don't have many friends, and partly because I find it quite tiring talking to other people, especially on the phone as I'm never sure when it's my turn to speak. I only have nine contacts in my phone; Mum, Dad, Sarah, Mikey, Nan, my Granny Eve and Granddad Jim, Uncle Simon, the Indian take-away (Dad called once from my phone), and the RSPCA, in case I come across an injured animal that needs rescuing.

I quickly answer my mobile.

'Hi,' Faith says. 'It's me.'

'Oh,' I say, forgetting Faith has my number.

'Just thought I'd call for a chat,' Faith says.

This worries me. I am not good at small talk and I am not used to people calling me on the phone to 'chat'. I begin to feel anxious.

'Did you get back okay?' Faith asks me.

'Yes,' I say.

'No one asked any questions?'

'No.'

'Okay...'

There's a pause at the end of the line. I start to scratch my arm.

'Are you all right?' Faith asks me.

'I was going to watch a nature documentary,' I say feeling agitated that I might not have time to finish the documentary if I have to stay on the phone to Faith.

'Interesting,' Faith says. 'What's it about?'

I begin to panic. I am hopeless at answering these kinds of questions, especially on the phone and especially when I am tired and have had an overwhelming day.

'I don't think we can be friends anymore,' I blurt out.

Faith is silent. I think she's going to tell me not to be stupid, or maybe get angry and shout at me. She doesn't. After a moment she says in a quiet voice, 'If you're sure that's what you want, Lou.'

'Yes,' I say, firmly. 'It's what I want.'

'Well,' I guess I'll see you around,' Faith says slowly. I can tell I have hurt her feelings but I can't take back what I've said and, besides, I am very anxious now. I am feeling short of breath and I have to get off the phone.

'Bye then,' Faith says.

'Bye,' I say, quickly hanging up and throwing the phone on the floor.

I sit on my bed, grip my pillow in both hands and try to breathe deeply. I dig my fingers into the fabric of my pillowcase. I feel that I am going to have a meltdown and I must not have a meltdown.

I continue to push my fingers into the pillowcase. I begin to feel a little better. I don't have to talk on the phone anymore. I don't have to talk to anyone who is going to make me feel tired or place demands upon me.

I still have time to watch my nature documentary.

THE NEXT MORNING when I am about to leave for school, there is a knock at the front door. I open the door to find Dad standing on the doorstep dressed like a postman. He's even wearing a red baseball cap and has a large post bag on his shoulder. He's holding a package.

'Hi, Dad,' I say.

'Hi Lou,' Dad says.

'Why are you dressed like the postman?' I ask.

'I am the postman,' Dad says.

'Since when?'

'Since yesterday.'

'You're working as a postman now?'

Dad frowns. 'This is the twenty-first century, Lou. A change of career is not at all uncommon.'

'But you used to be a P.E. teacher.'

'This is a very sought after position.' Dad looks at his feet. 'I did try to get my route changed but it wasn't possible...'

'What about Bernie?' I ask, thinking about our old postman who used to deliver the post on his bicycle.

'He's retired,' Dad says. 'Gone to Majorca. Planning to set up a pedalo business. I went to his retirement do.'

I imagine Bernie sitting on a beach in a deckchair wearing a bum bag and drinking pineapple juice through a green straw. He stands up every now and then in order to shout, *Stay away from the rocks!*

Once, a few months ago, I was walking along our road to school at the same time as Bernie was cycling with his post bag. He was cycling at about the same speed as I was walking which, I felt, was embarrassing for both of us. I then heard a strange creaking noise which I thought must be his bicycle but which I later realised were his knees.

'Good luck to Bernie,' I say.

'Here,' Dad says, handing me the package. 'It's for Mikey.'

I take the package which is shaped suspiciously like a cake tin.

'Thanks,' I say, putting the package in the hall. 'Do you have a bicycle?' I ask Dad.

'No,' Dad says. 'I'm on foot.'

This makes me think of Dad hopping along our road with his post bag. The expression should really be 'on feet'. I find it confusing.

'I hope to see you soon,' Dad says.

'Sure,' I say.

Dad looks happy. I wonder if he knows about Macro Steve yet. I decide not to tell him.

'Bye, Lou. See you at the weekend.'

'Okay,' I say. 'Bye Dad.'

Dad walks off down the drive with his bag. He's whistling to himself.

When I arrive at registration, Faith's already there. She's sitting at another table. She looks up at me when I walk in then quickly looks away. This makes me feel sad. I think about going over to her and telling her that I made a mistake but I expect that when I say it, it will come out wrong or sound insincere and that she might be angry with me.

It will probably be better if Faith finds another friend, someone who she can talk to on the phone all the time and share her make-up with and talk about boys to, as opposed to someone like me who likes to watch trains and talk about animals; who sometimes gets lost and who is easily exhausted by other people.

It's also better for me. I need my life not to be complicated and friendship is always complicated.

I hardly see Faith all day. She is very good at avoiding me.

We have P.E. after lunch, my least favourite lesson. Luckily it's only table-tennis which means we don't have to go outside. Sam and I are enjoying our game when I am hit in the back by a flying ball.

I turn around to see where the ball came from.

Lianne Parks walks over to our table to retrieve her ball.

'Sorry,' she says, in a sickly sweet voice, loud enough for our teacher to hear. Under her breath she says. 'We're gonna get you, freak,' before returning to her own table.

At the end of the day I go to my locker to collect my stuff. Someone has vandalised my locker. Actually, they have written a poem across it in black marker pen:

> Your dad's a pervert
> Your sister's a slut
> Your brother's a fairy
> And you are a nut.

A nut? Is that the best they could come up with? I guess they wanted it to rhyme. Dad doesn't work here anymore and Sarah can take care of herself but I'm worried about 'Your brother's a fairy'. Mikey is pretty well-liked at school. I would hate to think he is having a difficult time like I have a difficult time with Lianne Parks and Bryony Silver and Cherry Wiles and Bonnie Jackson, and the boys who think it's funny to trip me up on the school playing field.

I feel uneasy as I walk home. I keep looking behind me to make sure I'm not being followed. Lianne has already kicked me and punched me in the eye. I'm not sure what she means when she says she is 'Gonna get me'.

I walk home very fast. What with Faith not being friends with me anymore, and then being threatened by Lianne Parks during P.E. and the poem on my locker, this has not been a good day.

When I get in, I plan to sit on the floor and curl myself up as small as I can and rock backwards and forwards and maybe cry a little if I need to.

When I arrive home, Dad's car is there. Not parked half way down the street but actually on our driveway.

Mum's car is there too. This can't be good news.

There is also a small van blocking our driveway.

For a brief moment, I think that I may have it wrong. Perhaps Mum and Dad are getting back together. Maybe they're inside right now hugging and kissing on the sofa, their wedding album spread over their laps. (I don't think Mum burned the wedding album photographs.)

I realise this is unlikely.

The front door opens and two men appear carrying a large roll of carpet. As I approach, I realise it's our old carpet. The one with the burnt patch. It looks as though Mum finally decided to replace it.

The men nod to me and leave the front door open so I don't have to rummage around in my coat pockets for my key.

When I enter the house, I can hear raised voices in the kitchen. I can also hear music coming from Mikey's room. I know it's coming from Mikey's room as it's ABBA, *The Winner Takes It All*, one of Mikey's favourite ABBA songs although, worryingly, it's the song he plays when he feels sad.

I shut the front door behind me and tiptoe along the hallway. I can hear Dad's voice from the kitchen. 'I'm sure it was a mistake.'

I poke my head around the living room door. The new carpet is a light grey colour with darker flecks. The room smells like new carpet. I quickly back away.

'His feelings weren't a mistake,' Mum says crossly from the kitchen. 'He's taken it badly. I expect he felt he didn't have anyone to talk to.'

'If you're implying,' Dad says. 'That this is my fault—'

'Oh, no of course not,' Mum says sarcastically. 'I'm sure the fact that their family unit has been destroyed is having absolutely no effect whatsoever on our children.'

Uh, oh. This doesn't sound good. Mum and Dad are arguing.

'This is not the result of external circumstances,' Dad says. There's a short pause. I wonder if this remark has confused Mum as much as it has confused me. 'It comes from your side of the family.'

'Are you talking about Simon?' Mum says, raising her voice in a very threatening way.

'Yes,' Dad says.

Our Uncle Simon is actually Mum's first cousin. He never married and last Christmas he brought a 'friend' called Pete to our Christmas dinner. Pete owns a company that sells fruit pastes which are used as the bases for cocktails. Funny, the things you can do to earn a living.

'Sexuality is not inherited!' Mum shrieks.

Oh dear, this is bad. Dad has really gone and done it now. Sometimes he says such stupid things.

I am just about to walk into the kitchen when Mum says. 'And what about Lou? Are you going to blame my cousin for the fact that she's been truanting?'

I stop dead in my tracks.

'I didn't know that,' Dad says calmly. 'You didn't tell me.'

'I'm telling you now,' Mum says. 'You weren't here.'

I take a deep breath. I have been found out. I am too close to the kitchen to double back. I decide I must face my fate and the consequences of my decision.

I enter the kitchen.

Mum and Dad both turn and look at me. Dad is leaning against the cooker. Mum is standing by the fridge next to her gym timetable. She's holding a piece of paper.

'I guess you heard that,' Mum says to me as I walk in.

All I can do is nod.

Dad looks cross. 'You can't just not go to school, Lou.'

'I know,' I say.

'We could get into a lot of trouble,' Mum says.

I look very intently at the kitchen floor tiles. 'I understand. It won't happen again.'

Neither Mum or Dad know what to say. They are not used to me breaking rules.

'Things have been difficult,' I add, lifting my eyes from the floor.

Both Mum and Dad nod in agreement. They seem to be thinking about themselves. I decide this is my best line of defence. 'I've been under a lot of pressure,' I say.

'Don't push it,' Mum says.

Dad gives me a serious look. 'This mustn't happen again, Lou.'

'Were you talked into it?' Mums asks.

'No,' I say. 'It was my decision. I take full responsibility.'

Not that it matters anymore, seeing as she probably hates me anyway, but I don't want to get Faith into trouble. It was my decision to join her in skipping school.

Mum and Dad exchange glances. I'm not sure they believe me.

'We got a letter from school,' Mum says, waving the piece of paper.

'Oh,' I say.

'And it included this,' Mum says.

I look a little closer at the paper Mum's holding. I recognise my own handwriting. It's the two personal statements we were asked to write in registration.

'Your form tutor thought we should see it,' Mum says. She sighs. 'He thinks we should send you for an assessment.'

'What assessment?' I say, imagining myself surrounded by men in white coats with clipboards.

Mum and Dad look at each other again. 'We'll think about it,' Dad says finally.

The Winner Takes It All starts up again. It appears to be on a loop.

'What's up with Mikey?' I ask, thinking this may be a good moment to divert their attention away from me.

'He's upset about something,' Mum says, tucking the letter into her pocket.

'About what?' I say, hoping Mum forgets where she's put the letter.

'You'd better ask him yourself,' Dad says.

'Yes, why don't you go upstairs and see if he's okay.' Mum seems genuinely worried.

I leave the kitchen and go upstairs. I knock on Mikey's bedroom door. He doesn't answer. I try a few more times.

'Mikey?' I call through the door. 'Are you there?'

He doesn't come to the door. I decide to once again break the unspoken code of teenage sibling etiquette. I open the door.

Mikey is not in his bedroom.

I turn off ABBA still playing on Mikey's laptop which is on his desk next to a Mary Berry baking book, a box set of *Friends,* and a framed retro photograph of Madonna.

Mikey and I do not criticise each other's interests.

I close Mikey's bedroom door. I check the bathroom. He isn't there. I head downstairs. Mikey isn't in the living room. I notice his trainers are not by the front door where he usually leaves them.

'Mikey's not in his room,' I say, walking back into the kitchen.

Both Mum and Dad look surprised.

'He isn't anywhere,' I add.

'He must be somewhere,' Dad says.

'I told you he was upset,' Mum says.

'And his trainers are missing.'

Mum and Dad look at me. Now they are really worried.

'We should have handled this differently,' Mum says, visibly upset.

Dad rubs his head. 'I'll find him,' he says. 'He can't have gone far. I'll take the car.'

'I'm coming with you,' Mum says.

'I'm coming too,' I say, also feeling worried about Mikey. This will be my second rescue mission in three months. Last time we had to rescue Mum from Debenhams and this time we have to rescue Mikey, only we don't know where he is.

We hastily put our shoes on and leave the house.

When we get to Dad's car, I realise Kaylee is sitting in the front seat. She gets out of the car when she sees us all approach. She looks slightly scared, as if we have come for her. How did I not notice her when I passed Dad's car? Sometimes I notice little things that other people don't seem to notice but not the big things that everyone notices. Or maybe Kaylee ducked down and hid when she saw me coming.

'It's all right,' Dad says to Kaylee. 'We have to find Mikey. Did you see him?'

Kaylee nods. She looks from Dad to Mum. 'About twenty minutes ago. He came out of the house. I'm sorry, I didn't stop him, I—'

'It's not your fault,' Dad says, interrupting her. 'Did you see which way he went?'

'Left,' Kaylee says.

'Let's go,' Dad says.

There is an awkward moment when Kaylee tries to move around the car to get in the back seat so Mum can sit in the front.

'It's fine,' Mum says sharply, clearly more worried about finding Mikey than sitting in the front seat.

'No, it's okay,' Kaylee says, sidestepping around Mum and opening the back door.

'No really, it's fine,' Mum says, moving towards the back door at the same time as Kaylee so they nearly collide.

They both take a step back at the same time.

'Totally fine,' Mum says, gesturing to the front of the car.

'I don't mind,' Kaylee says, not moving.

By the time this has been sorted out Mikey could have left the country.

Eventually, Kaylee and I get in the back and Mum sits in the front.

If Mikey went left and not right, it means he can't be hiding out in the park at the end of our road. As we drive we see Mr Griffin. He's carrying a reusable shopping bag and walking Rocky. Dad slows down and lowers his window. 'I'll ask old Dundee,' he tells us.

Dad leans out of his window. 'I don't suppose you've seen Mikey?' he calls out to Mr Griffin. 'My son,' he adds, perhaps in case Mr Griffin has forgotten who Mikey is.

'Our son,' Mum corrects him.

'Our son,' Dad repeats out the window.

'In the red trainers?' Mr Griffin asks us.

'That's him,' Dad says.

'He got on the bus,' Mr Griffin says. 'I saw him when Rocky and I came out of the Co-op.'

Rocky barks as if to confirm this. I guess that in circumstances such as these it can be useful to have nosy neighbours who notice things.

'Ask him when,' Kaylee says from the backseat, trying to be helpful.

'What time?' Dad asks.

Mr Griffin looks at his watch.

'I'd say about sixteen minutes ago.'

'Thank you,' Dad says, rolling his window up.

Mr Griffin looks at us curiously before pulling on Rocky's lead.

We turn right at the end of our road.

'He's gone into town,' Mum says. 'Why has he gone into town?'

'We'll drive around and look for him,' Dad says.

Kaylee looks worried. 'The shops will be shutting. Where will he go?'

No one says anything but I know Mikey. He hasn't gone shopping. Mikey would not be wandering around the town centre or sitting on cold benches by the canal or hanging out in the skate park like other teenagers. He is Mikey. He likes baking and ABBA and *Friends,* and female divas with big voices.

I think that if I was feeling upset and wanting to get away from my family I might go and look at trains. I think about Mikey and all the things he likes and where he might go to be quiet.

'I know where he is,' I say.

Mum turns and looks at me. So does Kaylee. Dad looks at me in his rear view mirror.

'Where?' they ask.

We pull up outside the museum.

'Are you sure?' Mum asks me.

'I guess it's worth a try,' Dad says, turning the engine off.

'You used to bring us here,' I say to Dad. 'Mikey still comes sometimes. When he wants to get away from everything. He likes the bees.'

'I haven't been here for years,' Mum says.

The museum is set back from the road. Kaylee is peering at it through the trees. 'Is it even open?' she says, to no one in particular.

'Come on,' Dad says, undoing his seatbelt. 'Let's find out.'

'No,' I say sharply, causing everyone to pause. 'I'll go. You all stay here.' I think that the last thing Mikey would want, if he is inside, is me, Mum, Dad, and Kaylee all storming into the museum looking for him.

Mum and Dad don't look convinced.

I quickly open my car door before anyone has time to object. 'Wait here,' I say, jumping out and shutting the door.

I walk through the gates and onto the path that leads up to the museum. The museum is really a very large house that probably once belonged to some very wealthy people. I glance back over my shoulder. Remarkably, no one else has got out of the car. For once, it seems my family have listened to me.

I enter the museum. I am in the foyer next to the stand of information leaflets. There's a curly-haired woman at the front desk working at a computer. She has her glasses on a piece of string around her neck. She frowns at me.

'We close in fifteen minutes.'

'I'm only here to find my brother,' I say. 'Have you seen him? He's wearing red trainers.'

The woman shrugs. 'Whatever you're here for, we close in fifteen minutes. I've got to collect my dog from the grooming parlour. He doesn't like it, if I keep him waiting.'

I dart past the desk. I begin to climb the stairs that lead to the top floor rooms.

I pass the brown Russian bear in his huge glass case. I pause to say hello to him. He looks the same as when I last saw him; wary and slightly surprised. He's clutching the same tree branch.

I walk past the room that has all the other stuffed animals, birds and small mammals native to the British Isles. The Victorians had a thing for taxidermy. They liked to have mounted animals in glass cases in their homes. If they had these animals, it usually meant they were wealthy. Sometimes they liked to dress these animals up like people and make tea-party scenes.

I walk quietly up to the doorway of the room where the living honeybee observation hive is kept.

Mikey is sitting next to the glass hive watching the bees. I'm very pleased he's here. I am pleased because it means he's safe and we've found him. I'm also pleased because it means I was right. He was where I thought he would be.

Mikey doesn't look surprised to see me.

'Hi,' I say.

'Hey,' he says, still watching the bees.

'Where's the queen?' I ask.

'Here,' Mikey says, pointing her out. 'She's got a red dot.'

I watch the queen. She isn't moving much. All the other bees are milling around her, doing their various bee jobs.

'Everyone's worried about you,' I say.

'It didn't sound like it,' Mikey says slowly, not taking his eyes off the bees. 'They were arguing.'

'They're not arguing now,' I say. 'They're parked outside. Mum, Dad, and Kaylee too. We wondered where you'd gone.'

Mikey shrugs. 'I needed some time.'

I nod because I understand what 'needing some time' feels like.

'Are you ready to come back home now? We've got new carpet.'

Mikey sighs. He looks at me. 'Everything's shit, Lou.'

'It's different,' I say, trying to remain optimistic. It is thought that optimistic people live longer than pessimistic people. I always try to keep this in mind.

'I didn't want it to be different.' Mikey looks at the bees again. I know he's talking about Mum and Dad separating and Dad moving to his new flat and taking the deck chair and the pool table.

'It will be okay,' I say, trying to sound reassuring. 'Things always change. Nothing can stay the same. It's the universe. It's in a constant state of flux.'

'It's not just that,' Mikey says. 'I made a mistake.'

'What mistake?' I ask.

'There's a guy in my year,' Mikey says. 'We were hanging out together a lot. I thought he was into me, you know…'

I nod and decide to wait for him to continue.

'Well, anyway... We kissed and stuff.'

I quickly nod again. As much as I want to be understanding, Mikey is my brother, and I'd rather he didn't elaborate on 'stuff'.

'It was nice,' Mikey says. 'He was into it as much as I

was.' Mikey looks down at the table the living honey bee observation hive is sitting on. 'Next time I saw him,' Mikey says. 'He tried to make out like nothing had happened. He wouldn't talk to me.'

'I'm sorry,' I say.

'It's all right,' Mikey says.

I want to hug Mikey but I am not good at hugging. I feel bad that someone Mikey cares about has hurt him and made him feel upset. I feel bad because he's my brother and I love him.

I also feel bad for a moment because I think that Faith cared about me and I hurt her.

'They all know now,' Mikey says. 'I don't know how but—'

'I think it's good,' I say. 'You've got to be who you are.'

Mikey doesn't answer me. He stares at the queen again. 'I don't want to go back to school.'

'You have to *own* who you are,' I continue, trying to remember what Faith said to me. 'Just walk in and say, yep, this is me. If they don't like it, then fuck them. It's the people who are different who make the difference,' I add, thinking of Mr Lawrence.

Mikey looks up at me. He smiles a tiny smile. He's still sad but he knows I'm trying to be helpful. 'Thanks, Lou.'

We both stand. Mikey makes a fist and holds his arm out. I make a fist too. We touch fists. It's our way of hugging. We fist hug.

The curly-haired woman appears at the doorway. He arms are folded. She does not look happy. 'The museum is *closed*,' she says, tapping a pencil against her arm.

'We were going anyway,' I say.

Mikey and I head down the stairs. The Russian bear watches us from inside his glass case.

'Did you say Mum, Dad, *and* Kaylee are in the car?' Mikey asks as we walk out of the museum.

'Yep.'

'Weird,' Mikey says, shaking his head.

As we approach, Mum and Dad both get out of the car. They look relieved.

'Everyone all right?' Dad asks cheerfully.

Mikey and I both nod. Dad is not good in dramatic or emotional situations.

Mum puts an arm around Mikey. 'We were thinking about getting a pizza,' she says. This is Mum's way of trying to tell her teenage son that she loves him, that he's perfect just the way he is, that she's sorry things haven't been easy recently and perhaps he feels she hasn't been there for him but she's going to try and change that now.

'Pizza would be great,' Mikey says.

'Well done, kiddo,' Dad says, opening the car door for me and punching me a little too hard on the shoulder. This gesture of gratitude is because I found Mikey and ensured our rescue mission was a success.

We climb in the back next to Kaylee. She also looks very relieved to see Mikey, although this is possibly because she has just spent the last twenty minutes trapped in a car with her lover's wife.

Thinking of my dad as anyone's 'lover' is actually quite gross. 'Boyfriend' didn't seem like the right word for an adult who is fast approaching forty-seven and who owns socks that are older than I am.

'What pizza are you going to go for, Mikey?' Mum

asks as we begin to drive away. Mikey is staring out of the window. He hasn't said much.

Mikey glances at me. I smile because we both know Mum is wanting to make sure Mikey is still okay without asking if he's still okay.

'Ham and mushroom,' Mikey says.

Mum looks pleased. 'Good choice,' she says.

'I'll have pepperoni,' Dad says, making a left towards the pizza place. Clearly Dad and Kaylee are also getting pizza.

'Margarita,' I say.

'Who'd have thought,' Dad says.

Mum and Mikey both laugh. They are laughing because this is the only pizza I ever have.

Kaylee looks confused. She has missed out on the pizza joke. After a moment she says, 'Maybe I'll have the spicy chicken.'

There is a long pause. Now Dad and Kaylee *must* be coming for pizza.

'I was thinking of having the spicy chicken,' Mum says.

There is an awkward silence. Can Mum and Kaylee both have the spicy chicken? Is it weird that not only are they going to eat pizza together but they want the same pizza?

'I love the spicy chicken,' Kaylee says, seemingly oblivious of the awkward atmosphere. 'It's very…'

'Spicy?' Mikey says helpfully.

'Yes,' Kaylee says. 'Spicy.'

'Maybe we could share,' Mum says. 'Get a fourteen inch.'

Now this is getting very weird. Mum and Kaylee are acting like best buddies. They are going to share a pizza which, although practical, seems to me quite an intimate act, the sort of thing only people who like each other, or who can at least tolerate each other, might do.

I feel proud of Mum. It can't be easy for her to be nice to Kaylee, even though she has Macro Steve now. She's doing it for our sake.

It's a shame Macro Steve isn't here, although I doubt that he eats pizza.

Dad pulls up outside the pizza place and we all jump out, keen to order our pizzas. For a few seconds I forget that we aren't a family anymore, that some of us don't live together, that one of us is new and one of us is missing. Just for a moment, as we slam the car doors and pile into the pizza place, it reminds me of a time when we were normal.

Then I wonder if there is such a thing as a normal family.

Probably not.

When we arrive back at the house with our pizzas there is a person sitting on the doorstep, dressed all in black, wearing a hooded jumper with the hood up. For a moment I wonder if I have seen a ghost, a dark phantom, grim-reaper type ghost sitting on our doorstep.

As we pull into the drive, the ghost lifts its head and I realise it's Sarah.

'Sarah?' Dad says, sounding surprised.

We open the car doors. My legs are warm where the pizzas have been resting on my lap.

'I've got them, Lou,' Kaylee says, taking the pizzas from me as I climb out.

'I forgot my key,' Sarah says shakily as we approach.

Her face is puffy and she has streaks of mascara on her cheeks.

Often when I misplace things I get anxious and panicky but I have never known Sarah to get so upset over a key.

'Hey, Sugarplum,' Dad says to Sarah. 'Good to see you.'

Sarah sniffs. She nods and looks as though she might burst into tears again.

Sugarplum is Dad's pet name for Sarah. Both Mum and Dad called her Sugarplum, apparently even before she was born. They told us once that when Sarah started nursery and the staff asked her what her name was, she said Sugarplum. After that Mum and Dad thought they had better start calling her Sarah.

Apparently they called Mikey Bubby-kins for a while when he was a baby, which is also kind of cute.

When I asked Dad what they called me, he thought for a moment then said Stinker. We called you Stinker.

I asked him if he wouldn't mind not mentioning that to anyone, EVER.

Mum lets us all in. 'What is it, love?' Mum asks Sarah, following her through to the living room.

'It's Brett. We broke up.' Sarah flings herself onto the sofa and begins to cry. At least I think that's what she's doing. She's making strange hiccupping sounds.

Mikey looks worried.

Kaylee looks embarrassed. 'We'll go and sort the pizzas out,' she says, side stepping out of the room with the stack of pizza boxes.

Mikey follows her, perhaps deciding he can be more help in the kitchen.

Sarah has her face buried in a cushion. 'He never told me,' she sobs.

Mum and Dad look uneasy.

'Told you what?' I ask, feeling it would be helpful if we knew the rest of the story.

Sarah lifts her face from the cushion.

'ThathesgotagirfriendcalledMeganandtheyvebeentogetherfouryearsandshespregnantandtheybrokeupbuthesgoingtogetbackwithherandshesgoingtomoveinwithimandtheyrehavingababy.'

Sarah turns her face back to the cushion.

'Oh,' Mum says.

Dad sits next to Sarah.

Sarah turns away from the cushion and buries her face in Dad's shoulder instead.

Dad pats her head. Although trying to comfort her, he looks secretly pleased. I'm not sure if he's pleased that Sarah broke up with her fireman or pleased that she's allowing him to stroke her head.

'He's doing the right thing, love,' Mum says.

'He wasn't worth it,' I add, trying to be helpful.

I'm not always very good in situations where people need comforting. I tend to say the wrong thing.

Sarah looks up at me. She blinks. She seems surprised to see me. For a moment I think I have definitely said the wrong thing but then she says, 'Thanks, Lou. You're a great sister.'

She smiles at me then leans her head against Dad's shoulder again.

A great sister?

This is the sibling that has barely spoken to me since she hit puberty, the person who, before then, used to kick me in the car, convince me there were evil goblins in the garden and invent strange initiation ceremonies for me and Mikey in order for us to become members of her secret club. One of these initiation ceremonies involved me standing on one leg for two hours blind-fold. Another involved Sarah sticking pieces of sellotape to my arm then ripping them off very quickly.

I have no idea how to respond to this remark. I think I am experiencing a state of shock.

Emotional and psychological shock is a very real condition. I once watched an episode of a program about 999 calls that told me all about emotional and psychological shock. It can cause a weak or racing pulse, clammy hands, confusion, faintness and nausea.

I check my pulse.

It feels okay.

Mikey and Kaylee enter with plates and napkins and the pizza boxes.

'Well,' Mum says. 'How about pizza?'

'You can share my pepperoni,' Dad says to Sarah.

Sarah looks happy. She likes pepperoni.

'I'll get the drinks,' Mikey says, disappearing back towards the kitchen.

We each take a plate and try and work out whose pizza is whose.

Mikey appears in the doorway. 'I think you better come and see this,' he says.

'What?' Mum says.

Mum, Dad and me put down our pizzas and follow Mikey towards the kitchen. Kaylee and Sarah stay where they are. They must be hungry.

Mikey stops suddenly in the hallway. He points to the kitchen door. We all lean around him in order to see, from here in the dark hallway, what he's pointing at.

There in the middle of the kitchen floor is Hammy

quietly munching on what looks like dried cereal that someone must have spilt.

None of us move.

Dad quietly steps backwards. He empties the laundry basket which, for some reason, has been left in the hall. He creeps ahead of us, holding the basket out in front of him.

In one quick movement Dad places the laundry basket over Hammy.

We all cheer.

Dad bends down next to the laundry basket. He lifts one corner and scoops up Hammy in his hands.

He carries him triumphantly back to the living room.

'Quick,' he says to Mikey behind him. 'Open the cage.'

Mikey rushes forward and opens Hammy's cage. Dad places Hammy inside. The door is quickly shut.

Sarah and Kaylee are watching from the sofa. 'Wow. Well done Dad,' Sarah says.

'That's a relief,' Kaylee says. 'Well done. You're everyone's hero today.'

I can't say for sure but I think Mum rolls her eyes a teeny tiny bit.

Dad brushes his hands on his shorts. 'No problemo,' he says, looking pleased with himself.

We finally sit down to eat our pizzas.

I would like to say that Hammy looks happy to be home and pleased to be watching us eat our pizzas from inside the safe confinement of his cage but, to be honest, he actually looks pretty pissed off.

11

THE next day I'm standing by my locker at lunch time after putting my lunch box away when I hear the sound of a lot of people coming towards me.

I shut my locker and look up. There *are* lots of people coming towards me. What's worse is that they all seem to be looking straight at me.

Lianne Parks is in front of everyone else. She's closely followed by Bryony Silver and Cherry Wiles and Bonnie Jackson. Behind them are lots more people including a crowd of boys from our year.

'There she is!' Lianne says.

I begin to feel very uncomfortable.

Before I know it I am surrounded on both sides by kids, mostly from my year, but there are a couple of first year kids too who seem to have come along for the ride.

Everyone looks as though they are expecting something. They look excited, like they are about to have a go on a new roller-coaster. I once went on a roller-coaster at a theme park and decided I would never do so again. It felt like the skin on my face was falling off and my internal organs had got stuck in my throat. I don't feel these are normal sensations for a human being to experience.

Lianne Parks is standing very close to me.

I step back but the lockers are behind me and there's nowhere to go.

'There you are, *freak*,' she says, almost spitting on me.

'Told you we were gonna get you,' Bryony hisses.

I begin to feel panicky. This is mostly because there are so many people around me and I am prone to feelings of claustrophobia in these kinds of situations where there are lots of people close to me. This is why I never attend music festivals, or use lifts, or go shopping in the sales.

'Smash her up!' someone calls out.

I wonder whether this is now a situation in which I will have to remove my glasses. I also wonder what I have done to deserve what is inevitably going to happen to me within the next few minutes.

I suspect it has something to do with me just being me, or with my dad being in love with an eighteen-year-old.

I think about telling Lianne that it's the people who are different who make the difference but when I open my mouth to speak, I find I am having difficulty with words again.

'She looks like a goldfish!' Someone says. This makes them all laugh.

Lianne glares at them and they shut up. She turns back to me. 'Freak,' she says, this time under her breath. 'Your dad's a fucking perv. We don't want people like *you* here.' She makes a fist with her hand then draws her arm back.

I flinch and squeeze my eyes shut in anticipation.

'Excuse me!' A loud voice says from somewhere in the crowd. 'Coming through. Make way.'

I open my eyes to see Faith elbowing her way through the crowd of kids. I was about to be 'smashed up' and Faith has come to my rescue. I have no idea why.

Faith reaches Lianne and stops.

'What do you want, Goth girl?' Lianne says. She looks annoyed but also a little scared. It's true, Faith is wearing an especially large amount of black make-up today.

Faith looks towards the doors. 'Mr. Dodd!' she says loudly.

The crowd immediately disperses. Bryony, and Cherry link arms and move away very quickly. Bonnie runs off in the opposite direction.

Lianne looks around. When she realises there's no sign of Mr. Dodd and that her disciples have abandoned her, she scowls at Faith. 'You made that up,' she says.

Faith shrugs. 'No shit, Sherlock.'

'Get lost,' Lianne says to Faith. 'This is nothing to do with you.'

I try to agree with Lianne but instead I make a small stuttering sound. Both Lianne and Faith ignore me.

'I think this party's over,' Faith says to Lianne. 'Don't you?'

Lianne now looks unsure. She looks from me to Faith. Faith is much bigger than Lianne.

I try to stare at Lianne with the most intimidating stare I have.

'I wouldn't waste my time with a couple of freaks like you anyway,' she says finally.

Faith raises an eyebrow.

Lianne looks as though she's going to say something else but changes her mind. She gives us one final look then turns and walks away.

I have been saved by Faith.

Then it dawns on me, Faith is my angel.

Faith saved me and, today, she is my guardian angel. I didn't even have to get lost in the woods and find a temple in order for her to save me.

Of course I know Faith can't really be my angel, the same as I know Annabel and Neil can't really be my parents, and Cliff Richard can't really be Nan's angel. I also suspect the evidence that proves the existence of angels is a little patchy.

Faith and I stay where we are until Lianne has disappeared. Faith won't look at me. Neither of us says anything.

I look at Faith and I want to say that I'm sorry I told her I didn't want to be her friend anymore and thank her for being my angel today, but I can't say anything as I can't speak yet. It's as though someone has built a dam in my throat that no words can get past. They are probably still there in my brain swimming around as usual but somehow they can't get from my brain to my mouth.

After a moment Faith turns and walks away. I watch her until she disappears around the corner and I can't see her anymore.

I WALK SLOWLY home from school. I don't feel much like rushing as I usually do whilst saying my favourite train poem under my breath.

I use the cut-through because there are less people around. I walk on the path through the middle of the empty field. The ground is hard under my feet. The field has recently been ploughed. There are long lines of brown earth on either side of me. I wonder how many lines there are, but I feel too distracted to think about it for very long.

This has not been a good day.

I know I should feel happy that I didn't get smashed up by Lianne Parks, but I only feel sad.

I want to sit on the floor when I get home. That's all I want to do.

Somehow, though, it doesn't feel like the right thing to

do. It feels as though I should be doing something else. I have a funny feeling that this something else will be difficult.

I know the thing I need to do is to make up with Faith. I need to tell her I'm sorry for saying I didn't want to be her friend anymore, and to thank her for rescuing me today. I thought she would be angry with me but you don't usually rescue people you are angry with.

I decide this is one of those situations, like skipping school that afternoon, where I must take action even though I don't know what the consequences of that action will be.

By the time I get home I have formulated a plan.

Mum is still out at work, but I can smell something nice coming from the kitchen.

Mikey is washing up a large mixing bowl. He's wearing Mum's pink rubber washing-up gloves. The oven is on and I can see something inside which must definitely account for the nice smell. I'm glad Mikey is baking again.

'Hi, Lou,' Mikey says.

'What are you baking?' I ask.

'Jamaican Toto cake,' Mikey says.

I leave Mikey to his baking and his washing up and go upstairs. I mustn't waste time. I have a plan to execute.

I sit on my bed and reach for my purse. I think if I don't do it now I will never do it. I take the card that says *Ray's Taxis.* I dial the number.

It rings.

For a moment I think no one is going to answer, then I hear Ray's voice.

'Hello?'

'I need a taxi,' I say.

Sometimes when I am in a rush I forget that you are supposed to say things like 'hello' and 'how are you' and tell someone who you are, before saying what you need to say.

There is a pause on the end of the line.

I take a deep breath. 'This is Louise Coulson,' I say. 'From the station. You gave me your card and now I need a taxi. It's an emergency,' I add, suddenly fearful that Ray might be busy and that I won't be able to carry out my plan.

I immediately feel guilty for saying this because probably this is not a real emergency; it just feels like an emergency to me because I need to make things right and it's a big deal for me to do this.

'I know,' Ray says, sounding more friendly, if a little surprised. 'How are you?'

I screw my eyes shut and grip the phone. I don't have time for these kinds of questions. I hate talking on the phone.

'Very well,' I say quickly. 'But I need a taxi to go to my friend Faith's house because the bus will take too long and I have to tell her I'm sorry for not wanting to be her friend anymore and thank her for being my angel and saving me from getting smashed up today by Lianne Parks and this is very difficult for me to do and if I have to get the bus and change buses in town I'm worried I will get overwhelmed and not be able to tell her.'

I take another deep breath. Ray hasn't said anything. He must be busy. Perhaps he has other taxi jobs to do. Or perhaps he's at his allotment. I decide this was a bad idea.

'Okay,' Ray says, laughing. 'You'd better give me your address then.'

I'm very pleased that Ray is willing to help me but giving a man you met at a railway station your home address is not usually something you should do. Not under any circumstances.

I give Ray my address.

'Right,' he says. 'I'll be with you in fifteen minutes.'

I glance at my clock and change out of my school clothes and into my favourite jeans and sweatshirt. I pull the plastic plug out from the bottom of my china piggy bank which I've had forever. I add five pounds to what's in my purse so I have enough to pay Ray. I haven't taken a taxi by myself before and I'm not sure how much it will be.

I look out of my bedroom window and wait for Ray to arrive. I keep an eye on my clock.

After seventeen minutes, I see what I think must be his car coming slowly along the road. I quickly run downstairs and put my shoes on.

Mikey must have heard me running down the stairs because he calls out to me. 'Cake's ready!'

'I have to go out!' I call back. 'Save me some!'

I open the front door and Ray is there in the driveway in his taxi. He's wearing his peaked grey cap.

I shut the front door. I notice Ray has a license number in the window of his car that says he's a taxi.

For a moment I can't decide whether I should get in the front or the back. I decide on the front. It seems more sociable under the circumstances even if it isn't strictly the correct thing to do.

'Where to?' Ray says as I jump in.

'Twenty-six Laburnum Drive,' I say.

'Righty-o.'

Ray reverses quickly out onto the road. I wonder if

he knows where Laburnum Drive is. He isn't using a satnav.

Mum and Dad usually always use the satnav. Well, Mum does. Whenever we used to go somewhere new she would tell Dad to use the satnav and Dad would grumble but turn it on anyway. If Dad was driving, he would turn it off when he thought he knew where he was going and then we'd get lost.

'Do you know where you're going?' I ask Ray.

'I know Laburnum Drive,' Ray says, cheerfully.

I sit back and try to relax. I like Ray's car. It's very spacious and smells of toffee. I don't usually like the smell of cars, especially if they have air fresheners in them. The small of air fresheners makes me feel sick.

As Ray drives towards town, I feel nervous about what I will say to Faith when I get there. Will she even be in?

I tap my hands on my thighs and move my head from side to side.

Ray glances at me. 'Would you like a toffee?' he says, gesturing to the handful of individually wrapped toffees sitting in the hollow of the holder that's meant for hot drinks.

'Thanks,' I say, taking one and slowly unwrapping it.

'Does she like trains too, this friend of yours?' Ray asks me.

It is quite difficult to answer Ray's question with a large toffee in my mouth. I shake my head and move the toffee to my left cheek. 'She likes Nietzsche and Fleetwood Mac.'

Ray nods thoughtfully. We stop at the lights. 'We can't all have the same interests,' he says.

'No,' I say, thinking of me liking the bear and Mikey liking the bees. 'Although I'm not sure she's my friend anymore,' I add. 'We fell out and it was probably my fault.'

'Takes a lot of guts,' Ray says as we pull away. 'To do what you're doing. Whoever's fault it was.'

I say nothing as I am concentrating on my toffee. I'm not sure if Ray's right or if he's just being kind.

We drive past the park. Even though I have been to the park many times in my life as soon as I see it it reminds me of the time Faith and I hugged the willow tree in the rain.

'I fell out with my brother once,' Ray says.

'For how long?' I ask.

'Ten years.'

Ten years! This is a very long time. I have not been friends with Faith for three days which seems, to me, long enough.

'What was it about?' I ask. 'Why did you fall out?'

'Well that's just it. Neither of us could remember in the end.'

Ray turns right at the roundabout and I recognise where we are from when Faith and I took the bus to her house and I met Jonathan and we danced to Bruce Springsteen.

I think that I will thank Ray now for driving me in case I forget later. Sometimes I forget to say thank you and goodbye. I don't mean to do this. Mum says I must remember that other people need to know when an interaction is over.

'Thank you for driving me,' I say.

'It's a pleasure,' Ray says. 'I like to drive.'

We pull into Faith's road. I can tell Ray is looking at the house numbers. I'm looking too. I spot Faith's house at the same time as Ray does.

'There!' I say. 'With the plants.'

Ray pulls over. I take a deep breath so I don't rush immediately from the car.

'Here we are then,' Ray says.

I remember that I am in a taxi and that I need to give Ray some money. I can't see a meter.

I reach into my pocket and take out my purse.

Ray waves it away. 'This one's on me,' he says. 'You go do what you've got to do. Life's too short not to hang on to those who care about you.'

'Thank you,' I say, putting my purse away. I didn't forget to say thank you after all. I open the car door and climb out.

'See you at the station,' Ray says.

'Sure,' I say.

Ray salutes me. I shut the door and wave as he drives away.

I turn and face Faith's house. I walk past the plants and up to the front door.

I ring the bell.

I THINK THAT as soon as the door opens I will tell Faith I'm sorry.

I hear footsteps approaching from inside the hall. The door opens.

'I'm sorry,' I say.

'Sorry?' There's a woman in blue dungarees staring at me. She looks confused.

Now I don't know what to say.

'Is Faith in?' I ask.

The woman relaxes. She smiles at me. She doesn't look confused anymore. 'Come in,' she says, stepping aside.

'You must be Lou.' She's still smiling. It's a little scary. How does she know my name?

I dart quickly past her and into the hallway, afraid that she might hug me. Once I'm inside she shuts the door. I notice the framed fish skeleton is still hanging in the hallway where it was before.

'I'm Susie,' the woman says. 'Faith's step-mum.'

I nod. I remember that I know two things about Susie. She likes plants, and she once went to Mexico.

Susie has long wavy hair. It's a reddish brown colour. I like her dungarees. They look comfortable.

'It's lovely to meet you,' Susie is saying. 'Faith's told us all about you. We're pleased she's made friends at school.'

I just stand there nodding and looking stupid. I think that Faith probably didn't tell them about me not wanting to be friends with her anymore.

I hear a voice coming from inside the living room. 'Who is it?'

Another woman appears. She's much taller and she has very dark hair like Faith's, only shorter. She's wearing coloured leggings and a sweatshirt but her hair is perfectly styled and she's wearing very nice make-up. I imagine she came in from work, got changed but kept her make-up on. She's very glamorous.

'It's Lou,' Susie says. 'Faith's friend from school.'

The woman with the dark hair also looks pleased to see me. She holds her hand out. 'I'm Kate,' she says. 'Faith's mum.'

I nod again and shake her hand. I don't mind shaking hands with people, if that's what they want to do, but I have never met anyone's mum who has shook my hand before.

I try to think of what I know about Kate. I know that

she likes bridges and was once worried about her biological clock.

'It's very nice to meet you,' Kate says. 'You're welcome here anytime. Do you like Chinese food?'

'Yes,' I say, wondering why Faith's mum is asking me this strange question. 'But I always order the same things,' I add.

Kate laughs. 'So do we,' she says. 'You should come over on a Saturday evening.'

Susie is nodding in agreement.

'Every other Saturday,' Kate says. 'Or if Faith's with us and not at her dad's, we get Chinese food and watch a film.'

'Um, thanks,' I say, wondering if Faith will be quite so happy with this arrangement.

'Faith's in the conservatory,' Susie says as if she knew I was thinking of Faith. 'I'll show you.'

I follow Susie along the hallway.

'Don't forget Chinese food, Saturday evenings!' Kate calls after me.

Now Susie and I are in the kitchen. There are more plants on the kitchen windowsill, or perhaps they're herbs. There's a photograph of Faith stuck to the fridge. She's much smaller but I know it's Faith. She's on the beach standing next to a huge sandcastle with a man in sunglasses. I guess that must be her dad.

I can hear the faint sound of classical music playing somewhere in the house.

'The conservatory's the warmest room,' Susie says, pausing in the kitchen. 'It gets the sun. That's why the plants like it. I'm playing them Bach. They seem to like Bach. They didn't do so well with Vivaldi.' She smiles at me. 'Perhaps because I played them Winter. They got confused.'

I'm not really sure what to say to this. It seems a little crazy. Perhaps all families are a little crazy. Luckily I don't have to say anything as Susie opens the door that leads to the conservatory. It's full of plants. It looks like a tropical jungle. I like it a lot. I can hear the music more clearly now.

Then I see Faith. She's sitting in the corner on a rattan sofa that's covered in cream cushions, reading a book. She looks up as Susie and I enter.

'It's Lou,' Susie says.

Faith nods. She doesn't say anything, nor does she look particularly impressed or surprised to see me. I wonder if I have made a mistake in coming here.

'Nice to meet you, Lou,' Susie says, not seeming to notice Faith's relaxed reaction to me. 'I'll leave you two alone. Help yourself to snacks if you're hungry. See you later I hope.'

I nod, still watching Faith. 'Thank you.'

Suzy closes the door quietly behind her.

Faith shuts her book. At first I think it's called *Death in Vince,* but when I take a few steps forward I can see it's called *Death in Venice.*

'Hi,' I say.

'Hi,' Faith says flatly.

'What's your book about?' I ask, because this is what you ask when someone is reading something you haven't read.

Faith studies her book as if she hasn't seen it before. 'It's about a man,' she says slowly. 'He becomes infatuated with a boy. Through his obsession, he at last experiences the Dionysian, the drunkenness and intoxication that accompanies lust and desire. Then he dies.' Faith pauses. 'In Venice,' she adds. 'I've read it before.'

I decide it might be best to tell Faith why I'm here. 'I've come to tell you I'm sorry,' I say.

Faith sighs. She puts her book down on the sofa. 'You can sit down,' she says wearily. 'If you like.'

I sit next to Faith on the sofa. She looks different. I realise it's because she isn't wearing any black eye make-up and her hair is down.

'I made a mistake,' I say.

Faith studies the pattern on the sofa cushion. 'I appreciate you coming over, Lou. I do. But you said what you said for a reason. I don't want to be something difficult in your life.'

Faith's right. When she called it *was* difficult for me. I freaked out because she called me on the phone at a time when I needed to be quiet.

'I felt overwhelmed,' I say.

'Do you often feel overwhelmed?' Faith asks me.

I think of school, the times between classes when everyone is shouting and running and pushing their way through the corridors. I think of the bell ringing and of locker doors slamming. Then I think of when I'm outside school. I think of supermarkets and department stores and gyms and crowded restaurants and busy streets and sirens and bright lights and people folding newspapers and pointing and talking loudly on their mobile phones and how everything rushes towards me and around me and how I can't ever seem to shut it out.

'Yes,' I say. 'All the time.'

'Tell me about it,' Faith says.

'Everything around me happens too fast,' I say. 'It's difficult for me to slow it down. It's like I feel *everything*. It's too much. Sometimes I can't speak and sometimes I just need to be by myself.'

Faith frowns. She seems to be thinking.

'I see,' she says finally.

I imagine that Faith now thinks I'm a freak too.

'Why didn't you tell me?' Faith asks.

I just did,' I say, feeling confused.

'No,' Faith says. 'Why didn't you tell me *before*.'

'Oh,' I say. 'I don't know. I guess I thought you knew.'

Faith looks surprised. She strokes the cover of her book. 'I figured out a few things about you, Lou. But not everything. I'm not inside your head, you know.'

'No,' I say, imagining a tiny Borrower sized Faith inside my head.

'You need to tell me,' she says. 'If you can't talk - just say - "I can't talk right now. It's an intense time for me." Then hang up the phone.'

'Okay,' I say, not completely sure if this will work.

'If it's not a good time for you to hang out with me, you have to tell me.' Faith studies the sofa cushion again. 'I don't always feel so great myself.'

'The shadowy queen?' I ask.

Faith nods slowly. 'Right. The shadowy queen.'

'I get it,' I say.

Faith looks at me. 'Thanks for coming over, Lou.'

'That's okay.'

We both smile. We're friends again. I feel a huge sense of relief.

Outside it's dark and windy. The music stops and I can hear the tapping of a tree branch on the conservatory roof.

'And you'll understand if sometimes I have to stay in and watch a nature documentary?' I say, just to make sure.

'Totally,' Faith says. 'We can be friends without living in each other's pockets, right?'

The Borrower sized Faith moves from inside my head to inside my pocket.

'Yes,' I say. 'We can do that.'

Faith tucks her hair behind her ear. 'It's about being there for each other - when it really matters.'

I nod. Faith's right again, and this reminds me of today.

'Thank you for not letting Lianne Parks smash me up earlier.'

Faith shrugs. 'It would have been messy. My locker's close to yours. I didn't fancy cleaning off the blood.'

'Thanks.'

Faith laughs. My phone beeps in my pocket.

I have a message from Mikey. It's a photo of his Toto cake. I've also had a text from Mum. She's worried, and is wondering where I am.

'I have to text my mum,' I tell Faith. 'I'll ask if she can come and get me.'

'You can stay as long as you like,' Faith says, picking up *Death in Venice.*

I quickly text my mum. Thinking of my mum and Mikey, I have an idea. 'Why don't you come to mine someday?' I say. 'You can meet my family.'

'Sure,' Faith says, looking pleased. 'I'd like that.' She leaves her book on the sofa and stands.

I stand too but then I panic because I think Faith might hug me.

'I don't do hugs,' I say.

'I wasn't going to,' Faith says.

My phone beeps in my hand. 'Mum says it's fine,' I say. 'She'll come and get me later.'

Faith crosses the room and opens the conservatory doors. The tree branch taps against the roof again.

'Cool,' she says. 'Lets get something to eat.'

Acknowledgements

Thank you Mum and Dad for supporting me and letting me go 'my own way'. Thank you to to my sisters for always being an ear at the end of the phone wherever we are. Thanks Uncle Tim for championing this book and for understanding my love of literature.

Thank you Mrs Tennant, my secondary school English teacher, for telling me I should write.

Thank you to my teachers, both at London Met and at Birkbeck, for giving me the space to grow and learn as a writer; Julia Bell, Carolyn Hart, Sunny Singh, Trevor Norris, Tony Gardner and Anne Karpf.

Thank you to all my friends and class mates who have supported my writing journey. Writing can be a lonely occupation and you were a constant source of inspiration. Thank you Chloe Seager at Diane Banks Associates for your unfaltering belief right from the very beginning and all the hard work that contributed to the publication of Notes.

Thank you to my publisher Everything With Words and to Mikka, for taking a chance and for giving it all you've got.

Thank you lastly to Gary Mepsted for teaching me how to write, and for the tough love that made this book what it is today. Thank you.